STRINGS OF DECEPTION

Profiling the Heart, Book 2
Stephanie R. Caffrey

Cover Art Design by: Kelly Moran/Rowan Prose Publishing
Photo Credit: Adobe Images/Deposit Photos
First Edition
ISBN: 978-1-961967-72-4
Rowan Prose Publishing, LLC
www.RowanProsePublishing.com
Published in the United States of America

GET STEPHANIE'S OTHER BOOKS!

For Felix.

Acknowledgments

This book was probably the most difficult book for me to write to date.

When I started writing it in November 2024, I wasn't certain if the series would get picked up by a publisher. By Christmas, I had about 30k words written, but then right before the holiday, my nephew passed away. From then, writing became something my mind couldn't quite do. But I got here! This book is finished, and I really hope, dear reader, you enjoy this second installment of Profiling the Heart.

I couldn't have gotten here, however, without lots of help along the way.

Thank you to Kelly and Katie at Rowan Prose Publishing. You ladies have always believed in me, and your support has changed my life.

To my fellow authors in the trees—I've gotten to know a lot of you over the last few months, and it has been life-changing. Your support and encouragement means the world to me, and I'm so glad we're all part of this little family.

Thanks, as ever, to Laura. This book would not be what it is without your diligent help. Thank you for letting me text you my ideas, and for giving me amazing feedback. You mean the world to me.

Sharon, Jamie, and Sarah—you three have been my rocks this year. Chasing away the self-doubt, being shoulders for me to cry, and the best damn cheerleaders a girl could hope for. I love you guys!

Mom and Dad, Nikki and Kate—This has been a year, and I don't think any of us could have made it this far without each other to lean on. I'm so thankful for your support and your love.

Finally, to Matt, Arthur, and Beatrice—Thanks for being my everything.

Chapter One

MILLIE

October 5

Millie Driscoll was the first to notice Rebecca wasn't standing at the barricade like she was supposed to. After informing the team, they moved up their push into the house. She led.

As if the tape were in fast forward, the scene quickly skipped until Millie was descending the basement stairs. She could hear shouting. And crying. She hoped she wasn't too late. Please, God, don't let her be too late.

Palming her weapon, Millie slowly walked down the stairs. A man was yelling. Threatening. Reaching the bottom of the stairs, a man, Guillermo, was towering over Rebecca. He was about to strike, a large, blunt weapon in his hands. Acting on instinct, and all the training she went through, she aimed and pulled the trigger of her weapon.

The loud boom of the gun reverberated through the room, punishing her ears. Guillermo slumped to the floor. Millie made eye contact with Rebecca, who screamed—

Millie sprung up in her bed, drenched in sweat, a loud alarm blaring through her room. She brought a hand up to her chest in an attempt to still her heart. It was just a dream. Just. A. Dream. A dream she had been having recurrently since the end of May. Everything was fine. She was fine.

She was not fine.

She wasn't.

The loud alarm still sounded obnoxiously through her bedroom. It was insistent. She needed it to stop.

Wait.

It was her phone.

Running a hand through her long, curly black hair, she took another calming breath and looked at the clock on her bedside table. It was three thirty in the morning. While logically she knew a call at this hour was more than likely from work, there was still that little voice in her brain that screamed 'Family Emergency.'

Millie reached over to where she plugged her phone in next to her bed.

"Driscoll."

"Hey." The voice of her best friend and coworker, Trevor Ford, soothed any leftover anxiety from the nightmare.

"Hey."

"You okay?"

Millie smiled. It spoke to how well they knew each other that he could tell from just a single word how not okay she was. "I'm fine. Nightmare."

Trevor let out a slow breath on the other end of the line. "Same one?"

"Yeah."

"You did nothing wrong. You know that, right?"

Millie nodded, even though she knew Trevor couldn't see her. "I know, and it wasn't the first time I had to take out a perp.

However, it was the first time I had to take out someone who was close to someone I know. Someone I'm close to."

"Rebecca isn't mad at you," he stated it as a fact.

"Yeah, but it doesn't make my subconscious feel any less guilty, apparently."

"Do you need to talk to someone? Other than me, I mean?"

Trevor had been a great listening ear for Millie for the last five months. When she had spilled her guts about not sleeping well since they returned from Cove Creek, how the vision of taking out Guillermo in his basement while he loomed over Rebecca haunted her sleep, Trevor had sat there and listened and not once placated her with trite words.

However, five months later, and she was still haunted by her choices, Millie knew maybe she needed to do something more drastic.

"Yeah," she finally replied. "I think I might need to call one of the Bureau's therapists. Talk through this shit."

"It would probably be for the best," Trevor agreed.

Millie settled back into her bed, getting more comfortable now that her body was feeling closer to normal. "So, Ford. What's with the middle of the night phone call? If it was just to shoot the shit, remind me to kick your ass in the morning for interrupting my much-needed beauty sleep."

Trevor laughed. "No, I know better than to wake you up without a really fucking good reason. There's a case. It's one we have to travel to. So, pack your bags and make your way to the Bureau. Thomas is giving us an hour and a half to make it, so work quickly."

"Fuck. Is it The Butcher?"

"No, no, a new one. Something out of some small town in New Mexico. All I know is it's serial."

Millie leaned her head against the headboard of her bed. "Fuck. It's been a while. We haven't had one of these since..."

"Since Iowa," Trevor finished. "Yeah. I know."

Since leaving Iowa and returning to DC, most of the BAU's, the Behavior Analysis Unit's, work had been consulting on smaller cases and following up on leads for cold cases. There hadn't been a serial killer case. Which had been okay for her. She wasn't sure if she could handle another serial case. Apparently, she was about to find out.

"So, New Mexico in October. What should I be packing for?"

"Well, let me do a quick search." The line went quiet while Trevor looked up the weather. "Well, according to the all-powerful Google, we should pack long sleeves and light coats."

"So, our normal suits would probably be best."

"And maybe an overcoat, in case it gets cold at night."

Millie let out a long breath.

"You're going to be okay."

"You don't know that for sure."

"Millie," Trevor's voice was earnest. "You're going to be fine. You're one of the strongest people I know. There isn't anything you can't do. And if you're triggered? That's okay, too. We'll all be there to support you."

Tears welling up in Millie's eyes. He was right. Even if this was going to be the most traumatic thing she ever did, she wouldn't have to go it alone. Her team would be there for her.

She lucked out when she came out of Quantico and went straight into the BAU with Trevor. She and Trevor had met in Quantico and hit it off. At one point, Trevor had asked her out, but she had turned him down. She was focused on her goal and didn't want anything distracting her. Instead, they became best friends, and had been ever since. When spots for a profiler, her, and a tech pro, him, opened when they graduated, it seemed like fate. Sometimes she wondered what it would have been like to date Trevor, but ten years later, she didn't want to lose the person she was closest to if things didn't work out romantically between them.

The rest of the team was amazing, too, which was icing on the cake. Millie hit it off with everyone. Which wasn't a surprise. She always made friends easily and was more of a social butterfly than the members of her team who found it harder to socialize. As a result, they blended well together.

"You're right," she shifted in the bed so she moved to the edge to sit up. "I've got an amazing support system in place. I can do this."

"I better let you go, so you can pack."

"Psh. You know me. I have a go-bag in the back of my closet ready to go."

Trevor laughed. "You're right. I forgot who I was talking to. Our resident Girl Scout."

Millie chuckled. "Shut up. It's not like you don't have your own bag packed as well."

"Millie. We all do. That's just who we are."

"All Type A, overprepared, ready for anything."

"And anyone."

A comfortable silence fell between them.

"Seriously, I'll let you go. See you in an hour." Trevor didn't even wait for her to reply before hanging up.

Millie looked at her phone, not moving. She could do this. All she needed to do was get up, get dressed, and get her ass into a car to take her to the office. That's it.

She bit her bottom lip, pulling it between her teeth, and closed her eyes. The image of Guillermo falling to the floor of his basement came to life behind her eyelids. The look of shock on Rebecca's face as her father fell permanently etched in Millie's memory.

Her phone dinged.

She looked down at it.

Rebecca.

Becks - Are you going to be okay?

Now, hot tears cascaded down Millie's face.

Her friend must have gotten up with her fiancé, Matthew, when his phone went off. And instead of going back to sleep or helping Matthew do whatever he needed to do to get out of the house, she was texting her, concerned.

Millie - You know me.

Becks - I do know you, hence the previous message. Are you okay?

Millie - I am. Trevor already talked me down from whatever ledge I was on.

Becks - You know I'm just a message away if you need to talk. About anything.

Millie - Shouldn't you be helping Matty?

Becks - Are you kidding? That man has his routine down to the millisecond. I was just told I'm in the way. Hence the messaging.

Millie - First time he's going to be gone on a big case since you moved here. You gonna be okay?

Becks - Yeah. Between school and extracurriculars, Benji and I will be super busy. Won't even notice he's gone.

Millie - It's okay to say you'll miss him.

Becks - I'll miss you both.

Millie smiled down at her phone. The best thing that came out of the Iowa case in the spring was Rebecca and Benji. She was so glad that the universe brought them together. And even better, that Rebecca fell in love with a member of Millie's team and moved to DC to be with him. In the three months since Rebecca and her son had arrived in town, they had instituted a weekly girls' night.

While Millie made friends easily, she didn't have many here in DC. She was too busy with work to meet people and forge friendships. And when she did, they didn't have the patience for her lack of availability. More than once, she thought she had made a friend, but one too many plans canceled at the last minute had destroyed that. It had hurt at first, the constant rejection, but she got used to it.

And her dating life? The thought alone made her cringe. If making friends was difficult, meeting a man was even harder. Millie had tried all the different dating apps, but for some reason, her job was a turn off to all the men she kept meeting. Whether it was the gruesome nature of it all, or whether it was the fact she could read all their tells and call them all out on their lies, she wasn't sure. But she knew for a fact it had to be one of those two, since she never made it beyond the first date with any of these men to find out if they hated her schedule.

Trevor actually made fun of her once because she could scare off any man with just one date. He came up with the clever nickname, "Millisecond Millie" since, he claimed, she could scare off any man within a millisecond of meeting.

Was she offended by the nickname? Nope. Dating had become a game once they created a spreadsheet to track how long into each date she could get before the man she was out with got the inevitable "family emergency" call.

She didn't feel bad. Out of everyone on the team, Logan was in the longest, most stable relationship. Everyone else was perpetually single, or in a marriage that was crumbling by the second.

Well, until Iowa. Until Matthew met Rebecca.

Millie opened the rideshare app on her phone and put in the request. It always took longer in the middle of the night. Twenty minutes. That was enough time to get dressed and grab her bags.

She also needed bring a light coat. The almighty Google did say she might need it.

She opened her closet to extract the coat and the bags, and her brand-new burgundy dress caught her eye. She had purchased it on a whim during a summer sale. Its scooped neck brought the dress off her shoulders, which led into three-quarter sleeves. The empire waist of the dress flared out into an A-line skirt. It made her boobs look fantastic.

Millie hadn't had a chance to wear it yet, and she had no reason to pack it. No reason at all.

Except.

What if she met someone on this case? It wasn't out of the realm of possibility. Matthew, the team's most awkward member, the one who had sworn off love entirely, who didn't even want to hang out with anyone from the team, managed to find love during the last case.

If he could find love, anyone could.

She looked at the dress for a second longer before grabbing it and throwing it on her bed. It was getting zipped up into one of her suit bags.

Millie was deciding now to be an optimist.

This was her time to shine.

Millie rushed down the halls of headquarters, dragging her suitcase behind her.

Her fucking rideshare had been late. And when he finally got there, he took his sweet time driving through the city. She was pretty sure he hadn't hit the speed limit once. Not. Once.

She could see through the glass wall of the meeting room that she was the last to arrive. She was never the last to arrive. That was Logan's job. Well, more recently, Matty's. He had always been the first, but since becoming a stepdad and a fiancé, he had been taking longer and longer to leave.

Of course, getting the call in the middle of the night may have sped things up for him. He probably didn't wake the kid up to say goodbye.

Millie had no such excuses. She lived alone and had no one to answer to. She was, however, at the mercy of whatever bozo picked up her rideshare request. And apparently tonight it was one of those sloths who worked at the DMV in that one animated movie she watched while babysitting Benji a few weeks ago.

Pushing the door open to the room, she already had her apology on her lips. "I'm so sorry. You would think driving through the city in the middle of the night wouldn't be a problem, but I'm pretty sure my driver missed sitting in traffic, and he made up his own problems."

Thomas Fleming, the team leader, gave her a kind smile, his crow's feet crinkling up in the corners of his eyes. "It's alright, Millie. You're not much later than the rest of us. I think every rideshare driver was out to get us tonight."

"Not Jorge," Matthew spoke up. He was sitting next to Thomas, doing something on his phone. "He got me here in record time."

Jorge was Matthew's regular rideshare driver. The two of them had become more friends than anything, and Millie was incredibly jealous that not only did Matthew have a family now, he had reliable transportation for when he got called in to travel.

Making friends with a rideshare drive was another thing to add to her list of things to do.

"Now that we are all here," Thomas's booming baritone broke her out of her thought spirals. "Let's talk about the case."

Trevor picked up the remote to the projector and turned it on. Four women's faces filled the screen.

Logan Hayes, the last member of their team, let out a low whistle. "Fuck."

Thomas nodded gravely. "Calico Rock, New Mexico has seen four women murdered in the last eight weeks."

Millie sat up straighter in her seat. "Four women in eight weeks?!"

"That is correct," Thomas answered.

"What pattern, if any, is there in the times of discovery of the bodies?" Logan asked, taking notes on his tablet.

"They discovered each body exactly two weeks apart. Like clockwork," Thomas answered.

Thomas nodded to Trevor, who tapped on his tablet and switched the view on the screen to show a portrait of a woman. Her light brown hair was shoulder length, and her bright smile spread across her face.

"Victim number one was Jamie Sanders. Forty-two years old. Married with two kids, both in high school. She was taken on August 18. Someone walking her dog found her the next morning at the local park. She had defensive wounds on her arms, and she had skin cells under fingers, so she managed to get a piece of our UNSUB. She was stabbed twelve times in her torso. Most of those seemed to happen post-mortem," Thomas explained.

"Any hits off the skin under the victim's nails?" Matthew asked.

"Nothing in CODIS," Thomas answered. "Same with the partial fingerprint they were able to lift off one of the victims."

Trevor switched the photo on the screen to show another woman. Her salt and pepper hair was wildly curly and looked as if it had a life of its own. She also had a beautiful smile, and her eyes seemed to indicate that she was playful in life. Millie hated this part the most. Seeing these women in life. It made her angry at the person who stole it from them.

Thomas continued. "Victim number two was Sharon Cruise, fifty-one. Married, three kids, all out of the home. She disappeared exactly two weeks to the hour as Jamie. The owner of the local supermarket found her the next day behind the store when he came in to open. She also had defensive wounds on her arms and multiple stab wounds in her torso. Again, mostly post-mortem."

Trevor changed the picture. This woman was younger. Her brown hair was long and straight, reaching her shoulders. She was laughing in her photo, as if someone on the other side of the camera had told her a joke and caught her mid-laugh.

"Victim number three," Thomas spoke, "was Laura Hutchins, thirty-four. Married, two small daughters. She was taken exactly two weeks after Sharon. She was found the next day in front of the local aquatic center. Same MO as the other vics. Defensive wounds, skin under the fingertips, and multiple stab wounds. However, she had been brutalized more than the others. She had nearly twenty stab wounds."

"Something about her triggered our UNSUB more than the first two," Millie spoke up, not taking her eyes off the young mother. Two little girls are motherless because of this asshole.

Trevor clicked through to the final picture. She was a little older than Laura, but not by much. Her dark brown hair was pulled up into a ponytail to show off her undercut. She had a crooked smile and an expression that dared you to mess with her. Unfortunately, someone tried and succeeded.

"Victim number four," Thomas's voice was becoming raspier. He had confided in her once this was his least favorite part of the job. "Sarah Bigelow, forty. Married with one child, middle school age. She disappeared exactly two weeks after Laura and was discovered the next day at the same park as victim number one. Same MO. Defensive wounds and multiple stab wounds. Less brutalized than victim three, but more than the first two."

"How long ago since they found our last victim?" Millie was already running calculations through her head.

"Five days ago," Thomas answered.

The room erupted in indignation. Everyone talking over one another.

Trevor's voice rose above all of them. "Why did they wait so long to call us in?"

Thomas shook his head. "Hubris. They thought they could solve this on their own. They didn't want us feds stomping all over their territory."

"They realize we work with them so they can do the arresting, right?" Logan spoke up.

Thomas shrugged. "Who the fuck knows?"

"They have wasted nearly half of our cooling-off period to catch the fucker," Logan nearly growled.

"I know," was all Thomas said.

"The UNSUB certainly didn't make this easy. He dumped the bodies all over the fucking city," Matthew pointed out.

"But our victims all have the same demographics. They're all women around the same age who are all married and are mothers," Millie pointed out. "That's a really solid start."

"It is," Thomas said. "And we will have a chance to dig deeper into victimology and start working on a profile when we are on the plane. Trevor is sending you the files on the victims. You can study in flight. Wheels up in fifteen."

As everyone gathered their stuff and began filing out of the room, Millie pulled up the victim files and opened up the file on victim number three, Laura. She opened up the photo Trevor had shown earlier, the one where she was laughing at whatever she saw behind the camera.

Something about Laura called to her. Maybe it was that she was so young, or that she had such young children. But she knew this would be the victim she would make sure she followed through victimology with. She wanted to talk to her family and learn about the life she led.

She wanted to give this woman a voice and bring her justice.

Chapter Two

TREVOR

October 5

Trevor stretched his arms above his head and checked his watch. They had been in the air for almost two and a half hours. They still had two hours to go. He had fallen asleep almost instantly once the plane was in the sky.

Thomas's phone call telling him they had a case and needed to get to the office woke him up at the wrong part of his sleep cycle, and he had been dragging ever since.

He glanced over at Millie, who had taken the seat facing him. They always sat in the same seats on the plane. It had been their tradition for the last decade whenever he would come out with them, which was becoming more and more often.

His job was supposed to be all things technology related, especially relying on his hacker skills. However, he had done so well at Quantico in his profiling training, they also brought him out with him into the field occasionally. Which he didn't mind. Being left behind was beginning to feel more and more like he was being left out. He had a lot of FOMO when he was stuck in his room of screens.

Plus, he got to spend more time with Millie.

She was sound asleep in her seat, her head tilted back, her face toward the ceiling of the plane, her mouth open slightly as she was breathing heavily. Her long black hair draped over one shoulder.

Trevor was glad she could get some sleep. He knew she hadn't been sleeping well, and he was certain it was worse than she was letting on.

Trevor was trying to be supportive of Millie's problems following what happened in Cove Creek, however, he couldn't relate. He'd never had to discharge his weapon in the line of duty, let alone killed someone. That was a perk of his job, at least. Being behind a computer screen left very little opportunity to find yourself in the line of danger.

Trevor reached over and pulled his tablet onto his lap. He needed to get some files updated and ready to push to the rest of the team before they landed.

The local law enforcement was being very helpful, which was nice, considering they seemed to be very hesitant to call his team in.

Waiting for four victims before calling the FBI was pretty bad. A lot of the time they got called in after a second victim with the same MO was discovered within a short period. The Cove Creek police had waited for three, but the cooling-down period was much longer, and there wasn't a tremendous sense of urgency until the window started closing.

Calico Rock's victims were being killed at a predictable pace in a very short time frame. This UNSUB showed no signs of slowing down.

The level of fear the women of that city must be feeling right now had to be off the charts.

And for the local law enforcement to waste nearly half of the cooling down period was incredibly frustrating, and irresponsible.

But Trevor would try to let that go. The local police were helping now. They had sent over everything they had on the four cases.

The files were a mess. Nothing was organized. The files were all in different formats, and with different shorthand being used.

They had assigned a different fucking detective to each of the victims to, as they put it, "lighten the load."

No wonder they hadn't caught this asshole yet. Merely skimming the files showed they were not talking to each other. Facts that should have been concrete were being presented as new in each file. No one had drawn any conclusions regarding victimology.

Fuck, Millie had drawn the similarities of the victims out within five minutes of knowing the case. If they had all been working together, they might have been able to find something, anything, by now.

Trevor opened the first of three runs of the DNA found under the victims' fingernails. The good news was, all four victims had the same DNA under their nails. The bad news was they couldn't find a match in any of the systems. The DNA was male, which was a good lead, but not unexpected. The violence in the killings definitely led to the UNSUB being a man. Unfortunately, he was a man with a clean record. And one who never did any of those mail-in genealogy tests. Which was unfortunate. If he had bought into the trends, their lives would be so much easier. None of his close relatives had even taken any of the tests. It was quite frustrating.

They also knew he was white. Which in New Mexico would narrow it down, but not a lot. When he saw the UNSUB was white, he definitely breathed a sigh of relief. As a Latino man, he dreaded the idea of looking for a serial killer who was also Latino.

Especially after their last case ended up with a middle-aged Latino as the serial killer. Which he had not seen coming.

Trevor was usually pretty good at following the facts and figuring out who the UNSUB was. Hell, they all were. However, the case in Cove Creek threw them all for a loop. They followed one too many red herrings, and two more victims ended up getting killed right under their noses.

They were going to do better this time.

They had to.

They had nine days to catch the asshole before he killed another woman.

It was imperative.

Millie stirred across from him, getting comfortable.

Trevor smiled to himself. One thing he admired about Millie was her ability to sleep anywhere. It was one of her special talents. When they were at Quantico together, they would stay up late studying, and somewhere, in the middle of the night, he would look over and Millie would be fast asleep on the uncomfortable wooden chairs with her head on the table at the library.

The memory made him smile. Her jet-black hair was such a contrast to the light wood of the table.

He was pretty sure it was one of those late-night study sessions that made him fall in love with her in the first place.

Not that anything ever came of it.

Trevor had asked her out once, somewhere near the beginning of week six at the academy.

She turned him down.

It was fine. They spent the last twelve weeks of the Academy getting closer. Trevor felt like he had won the lottery when they were both able to move into the BAU. He had never been happier. Joining with his best friend made the whole thing less intimidating.

The only downside was that he started out being stuck in the computer room, only occasionally spending time with the rest of the team. It took a while to bond with everyone, but Millie always included him when the team went out for drinks.

Millie let out a loud snort and startled herself awake. She looked across at him and smiled. "How long was I out?"

"Couple hours."

"How long until we land?"

"Couple hours."

Millie laughed, and Trevor's chest warmed. He knew if she was laughing, she was going to be okay. "Halfway there."

"Long flights are the worst."

"At least flying private, we don't have layovers."

"Major perk of this job, for sure."

"So glad Thomas fought for our jet during the last budget meeting."

"Love that for us."

Trevor laughed, shaking his head.

"What are you looking at?" Millie gestured to his tablet.

"The files the police sent us."

"Anything useful?"

Trevor shrugged. "Not sure yet. They decided to work efficiently and split the work between four detectives. Each one investigated a different victim."

"Fuck's sake." Millie groaned. "So, we have to wade through a mountain of shit to find anything useful."

"Exactly."

She rubbed her face. "Please tell me they at least drew conclusions between the victims."

Trevor gave her a pointed look. "What do you think?"

"I think we have nine days before this asshole kills again, and they have made our job infinitely more difficult."

"Glad to see we made it to the same conclusion."

"I can already feel the migraine coming."

Trevor reached across the aisle and placed a comforting hand on her leg. "We'll get through this, and we will catch the guy."

Millie gave him a weak smile. "I can't help thinking about the last serial we worked. We fucked that investigation up so badly, two more men died right under us. I don't think I can take it if that happens again."

"This case is completely different from that one. Cove Creek's killer didn't have a set timeline. He killed on a whim. We never knew when he would kill again, and he switched up his time frame as soon as we got into town, lining up more with a spree killer than a serial. Calico Rock's killer is textbook serial. He has a pattern, and he is following it. We know that we have nine days until he abducts and kills another woman. And we won't squander those days."

"What if he panics when we get there and he goes off script?"

Trevor squeezed her knee. "Look at me."

Millie looked at him. Dark circles stood out sharply against her porcelain skin. Yeah, she was definitely holding back about how bad her sleep has been lately. Trevor wanted to pull her into his arms and tell her she was going to be okay. Instead, he met her gaze and talked to her in a firm, yet gentle, voice.

"He won't. I can already tell he is compulsive and won't stray. His MO has been consistent across four murders, with only slight variations. The man is compelled to kill, and once we figure out what his trigger is, we will catch him."

"You sound so confident."

"That's because I am. You should be, too. We're one of the best teams around. We are fucking good at our job. We've got this."

Millie held his gaze a little longer. Trevor could almost see the gears working in her head, trying to figure out if she believed him. He wouldn't blame her if she didn't. He wasn't entirely certain he believed himself.

Finally, Millie broke his gaze with a sigh. "You're right. There is no point in catastrophizing at this point. We haven't even landed yet."

Trevor broke into a wide smile. "That's the spirit. You could make a connection between the victims with only the initial report. I'm going to count that as a good sign."

Millie nodded. "Good first step. We're going to need to work quickly to build a profile if we're going to catch him in time."

"One step at a time. I'll forward you some of the police files. You can help me go through them and see if you can catch anything."

Millie gave him a smile that lit up her entire face, which Trevor thought made her look absolutely beautiful. "That would be great."

Trevor sent her the files, and they sat in their respective chairs and began sorting through everything, hoping to connect some lines. All the while, Trevor couldn't help sneaking glances at Millie, making sure she was doing okay.

Trevor and Millie made their way to the aquatic center, where victim number three, Laura, had been found.

After they had landed in Calico Rock, the team had checked into their hotel. While it wasn't super run down, it wasn't as nice as the bed-and-breakfast they had stayed at in Iowa. The motel was a retro-looking L-shaped building with the doors exposed to the outdoor courtyard. The owner had tried to make it look like it was straight out of the nineteen fifties, trying to cash in on nostalgia chasing tourists traveling down Route 66. Millie and Trevor's rooms were right next door to each other, and when Trevor went into his, he rolled his eyes at the dated decor.

They didn't stay long in their rooms, instead heading straight to the local PD, via a stop to get snacks at a gas station.

Trevor knew what he wanted and made a beeline for the soft drinks to grab something diet with caffeine. After making his selection, he made his way to the counter to check out when he caught Millie out of the corner of his eye. She was talking with a man who had his back toward him. He had hair pulled back in a ponytail, and grungy looking clothes.

Millie was facing him, and he could tell she was trying to brush off the man and his intentions. This happened quite often when they were out. Millie was a beautiful woman, and men often tried to flirt with her. And just like all the other times, he watched as Millie shook her head, and pushed past the man to make her own purchases.

"You good?" Trevor asked as she approached the register.

"Yeah. I'm fine. Nothing I haven't dealt with before."

After buying their snacks, they made their way back to the cars and finished the trek to the police station.

There, they found the conference room and the four detectives working the case, ready and waiting for them.

They were currently in the car with the detective who had worked on Laura's case, Detective Bill Jacobs. "Who discovered the body?" Trevor asked as they pulled to a stop next to the drop location.

"A man out on his morning jog. The Center had already closed for the season, so there was no one coming to open it. The jogger said he was coming up over the incline to the west over there and saw her lying on the ground." Detective Jacobs pointed out the windshield toward the west, where the road descended slightly.

"Can you show us where she was found?" Millie was sitting in the passenger seat of the car, her sunglasses pulled down over her eyes, shielding her from the harsh New Mexican sun.

"Absolutely." Detective Jacobs turned off the engine of his SUV and undid his seatbelt.

Trevor and Millie followed suit, and all three stepped out of the car into the warmer than expected day. Google said light jacket, but they must have been going through summer's last gasp as it was currently about eighty degrees. Trevor was regretting the long sleeve dress shirt under his suit jacket.

"He found her over here." Detective Jacobs led them over to the entrance of the aquatic center. There was a little counter and a turnstile on either side of it, which allowed entrance into the aquatic park. "She was propped up against the counter, kind of slouched against it, right here."

Trevor and Millie came to a stop in front of the counter. He looked back in the direction the jogger was coming from and frowned.

"You said the jogger spotted the body when he crested that hill there?" Trevor pointed back in the direction Detective Jacobs had indicated before.

"That is correct."

"Millie, can you sit against the ticket counter for a second? I want to see something."

God bless Millie. She didn't even question him. She just dropped to the ground and pushed herself against the counter. She even slouched a little. Trevor turned and jogged over to where the hill just began to crest and turned back around.

"I can't see you."

"What?" Millie shouted back.

Trevor jogged back to Millie and Detective Jacobs. "I couldn't see you from there. You're too far in. The sides of the building sort of block you. The jogger would have had to have been almost right on top of the victim before he saw her. Even then, he would have had to be glancing that way."

Millie frowned. "So, the jogger lied?"

Trevor shrugged. "Maybe? I don't know. It seems like an odd thing to lie about, really. What was the jogger's name? We're going to want to follow up with him."

Detective Jacobs pulled out his phone and scrolled for a second. "Huh. That's weird."

"What's weird?"

"I wasn't first on the scene when the body was called in. Third dead woman in six weeks, you know? Rushed out here. There were two other officers on the scene, and I know they took the guy's name and put it in the file. He was gone by the time I arrived. But now all of his information is gone."

Trevor frowned. "Gone?"

"Deleted, I guess. I can't find it."

Trevor and Millie exchanged a look. This was the opposite of a cut and dry case.

"Can you get it back?" Millie asked.

Trevor shrugged. "I mean, maybe? The odds are I can. It will take a little work, but nothing too challenging."

"Guess we know what the first thing you'll be working on when we get to the precinct again," Millie said.

Trevor shook his head. "What's really bothering me is the fact that the jogger lied about how he discovered the body and then someone went through the process of deleting his information from the file."

Millie frowned. "Yeah, talk about a big ol' red flag. We need to get his name back so we can question him about it. He could be a suspect."

Trevor nodded. "I agree."

"Is everything okay here?"

A man approached the trio from the opposite direction the supposed jogger had arrived. He was wearing a well-loved Metallica T-shirt and a pair of cargo shorts. His dark brown hair fell to his shoulders and was parted to one side. He wore a beard that was shaved close to his face, and it looked like he had applied black eyeliner around his eyes. He looked vaguely familiar, but Trevor couldn't quite place where he had seen him before.

"Everything is fine, sir," Detective Jacobs replied, flashing his badge. "You can continue on your way."

The man ignored the detective and set his gaze on Millie. "Isn't this where the body was found a few weeks ago?"

Millie cocked her head to the side, narrowing her eyes at the man. "Wait. You're the man who was hitting on me at the gas station an hour ago. What the fuck are you doing here? Are you stalking me?"

The man laughed a little, shaking his head. "No, no. I'm not some creep. I live just over there, and I noticed the car stopped in front of here. The aquatic center is closed for the season, so I decided I'd better check it out. I didn't know you were the cops."

Millie reached into her pocket and pulled out her badge. "Special Agent Driscoll with the Behavioral Analysis Unit with the FBI, and this is Agent Ford. What can you tell me about the day they found the body?"

The man shrugged. "I don't know. I wasn't around. I was already at work when they found her."

"Where do you work?" Trevor asked.

"Construction. Right now, we're doing a job on the west side of town. New bank going up. I'm there before the sun even wakes up."

"Why aren't you there now?" Millie interrogated.

"Day off." The man did not once take his gaze off of Millie. It was beginning to unsettle Trevor. There was something about him that made Trevor uncomfortable, and it wasn't just how he fixated on Millie, but he couldn't put his finger on it. But he was sure it had something to do with the fact they had already run into this man once before.

"Did you notice anything suspicious about the area when you were leaving for work? A car driving suspiciously fast or slow? Someone parked outside the aquatic center?" Millie was not wasting this man's rapt attention on her. Trevor was proud.

The man shook his head. "No, like I said, I'm working on a job on the west side of town. I didn't even drive this way. I'm sorry I can't be much more help."

Millie reached into the pocket of her suit jacket and pulled out a card, handing it over to the man. "Here's my card. Call me if you think of anything."

The man took the card, glanced down at it, and slipped it into the pocket of his cargo shorts. He lifted his gaze back to Millie's and gave her a crooked smile. "Will do."

"And for the record, what is your name?" Millie asked.

"Sebastian. Sebastian Sable."

"Thank you, Mr. Sable." Millie's tone was dismissive.

Trevor tried to hide the smile that was trying to sneak in. She was pretty hot when she shut shit down. It was probably one of his favorite qualities she had.

"You're welcome, Special Agent Driscoll. I will definitely contact you if I remember anything." His tone bordered on smarmy, and he ended his statement with a wink.

Not waiting for a response, Sebastian turned around and began walking down the sidewalk in the direction he had come from. He made it about ten feet before he turned around again and shot Millie a wide smile.

Trevor looked over at Millie and frowned. Her cheeks were turning a little pink, and she was ducking her gaze away.

Trevor swung his gaze back toward the retreating back of Sebastian.

Fuck.

Chapter Three

MILLIE

October 5

Millie laid her head down on the table in front of her in defeat. They had been going over the evidence for about five hours now, and nothing was going as easily as they had hoped. In fact, the only good thing that came out of the morning was meeting that man, Sebastian. But that was more of a personal thing than having to do with the case. He was quite easy on the eyes, though maybe slightly on the young side.

As he was talking to them, she couldn't help but briefly fantasize that maybe this was her chance to meet her Rebecca. It couldn't have *just* been a coincidence that she had seen him twice in one morning. It had to be some sort of fate.

Or he was stalking her, which she had to admit, could be likely. As much as Rebecca and Matthew talked about divine intervention leading to their being together, that wasn't something Millie subscribed to.

Once he left, and they went back to investigating the crime scene, Millie was able to put him out of her mind.

She was focused on the case, which really should have been easier than it was. She thought that because she could easily connect the dots between the victims, they would waltz in, look at the evidence, and easily build a profile.

Nope.

The jogger lying about spotting the body was the tip of the iceberg when it came to the shitshow this case was turning out to be.

Matthew and Logan came back to the precinct after visiting the site of victims one and four, the park. Matthew was amazing at reading crime scenes, and he had the same niggling feeling Trevor had at the aquatic center. Something was off. And when he and Logan asked the detective they were with for information about the dog walker.

Gone.

Deleted.

Just like the jogger.

What the fuck was going on?

Thomas returned from the supermarket, and that entire story checked out at least. The owner had found the body. He noticed nothing out of the ordinary that morning. While he had cameras in the back alley, something had interfered with the feed sometime around midnight, and they didn't go back on until about five in the morning.

Whoever this UNSUB was, he was tech savvy, to say the least. To disable the cameras at the dump site, to go back into the police records and delete information...

"Careful, don't give yourself a concussion." Matthew's voice came from her right as he dragged the chair next to hers out from under the table and settled himself down.

"Why is this case already giving me a migraine on day one?"

"Because we would be out of our jobs if it were easy."

Millie raised her head off the table and looked at Matthew. "So, we agree the jogger and the dog walker have to be the same person, right?"

Matthew let out a long stream of air. "I mean, yeah. They have to be. And different people arrived at both the calls…"

"They wouldn't have been able to make the connection that the man was exactly the same."

"So obviously same man, two different names?"

Millie shrugged. "That's what I would say. If he's smart enough to fuck with the technology, he wouldn't be dumb enough to give the same name."

"Different detectives worked the different victims." Matthew pointed out.

"But he couldn't have known that was what was going to happen."

"But maybe he did?" Logan spoke up from across the table.

"What?" Millie asked.

"Maybe he did. He's obviously able to get into the police records and change them, so why would it be any stretch of the imagination to think he had some sort of tap into the precinct? He would be able to see what everyone was planning. By victim three, it might have looked obvious they were assigning different detectives on the cases and took a chance when he dumped the third victim."

"Real name or alias?" Matthew asked.

"Alias, for certain."

"Killers often try to insert themselves into the case. In order to maintain that control. Look at the Zodiac." Millie mulled over the possibility.

"Where did Trevor go?" Matthew asked.

"He and Thomas are setting up a computer room with someone from the precinct. He has a lot of digging to do to find where our UNSUB is breaching the records, and a tablet isn't going to cut it," Millie explained.

The ringing of her phone cut through the room. She looked down at it and frowned. Unknown number. She pushed the button and held the phone up to her ear.

"Hello?"

"Special Agent Driscoll?"

"Yes?"

"This is, um, Sebastian. Sable. From earlier?"

The man from the aquatic center, and the gas station Millie's heart picked up a little. Act. Cool. "Oh yes. Hi. Can I help you?"

"So, I think I remembered something about that morning."

Millie sat up straighter in her chair. "You do?"

"Yeah. I was at home, and it hit me. And I had to call you right away."

"Well, what was it you remembered?"

"Can you meet me for dinner?"

Millie's heart sped up, and butterflies erupted in her belly. Was he asking her out on a date? Surely, she was mishearing him. "Excuse me?"

"Well, I think it's better if I tell you in person."

"I don't know..."

"C'mon. You have to eat, right? And you have to admit that we had a connection earlier. Right? You had to have felt it, too."

Millie's face warmed. She had felt it. When his gaze met hers after she gave him her card. His smirk. There was definitely something there.

Apparently, she had a thing for guys with long hair and eyeliner. Who knew?

But he was a stranger. And she knew absolutely *nothing* about him. There was a serial killer at large, and he was definitely in the demographic...

"Okay." Millie wasn't sure where that came from. She apparently *really* had a thing for guys with eyeliner.

"Really?"

"Yeah." She was more confident in her answer.

"Sweet. That was easier than I thought it was going to be. I spent about an hour getting up the courage to call you and ask you out."

You're not the only one surprised how easy it was to get me to agree to meet you, Millie thought.

"I thought you said you had something to tell me about the case?" She said instead.

Sebastian chuckled. "Yeah, that was sort of my in. Are you going to back out on me? Now that you know the truth?"

Millie smiled. "No. Just tell me where to meet you."

"There's a little Mexican restaurant downtown. El Mariachi's. Meet me there in ten?"

"I'll be there."

She hung up the phone and looked up to see the two men at her table staring at her.

"And...who was that?" Matthew asked, a shit-eating grin spread across his face.

"Nobody." Millie kept her tone terse, nonchalant.

They didn't buy it.

"It didn't sound like nobody," Logan hedged.

"Nope. It was nobody. Wrong number." She gathered her stuff together and formed it into a pile, and placed it in the middle of the table. "I'm just going to, um, go ahead and leave. Get some dinner. Unless you need me here?"

"Go, take your dinner." Matthew dismissed her with a wave of his hand.

"Thanks. I'll only be gone an hour."

Logan smirked. "We wouldn't tell if you were gone longer." And then he had the absolute gall to fucking wink at her.

Wink at her!

"I'm going. Tell the rest I'm at dinner. I'll be back in an hour."

She didn't even wait for a reply before leaving the room. She could hear the snickers of Matthew and Logan as the door closed behind her.

Let them laugh.

She had a date with a sexy man with guyliner to look forward to.

Millie pulled up to the restaurant, El Mariachi, with a few minutes to spare.

She took the time to compose herself. She was still wearing her work clothes, the same ones she had traveled in, and she was running on fumes. What was she thinking agreeing to meet with a man in this state?

She knew what she was thinking. She was thinking that the man was kind of hot in a goth sort of way. She could tell through that worn Metallica shirt he was ripped, and the long dark hair and the eyeliner only added to the attractiveness.

And it didn't seem like he knew anything about the case. Which a little voice in the back of her head told her was problematic, but she told that voice to shut up. So what if he lied to get her to dinner? Not having any evidence to add to the case simplified things. He was just a local man.

Just like Rebecca was just a local woman and look at how that turned out for Matthew.

The little voice in the back of her head really was a bitch.

Millie shook her head. No. This was just a fucking sexy man...who just happened to live near the dump site of one of the bodies. And was maybe, sort of, following her.

Millie closed her eyes. This was a bad idea. A really, really bad idea.

Just as she was about to change her mind and drive away, she opened her eyes and saw him walking in. Sebastian.

Fuck. His name was even sexy.

Sebastian had changed out of his worn-out t-shirt and cargo shorts and was now wearing form-fitting black jeans and a charcoal gray button-down. He had pulled his hair back into a ponytail, and he had reapplied his eyeliner. She pulled out her phone and snapped a discrete photo of him and sent it to Rebecca.

Millie - It's totally a bad idea that I'm going to walk into a restaurant to meet this man not even twenty-four hours after landing here, correct?

Becks - Fuck. He's like something out of those vampire romance novels I read.

Millie - Tell me to drive back to the police department and work on this case.

Becks - Go inside the restaurant and wrap yourself around him like a baby koala.

Millie - You're no help.

*Becks - *gif of a koala wrapped around a person's leg as they tried to walk**

Millie looked back up at where Sebastian was standing in front of the restaurant, waiting for her, and she made the decision.

Millie - I'm going in.

Becks - I love this for you. Text me when you get back to the precinct so I know you weren't murdered.

Millie - You do know I'm here on a case about a serial killer who kills women my age, right?

Becks - I said what I said. *kissing face*

Millie rolled her eyes before tucking her phone away.

She was going to do this.

She was.

She really, really was.

She tucked her phone into her pocket and got out of the car. Walking over to Sebastian, she plastered on a smile, even though she was still debating whether or not this was a good idea.

"I'm sorry. I didn't have a chance to change before meeting you." Millie cringed. *What the hell was that?*

Sebastian looked toward her and flashed her a smile that made her weak in the knees. "It's fine. I didn't expect you to. I gave you what? Ten minutes? You're obviously here working. I didn't think you would run back to wherever you're staying to change."

"You changed." Millie pointed at his new outfit.

"Well, yeah, I had to impress a really attractive woman. First impressions count, you know."

"We've already met today, remember? Twice. That was technically your first *and* second impressions."

Sebastian flashed her a crooked smile. "Well, those first two impressions must have been fantastic if they got you to agree to come out with me." He gave her a wink, but didn't give her a chance to respond. "C'mon. They have the best queso."

He held out his arm as if he were right out of the Regency era. Millie couldn't stop the blush rising on her cheeks. But of course, she slipped her arm through his, because she was a woman who had had fantasies like this.

Sebastian led them into the restaurant, and they were seated almost immediately. She looked around the small restaurant and smiled. She loved places like this. Locally owned restaurants full of local charm. And authentic food. Millie hadn't even realized she was hungry until the scent of warm tortillas and savory meats filled her nostrils.

This one was a little bit of a hole in the wall. Dim lights and low mariachi music set the atmosphere. Sombreros hung from the walls, and ceramic cactus statues littered the surfaces. All of it screamed kitschy, and she loved it.

Settled into their seats, Millie picked up her menu. "What's good here?"

"The queso. You should get a burrito and have it smothered in the stuff. It's literally the best thing I've ever eaten."

Millie smiled. "Noted. Choice made."

Sebastian flashed her what she had begun to consider his signature crooked smile. It just barely cleared the category of smirk. "Easily influenced? I don't know if I should be flattered or worried you're one of those women who doesn't hold any opinions of their own."

"Not easily influenced. More like exhausted because I've been up since three in the morning, East Coast time, and have been going ever since. Sometimes it's nice not to have to make choices for myself."

Sebastian nodded. "I can respect that. Sometimes I wish I didn't have to make all the decisions." He leaned forward, resting his forearms on the table in front of him. "When faced with a really tough decision, do you ever look around for an adult, and then realize, shit, I'm the adult?"

Millie laughed. "All the time. I'm thirty-eight years old, and sometimes I find myself calling my mother before I make key life decisions."

"I wonder if you ever grow out of never feeling quite grown-up enough. Like, when I'm eighty, will I still be looking around wondering where the adultier adult is?"

"That's a really interesting question. I'll have to call my grandmother and ask her. She's nearly ninety, and now I'm wondering if she's ever like, 'Where is the person who is older than me? Fuck. They're all dead.'"

Sebastian let out an uproariously loud laugh, and pride rose in her chest. She had never gotten a reaction like this from someone she was on a date with. Was this date a success? Was Millisecond Millie no more?

Sebastian sat back in his seat and folded his arms across his chest. "You're hilarious. I was honestly worried all day about asking you out. I Googled what the BAU was, and when I learned it was basically full of people who can psychoanalyze you, I thought you might be uptight and boring."

"Fuck. You really tell it like it is, don't you?"

"I pride myself on being open and honest, even if it hurts people's feelings."

Millie frowned. "You're not one of those 'Fuck Your Feelings' assholes, are you? Because if you are..."

"No. No, definitely not one of those, but I won't mince words. I learned growing up that life is hard and brutal, and I don't have time to sugarcoat shit in case it hurts their feelings. So, yes. I asked you out, taking the calculated risk that you would be boring as hell, and have a stick up your ass. I'm glad to see that I was wrong."

It was Millie's turn to lean across the table and rest on her forearms. "And you're not worried that I'm going to read all of your thoughts from your face, and completely figure out who you are as a person without you having to tell me much more than a few key details?"

Sebastian leaned forward, his head mere inches from hers. She could feel his breath on her cheek. "Honestly? I find it incredibly hot. Does that talent transfer to the bedroom?"

Her cheeks burned. And places in her body that had been long dormant tingled. She twisted her mouth into a smirk of her own. "Wouldn't you like to know?"

Sebastian let out a small laugh. The warm, vaguely minty, air expelled from him ghosted across her face. "I'll just have to play my cards right, won't I?"

Millie drew her lip between her teeth before leaning back with a shrug. "Maybe. Just know I don't sleep with a man on the first date."

Sebastian leaned back, mirroring her posture. "Noted. We'll just have to make sure we have a second date, then. What are you doing for dinner tomorrow?"

Millie laughed. "This date isn't even over yet, and you're already asking me out for a second date? What if by the end of this one you decide you no longer want to be with me?"

"Consider me an optimist."

They were interrupted by the waitress arriving to take their orders.

They filled the silence waiting for their food with small talk about their days. His was pretty mundane, and she couldn't disclose any details of hers.

When their food came, she had to admit he was right. Ordering a burrito smothered in the queso was the best choice. It was amazing.

"How long have you lived in Calico Rock?" Millie asked about halfway through their meal.

"All my life," Sebastian answered. "Grew up here, started working construction out of high school. I take jobs in the neighboring cities, but we're currently having a bit of a population boom, so there's been no shortage of new builds popping up around the city for me to work on."

Millie nodded. "That sounds like a nice, stable life."

"It is."

"Are your parents still around?"

Sebastian shook his head. "My dad was never in the picture, and my mom passed earlier this year. Breast cancer."

"I'm sorry."

"It's okay. I was there with her until the end. I got the closure I needed."

Millie's heart ached for him.

"What about you?" he asked, shifting gears. "Have you always lived in DC?"

Millie shook her head. "No. I'm from California. Moved to DC for the Academy."

"Are your parents still out there?"

"Yeah, and my brother and sister, and their families."

"That must be hard, being so far away from them."

"It is. But I get out there a lot to visit. A few times a year. I'm the favorite aunt. I bring all the fun. And the presents. Can't forget the presents."

"Oh, you can never forget the presents."

"Do have any nieces or nephews?"

"Only child. But I have friends who have kids. So, I'm like the favorite faux uncle."

Millie smiled. "I love that."

The rest of the meal went quickly, filled with small talk. At the end, when the check was delivered to their table, he paid it. She thanked him graciously. When it was time to leave, he stood up and pulled out her chair for her.

"Thank you for the meal." They were outside the restaurant, facing each other.

"It was my pleasure. Text me when you're free tomorrow, and we'll do it again. Date number two." He waggled his eyebrows suggestively, which made her laugh.

"Okay. I'll do that."

Without hesitating for a second, he leaned forward, capturing her mouth with his. Caught off guard, Millie didn't return the kiss. She stood there, shocked. She barely knew this guy, and he was kissing her. She had been on lots of first dates. *Lots* of first dates, and none of them ended with a guy so fucking confident that they kissed her. Millie liked Sebastian, but this was a lot.

Seemingly unfazed by her lack of response, Sebastian pulled back from the kiss, but kept her close to his body. She could feel that their non-kiss had sort of excited him, and she was both proud she had that effect, and a little weirded out.

He brought his mouth to her ear and whispered, "I'm looking forward to our next date."

Millie had to admit that was actually kind of hot. She had never felt so wanted in a very long time. Now, she probably wouldn't turn down a kiss from him.

Instead, he gave her a salacious wink before walking back to his car. Leaving her there in front of the restaurant hot, bothered and wishing like hell she had taken part in that kiss earlier, because that's all she wanted to do now.

Chapter Four

TREVOR

October 5

Trevor leaned back in the very uncomfortable chair the rookie who helped him set up the room, Officer Jones, gave him to sit in while at the precinct. He really missed his ergonomic chair back at the Bureau. At thirty-eight, he really needed the lumbar support, not whatever this was. It was the opposite of back support. Back torture?

Rubbing his hands down his face, he closed his eyes to give them a break. Ever since returning from the crime scene earlier, he had been in this makeshift command center, staring at multiple screens as he ran endless searches and programs designed to trace phone numbers.

It was a good thing he was great at multitasking.

If he ran things one at a time, they would waste valuable time. The countdown was ticking.

Literally.

He and Thomas took the time to set up a literal countdown clock. They knew, down to the second, how much time they had before the next victim would be taken.

Trevor didn't know if it was helpful or harmful, but he knew it was what they needed to light a fire under their asses and not take their sweet time with things. They weren't in a hurry during the last case, and look where it led them.

Glancing at the programs running, he realized he still had a long way to go, so he decided now would be a good time to get up, stretch his legs, and maybe grab a bite to eat.

He sent a text to Officer Jones, who must not have been very far away. The door to the room opened up less than a minute after he sent the text.

"What's up?"

Trevor gestured at all the stuff in the room. "Can you just sit in here and make sure no one touches anything? I'm going to find some food."

"Yeah, no problem. If you wanted, I could pick some food up for you, that way you don't have to leave the room. My captain said it's my job to make sure you all are comfortable."

Trevor shook his head. "Nah. I need to stretch my legs. But thanks. I'll keep that in mind for next time."

"So, I just, sit in here?"

"Yes. Don't touch anything. Don't let anyone else touch anything. The programs are automated, and they know what to do."

Officer Jones gave Trevor a mock salute. "Aye aye captain."

Trevor rolled his eyes and looked at the screens one more time to make sure they were going to be doing what they should be doing, opened the door to what he was pretty sure was a larger than average closet and walked toward the main conference room.

Inside, Thomas, Logan and Matthew were working away dutifully on the case. Missing was Millie.

"Hey," he greeted.

"Hey," Thomas answered. "Any progress?"

"Not yet. I've got stuff running. But it should be soon. I needed to take a break. My eyes were starting to strain, and my back was protesting against the fucking chair. Plus, I'm starving."

"We were just about to order in some pizza. Want in on it?" Logan asked.

"Sure! Pizza sounds amazing right now. I can't even remember if I ate lunch today."

"Pretty sure none of us ate lunch today," Matthew said.

"Where's Millie?" Trevor asked.

Logan and Matthew shared a look, grinning.

"What was that?" Trevor gestured between the two of them.

"What?" Logan asked, turning back toward Trevor.

"That look you two just shared."

"For fuck's sake, you two, just put him out of his misery and tell him." Thomas sounded exhausted and as if he was in no mood for their antics.

"She's on a date," Matthew answered.

Trevor frowned. "A date? With who? We've only been in town for a handful of hours."

All three men shrugged.

"Don't know. She got a phone call, and then she was getting up to go meet him somewhere," Matthew explained.

Trevor's jaw dropped open. He looked at Logan and Matthew as if they had grown an extra head. "Are you guys out of your fucking minds??"

"What?" Logan asked.

"We're here investigating an asshole who is murdering women. And you just let her go off on her own and you didn't bother to get a name or location of where she's going?"

Logan and Matthew at least had the wherewithal to look sheepish.

"She'll be fine," Matthew said. "What are the odds that the man she's meeting is the serial killer?"

"I don't know, man whose fiancée's dad ended up being the serial killer, why don't you come up with those odds for me?" Trevor's voice was harsh and firm, and a little mean, but he couldn't help it.

"Fuck, low blow, asshole," Matthew retorted.

Trevor sighed. "I'm sorry."

"Look, Millie is a very capable woman who has gone through all the same training we have. If the man she's on a date with gives off serial killer vibes, or any bad vibes at all, she'll sense them, and leave," Logan said.

Trevor pulled out his phone and opened it.

"Put that away," Thomas chastised.

"What?"

"I know what you're doing, so stop it. Millie would not appreciate you using your technological voodoo to trace her phone and spy on her. Trust. Her."

Trevor sighed, but put the phone back in his pocket. "Fine. I'll trust her, but I don't have to like it."

"Good. Let's worry about what's important. What do we want on our pizzas?" Logan pulled out his phone. "There's a local place that delivers, and from the pictures online, the pizzas look amazing."

Since none of them were picky, ordering a pizza didn't take very long, as they all agreed on the same thing. As they waited for the pizza, Trevor lamented the fact that they had relegated him to a closet for this case. Alone.

He knew it was for the best. He would work better and more efficiently from the closet/office that they set up for him. However, it was so isolated, and he would have very few chances to chat with his friends.

"So, what's on the agenda for tomorrow?" Trevor asked.

"Victims' families," Thomas answered.

Trevor felt his chest tighten. Talking to the victims' families was his least favorite thing. Maybe with the tech-heavy element to this case, he could stay behind. Even though he and Millie typically partnered up for things like that, she could always team up with Thomas.

And now he was feeling guilty for wanting to abandon her and the case.

He wasn't,

Trevor just knew where his strength lay. And he also knew which victim Millie had latched onto. The third victim. Laura. He could tell she felt a connection to her. It was probably because they were about the same age. And knowing her connection to that victim, he didn't want to go talk to the family. Talking to a husband who brutally lost his young wife, the mother to their two young children...his heart was aching already.

If Millie asked him to go with her, he would. But otherwise, he was going to hang back and work on tracing the hack.

Thomas's phone chimed, and everyone in the room turned their attention to him.

For the last several months, he had been getting messages from a mystery person taunting him.

At first, the messages had been pretty harmless. Just idle threats and bravado.

And then the mystery texter actually killed someone.

Last month, he sent them a picture of a woman he had killed, Claudia Richmond, aged twenty-one. He had strangled her before stabbing her multiple times post-mortem. At the scene of the crime, he had left a single rhododendron. Later, they had looked up what the rhododendron meant in the language of flowers.

Danger and caution.

The mystery killer, who the press was already naming The Blooming Butcher, was warning them. And they knew this was only the beginning.

As much as they wanted it to be their full-time investigation, the local PD was just using them as a consultation right now, since it was only the one killing. Until he killed again, Thomas's superior told them it was hands off. Just keep tracing communications.

Thomas looked at his phone, and his shoulders immediately relaxed. "It's Carla." Carla was Thomas's estranged wife.

Trevor relaxed, not only glad it wasn't The Blooming Butcher, but glad Carla and Thomas were communicating with each other. He always admired their relationship. When it started falling apart, he wondered if they couldn't make it work, could anyone really?

Matthew's finding Rebecca restored some of his faith in love. But only just a little.

"Who would have thought the sound of the boss's phone would be a fucking trigger?" Logan laughed.

"Certainly not me," Trevor said. "The asshole has been quiet since the body drop. Think he was a one and done?"

Matthew shook his head. "No. That rhododendron was very clearly not only a message but also a signature. Killers don't create a signature unless they're planning to do it again. He taunted Thomas for months before he killed for the first time. It's been a month since his first kill and his last contact. He's due to be getting back in touch soon."

"I wish the fucker would use a stationary number so we could at least lock him down. The first victim was in Connecticut, but who even knows if that's where he lives?" Trevor said.

"My money is on the fact that he's nomadic. He'll kill again, but it will be in another state, but along the same corridor," Logan contributed.

"You're probably right." Trevor ran his hand down his face. He was already exhausted, and they were still going to be working all night. "Tech savvy killers are not working out in my favor."

"Yeah, where are the good old days of people cutting out words from the newspaper and pasting them into letters to send to the newspapers?" Matthew joked.

"Not a good example, Grant. They never caught the Zodiac." Logan pointed out.

"You're right, but still give us an analogue criminal."

"Or, how about a criminal who commits their crime in the view of a security camera?" Trevor added.

"Yes! If only, if only, we could have a case as cut and dry as all of that." Thomas sounded wistful.

"My job would be easier, for sure. Instead, our current UNSUB not only dumped the bodies either out of sight of the cameras or disabled all nearby cameras, he also snatched the women out of sight of the cameras."

"Local man knows where they all are, which makes him able to plan ahead?" Logan leaned back in his chair, crossing his arms across his chest.

"Makes the most sense. Eight weeks, a different victim every two weeks definitely doesn't scream transient." Matthew leaned forward in his seat, taking notes in a notebook as they talked.

The beginnings of building a profile was always a little in flux, but it was always good to keep notes. To keep track of what they were throwing out into the void. Whether any of these things stuck around for the final profile was up in the air. But when it came together, it always felt like magic to Trevor.

"The victims' ages ranged from mid-thirties to early fifties. Are we thinking similar ages for the UNSUB?" Thomas threw out.

Matthew sighed. "This is a tough one. Until we figure out motive, it'll be hard to say."

"What are we thinking in terms of motive?" Trevor leaned forward in his seat. "They found all four women with defensive wounds and DNA under their fingernails. They were not only stabbed to death; they were excessively stabbed to death. Crime of passion?"

"I'm thinking the victims were proxies. They represent something that may have hurt our UNSUB in the past, and they triggered the response. The question is whether he picked the victims at random, or if he planned to kill them all along."

The door to the conference room opened, and Millie walked in. She didn't look at anyone, just walked over to her seat and sat down.

"How was the date?" Logan's voice held a lilt of teasing in it.

Millie had just sat down in her chair and her gaze snapped up to meet Trevor's. Her cheeks grew red as her gaze caught his. She quickly looked away before answering. "It was good, actually. We're going to meet up again tomorrow."

Trevor felt his chest tighten with the revelation. The feelings he kept suppressed in order to maintain his friendship with Millie were threatening to rise to the surface in the form of intense jealousy.

Fuck.

Logan let out a long whistle. "Damn, girl. Working fast."

"Shut the fuck up, Logan," Millie chastised. "Are you giving me shit because I'm a woman?"

"No, I'm giving you shit because you're my friend."

"Yeah, you guys all gave me shit when I started seeing Rebecca," Matthew pointed out.

They did. They were relentless and mean.

But for once, Trevor didn't feel like teasing his friend about her love life.

He took a deep breath and shoved the jealousy back down, far, far down.

"So, who is this guy?" He sounded normal and casual, right? Like a supportive best friend. He totally did. He was selling this. He really was.

"You, um, you've actually met him," Millie said, not even really looking him in the eye.

Trevor cocked his head to the side. "Detective Jacobs? He's like fifty. Didn't think he would be your type."

Millie snapped her gaze up to his, like she was trying to see if he was being serious. When she saw he was, she started laughing. "Oh my god. No, not Detective Jacobs. You're right. He is not my type, and I'm pretty sure he's married."

"Then who? He was the only one..." and then it hit him. "The dude in the Metallica shirt from the crime scene?"

The mood in the room palpably changed.

"What do you mean, the man who was at the crime scene earlier?" Thomas leaned forward.

"He came over to see what we were doing. He lives near the crime scene. Said he was concerned we were vandalizing or breaking in."

No one said anything.

"What?" Millie asked. "He's a local man who works in construction. He is a really nice guy. And technically, I met him at the gas station. He just *happened* to be at the crime scene when I met him a second time."

"What's his name?" Logan asked.

"No."

"What?"

"No, you're not going to background check him. You're going to trust my judgment and move on."

"Millie, we're not going to background check—"

"When Matty started crushing on Rebecca, you said nothing. Nothing. You let him pursue her even though the case revolved around her. And now, I meet a nice local man to have a little bit of fun with. You're all acting like I'm dating the fucking UNSUB. No."

She didn't even wait for a reply. She stood up from the table and stormed out of the room.

Everyone swiveled to Trevor, looking at him expectantly.

He sighed, pushing himself away from the table. "I'll go check on her."

As he walked down the hallway to go look for Millie, he steeled himself to give her the pep talk that he didn't necessarily want to give.

Chapter Five

SEBASTIAN

October 5

Sebastian stepped out of the shower, feeling very satisfied. He made good on his promise to Millie after they finished dinner.

Wrapping the towel around his waist, he walked back into his bedroom and jumped up on the bed. Leaning against the headboard, he crossed his legs at the ankles and grabbed his phone from the nightstand next to the bed.

Opening the camera app, he posed for a selfie. His long dark hair hung wet around his bare shoulders. He pouted at the camera, snapping the picture. Satisfied, he sent it to Millie with no words. He let the picture speak for itself.

Sebastian exited the messaging app and opened the browser on his phone and typed in behavioral analyst into the search bar.

Lots of websites came up, but he clicked on the link about studying at the academy at Quantico.

Millie was incredibly hot, way out of his league. And in addition to her looks, she had an amazing personality that clicked with his.

Calling this afternoon was a risk he didn't normally take, not lately at least. Using the case as a ruse to talk to her took some of the pressure off asking her out. Honestly, he was shocked she had said yes.

The date tonight had gone well, but now he felt pressure to keep her attention. She was so fucking smart. He was so happy she had agreed to a second date tomorrow. Not only because she had implied she would sleep with him, but also, he couldn't wait to spend more time with her.

Scrolling through the website, he looked for anything that would indicate what sorts of classes someone would have to take to become an FBI agent, specifically a behavioral analyst.

Sadly, Sebastian found the website lacking.

That was okay. He could find other ways to learn.

He wanted to learn everything he could about what she did so he could ask her specific questions about her job.

He had to make sure that he didn't fuck up tomorrow. Everything needed to be perfect.

Sebastian opened the drawer of his nightstand and pulled out the notebook and pen he kept in there. Opening to a blank page, he began to write. Making plans. He would have to make sure he did all the right things, said all the right words.

Everything was riding on this next date. He couldn't screw this up. His track record wasn't great when it came to women. Mostly one-night stands or failed first dates.

Maybe if he planned it out, he wouldn't fumble. He could come off as the type of cool guy Millie typically dated in Washington, DC.

After writing out his plans, he looked back at the page and smiled.

Tomorrow, first thing in the morning, he would start putting these plans in motion, and they would be epic.

Chapter Six

MILLIE

October 5

Millie slammed the door of Trevor's closet/office. Halfway through her storm out, she realized she didn't really have anywhere to storm off to. She decided the easiest and best place would be Trevor's closet. He wasn't in it anyway.

"Whoa!" a voice from over by the desk shouted.

A man in his early twenties, sat in full uniform in Trevor's chair. He had sandy blond hair and blue eyes.

"Who are you?" Millie asked.

"Officer Jones, I helped set up the room. Agent Ford asked me to hang out here while he got some food."

"Oh. I'm sorry. I wasn't expecting anyone to be in here."

Officer Jones winced at her tone before standing. "Since you're here, I'll just, um, I'll take off." Without waiting for a response, he pushed past her and exited the room.

She watched him leave, and once she was alone, really alone, she felt her anger return. She didn't understand why she was so angry about the ribbing her friends were giving her. They did it all the time. They did it to Matthew during the last case, when he met Rebecca. So why did this feel different?

Because you're a woman, and you're constantly having to prove your worth in a man's world, the voice in the back of her head piped up.

And it wasn't wrong. She was the only woman on the team, always had been, and it always felt like she had to work twice as hard as the rest of the members of her team to prove that she could do it. That she could be as good at the job as the rest of them.

It shouldn't be this way. It was the twenty-twenties after all. However, it was the truth. She really should have expected they would treat her differently than her male colleagues in the same situation.

If she were a man and met a woman at a place that was tied to a case, no one would bat an eye.

Case in point: Matthew and Rebecca.

But suddenly, because she was a woman, it was a big deal.

The double standard stung.

Millie's phone pinged. She pulled it out of her pocket and looked at the screen.

Sebastian.

She opened the message and blushed.

It was an impressive picture of him.

Very sexy.

Very bold.

This man was screaming desperate. He was trying *really* hard to impress her, which felt like a red flag, honestly. Or maybe she was overreacting? Was this what happened when a man doesn't run out ten minutes into a date and *wants* to see you again? She was so out of her depth. She needed a second opinion.

So, she forwarded the picture to Rebecca.

Her phone rang.

"Ho-ly shit!" Rebecca's voice came through loud and clear through the phone the second Millie answered it.

"Language. You have little ears."

"No, I don't. He's on the phone with Matty. He can't hear me. Is this the guyliner guy?"

"It is."

"He is hot."

"I know."

"How did the date go?"

Millie smiled. "It went really well. We're having a second date tomorrow."

Rebecca let out a whistle. "Wow."

"What? What was that tone? That sounded strangely like the tone the guys were using earlier."

"Nothing. It's just. Don't you think things are moving quickly?"

"Pot. Kettle."

"Not really. Matty and I didn't go on a date the day we met. And we certainly didn't go on a second immediately after. We moved quickly, but not that quickly."

Millie sighed. "See, now I feel like you're validating all of my feelings. This is weird, right? Him sending me half-naked pictures of himself? Kissing me and pressing his erection against me on the first date?"

"All of that is not weird. Honestly, him calling you and asking you on a date instead of just sending you an unsolicited dick pic is refreshing. Wholesome, even. Everything else is pretty much par for the course if you are dealing with a very forward man."

"I'm so out of my depth here, Becks. And it's been so long, and he's so hot. And I don't think I'm looking for anything serious with this man, but..."

"You're, and he's willing?"

"He's very willing. And look at him. He's hot!"

"I know. I have eyes. If this is all just to let off steam and scratch an itch, I totally get it, and I will stop worrying and lecturing. But I do want you to be careful with your heart. I don't want to judge a book by a cover, but he looks like the type of man who will sleep with you and never call you again. As long as you're both on the same page, you should be fine."

Millie didn't know if she should be hurt by what her friend was saying. "What does that mean?"

"Look, Millie, you wear your heart on your sleeve. You are so kind, and you form attachments easily. I just don't want you to attach yourself to Sebastian only for him to break your heart after you have sex with him."

"Wow. I expected this from the guys, but not from you."

"What?" Rebecca sounded genuinely confused.

"The internalized misogyny. Just because I'm a woman, I can't separate my feelings from sex."

"That isn't what I'm saying." Rebecca sounded hurt, and Millie felt bad about what she had said.

"I'm sorry. The guys were ragging on me for the same things. The fact he showed up at the crime scenes, which I will admit, is also giving me some pause, but he's technically not a suspect or a witness, he just lives nearby and knows nothing about the case. They've worked me up, and I'm taking it out on you, and I'm sorry."

"Look. I am not chastising you for your choices. Fuck a new man every night. I don't care. I just care about your well-being. I know you, Millie. You're very open. And I just don't want to see you get hurt."

Millie sighed. "I know. I know. I'm sorry. If these men would just not be assholes, then everything would be so much easier."

"I'll talk to Matty. Tell him to go easier on you."

"That's okay. You don't need to do that. I'll be fine. I just need to not be so sensitive about the whole thing. I'll put on my big-girl panties, so to speak."

"If you're sure. If you change your mind, let me know and I'll talk to him. That would take at least one person off your back."

"Thanks."

"So...."

"So?"

"Other than him being extremely hot, the date went well?"

Millie smiled. "Yeah. It went well. Conversation came smoothly. He didn't run screaming when he learned what my job was. So, I'll call that a win."

"That's great! I know I gave you a hard time about jumping in and moving quickly, but I'm glad you're going out with him a second time. You don't get many second dates."

"I don't. I guess the men in New Mexico are made a little differently than the ones in DC."

"Yeah, they appreciate a smart, capable woman."

Millie's heart swelled at the compliment. She and Rebecca had only been friends for a short time, but it felt like they had known each other longer. Meeting Rebecca had been good for her. She needed a good friend who wasn't a coworker. Someone outside of the field. Someone she could talk to about things that were not work. It was nice.

"Thank you, Becks. Talking to you has made me feel significantly better."

"You're welcome, Mills."

The door to the closet opened, and Trevor peeked his head in. He visibly relaxed when he caught sight of her. "Oh, thank God, you're in here."

"Hey, Becks?"

"I heard him. I'll let you go. Call me after your date tomorrow."

"I will. Love ya."

"Love ya back."

Millie hung up the phone and gestured for Trevor to come all the way in.

He entered the closet and shut the door behind him, leaning against it. If it were anyone else, she would have felt like he was trapping her inside. But this was Trev. He was just giving her space.

"Rebecca?" he asked.

She nodded. "Yep."

Silence filled the small room, neither one really knowing how to broach the subject that was filling the room. The elephant, so to speak.

"I was worried you had left the building and gone back to the hotel." Trevor's voice was soft, almost too quiet to hear.

"No, I wouldn't do that. I just needed a place to calm down. Somewhere I wouldn't be tempted to throw something at one of your heads."

Trevor smiled. "Maybe we deserved something thrown at our heads."

"You totally did."

Trevor didn't move from the door, and Millie appreciated him giving her space. But she also wanted him to come closer. The space between them almost felt symbolic.

She didn't like it.

Closing the gap between them, she stopped right in front of him. He knew what she wanted. Stepping away from the door, he wrapped his arms around her, pulling her tightly to his chest. She sighed, taking in the rich sandalwood and citrus smell that was just him. She wasn't sure if it was a soap or cologne, but it had been a combination that was distinctly his since they met, that one whiff of him calmed her down and comforted her.

"I'm sorry," he whispered against her head, which was tucked nicely under his chin. "I didn't mean to make you upset earlier. I know you're capable of taking care of yourself. We all know that. It just threw us off a little bit to hear you going out with a man you met at a crime scene."

"I know. Logically, I know you all know I'm capable and can take care of myself. I don't know if I'm just being super sensitive lately about being the only woman on the team because of everything going on in the world, or I don't even know."

"You're allowed to feel however you're feeling. Your feelings are valid. Don't let us trivialize anything. Please tell us when we're being out of line."

"Oh, you know I'll let you all know when you fuck up."

"Yes. And that's what we love most about you."

Millie closed her eyes and focused on the soft beating of his heart and his unique scent, allowing them both to calm and soothe her. She was so lucky they had met during the Academy and that they were working together. Being the only woman on the team would probably be intolerable without him.

Trevor pulled back, and Millie held back the sounds of disappointment that threatened to leave her. He didn't move too far away from her, though. He looked down at her. She was only a few inches shorter than his five foot ten. She met his gaze.

"So, tell the truth. The date?" Trevor's eyes were soft and curious. He genuinely wanted to know.

"Best date I've been on in years."

Trevor's mouth quirked into a half smile. "Really?"

"Really. Get this. He found my job, wait for it, fascinating, and not in a 'I'm just saying that to shut you up' sort of fascinating."

Trevor laughed. "Does he fully understand what a behavioral analyst is? Because I've been on dates with women who just sort of nod along until I accidentally read them, and then they hate it."

"He asked if my superpowers, his words, not mine, transfer to the bedroom."

"Fuck. And that was appealing to him?"

Millie nodded. "Very."

"Don't mind me taking notes. Is that the sort of thing that would be a turn-on or a turnoff to women?"

"Definitely a turn-on."

"Will definitely use that for my next date. Maybe I'll get a second date."

"It's definitely why he got a second date."

Millie could tell the second everything clicked in Trevor's mind.

"Millie Driscoll. Are you going on a second date with Metallica Man because you're horny?"

"So. Horny, Trevor. You know I need a connection with someone before I sleep with them, and you also know I've been having shit luck with the men in DC."

"Millisecond Millie," Trevor muttered with a smirk.

Millie glared at Trevor, but there was no venom in the look. It was playful. "Yeah, Millisecond Millie. If I were a man, that would be a very offensive nickname, you know."

Trevor's laugh was loud and genuine, making the laugh lines next to his eyes stand out. "You're right. But you're not a man, so it's just funny."

"Thanks a lot." Sarcasm dripped thickly from that statement, but Millie was smiling. She felt so much lighter than she had earlier.

This is what she needed.

She loved Rebecca, and they were good friends, but it wasn't like this. She and Trevor had known each other for over a decade. He was her other half. Millie didn't know what she would do without him in her life.

Which is why she rejected him when he asked her out during the Academy.

"Feeling better?" Trevor asked once their humor faded.

"Much, thank you."

"You know we were just giving you shit because we see you as one of the guys, right? We gave the same shit to Matthew. Remember, we even questioned whether he should even date Rebecca because of the case, and how connected to it she was."

Millie sighed. "You're right, and I do remember that, because I gave a lot. But it felt different when you did it to me. Like you were worried I was dating the serial killer, and that I was going to get killed. We can't just suspect everyone we meet. It's not a large city, Trevor."

Trevor scrutinized her, and he looked like he wanted to say something, but he stopped himself. Instead, he just sighed and nodded. "You're right. No more wondering if Metallica Guy is the UNSUB. Can I judge him for the fact that he is in his thirties and still dresses like he's in his teens? Is that acceptable?"

Millie smiled. "Sure. If you have to tease me about something, tease me about that."

"You're going to regret giving me that permission, Driscoll," Trevor teased.

"I regret many things when it comes to you, Ford. I think it comes with the territory."

"But you love me anyway."

"Of course, asshole. Come here." She gestured him forward and opened her arms, which he stepped into immediately, wrapping his arms around her tightly, burying his face in her neck. And there was that smell again. She needed to figure out what he used and buy a bottle to sniff whenever her anxiety was high.

That's weird, Millie, she chastised herself. Those were some real stalkery thoughts coming into her brain. Don't become the people you catch, Driscoll.

They pulled apart and smiled.

"What's the plan for tomorrow?" Millie quickly ducked her head away by turning toward the computer screen set up Trevor had in his closet office.

"Victims' families." Trevor cleared his throat, his voice coming out gruff and gravelly.

Millie nodded, still facing away. "So, you and I will go talk to Victim Number Three's family?"

Millie heard Trevor shift behind her, as if he were moving from foot to foot. "Well, I was thinking maybe you could take Thomas with you and I could stay here and keep running programs to see if we can figure out whether or not we can trace this guy."

"Oh." The disappointment she was feeling reflected sharply in that one word. Millie cringed. She didn't mean to sound so disappointed. She really didn't. But it was a tradition for them to question people together, to build a victimology. Logically, she knew his job was to do the computer tracing stuff, but their team was so small, and he usually did a little bit of everything, especially if the case involved little digital tracing.

However, this one involved all of the computer tracing, and Trevor had his work cut out for him.

"I mean, I guess I could go with you..." Trevor started.

"No, it's fine." Millie spun around to face him, working to mask her disappointment on her face, and knowing that trying to hide your genuine emotions from a Behavioral Analyst was futile, but still she tried. "I know you have a lot of work to do. Like a lot of work. I'll go with Thomas or one of the local PDs. It's not a big deal."

Millie could read the conflict on Trevor's face. He wanted to change his mind and go with her. She could see it. "It's not a big deal. I can set some programs up..."

"No, it's fine. Honestly. Please don't change your plans because of me."

"I know that this will be difficult for you, talking to the vic's husband, learning about the little kids..."

"Yeah, it will be, but I'm a big girl. I can handle it without you holding my hand." The words came out harsher than she intended. Luckily, Trevor knew her well enough to know she didn't mean the tone.

"I know you are," he said gently. "I just want you to be comfortable and to be successful. I don't know if the others clocked it yet or not, but—"

"I am drawn to Laura," Millie finished.

"Yeah."

"Yeah, and I don't know why, but when you put that picture up of her, with her mid-laugh, something spoke to me. I need to catch the bastard who did this to her."

"It's because you are similarly aged to her, and it's the kids."

"I fucking hate it when kids are involved."

"I know."

Millie ran a hand down her face. She was exhausted.

"I think we're going to wrap things up here early tonight, have everyone get some rest and hit the ground running tomorrow." Trevor could always read her.

"But we have a limited window."

"That we will squander if we aren't fully rested and running on all cylinders. We'll sleep tonight and start again tomorrow."

Millie was about to argue again, but her phone notification interrupted them. She pulled her phone out and looked at it, frowning.

"Who is it?"

Millie shook her head. "I don't know."

"What do you mean you don't know?"

"Unknown number."

"Spam?"

Millie shrugged as she unlocked her phone and opened the message. Her frown deepened.

"What is it?" Trevor's voice lost all playfulness. It was all business now.

"Not spam, that's for fucking sure."

"What does it say?"

Millie cleared her throat, trying to rid it of the panic and dread that were rising inside her. "'**Hey there, beautiful. Can't help but notice you're the only female on your team. Who did you have to fuck to get that position? I bet you're feisty. Can't wait to find out when we meet. Tick Tock.'** And then there is a little bomb emoji."

Trevor pushed past her and sat down at one of the computers, pulling up something on the screen. "Read me the number."

Millie read him the number as he quickly typed it in and began a trace.

"Motherfucker!" Trevor yelled, slamming his hands down on the desk in front of him.

"Untraceable?"

"Fucking spoofed the number. Unless the local elementary school is sending you threatening texts."

"How did he even get my number?"

Trevor shook his head. "Easy enough. It's not a secret. All our numbers are out there. He's tech-savvy. We know this. Quick search of our team, figure out your name, find your number. It's cake to someone like this guy who can hack into the police department's files."

Millie stared down at the message on her phone. "Did any of the other victims get messages prior to their disappearances?"

"First, don't lump yourself in with the victims. You are not a victim."

"I think the UNSUB is going to disagree with you about that."

"Second," Trevor continued, ignoring her interruption, "I don't know. It wasn't in any of the reports I've looked at so far, but I haven't looked at all of them thoroughly. Was it in Laura's?"

Millie shook her head. "No, the husband said nothing in his statements about her receiving messages prior to her disappearance."

"What if these women didn't say anything about receiving them? They just ignored it, brushed them off?"

"Or what if the initial message threatened harm to them or others they loved if they told?"

Trevor began typing on the computer again. "We need to get the phone records of all four victims."

Millie never took her eyes off her phone and the message. "Millie."

She looked over at the Trevor. "What?"

"You should go tell the team. It's going to be a long night."

Millie nodded. Of course, it was going to be a long night. They had a new lead to chase, a timeline to adhere to, and now they had the next victim.

Her.

Chapter Seven

TREVOR

October 6

Trevor jolted up from where his head had fallen on the desk in front of him. He must have nodded off sometime during the night. He hadn't meant to, but he was only human, and humans needed sleep to function. He scrubbed his face with hands. He felt disgusting, his mouth tasted stale, and his head ached.

No one went back to the hotel the night before. As soon as the team saw the message sent to Millie's phone, everyone had perked up despite being up since the middle of the night DC time. All thoughts of calling it an early night gone.

It didn't take long for Trevor to get the phone records for all four victims. He sent them to the team, and they spent the night combing through them.

Messages had been sent to all four women in the days leading up to their disappearance, which wasn't what surprised them.

No, what surprised them was that the messages weren't all threatening. They were quite the opposite. They were friendly, and the women, every single one of them, responded to them.

Every. Single. One. Of. Them.

The last message that was sent the day they disappeared was all the same.

Let's Meet Up.

It wasn't immediately clear whether they had told anyone they were communicating with the UNSUB. Likely not, as the families would have told the police, the victims were supposed to meet up with someone on the day they disappeared. They read through all the reports back and forward, and there was nothing about the texts in any of them.

Each victim had received a message about something different in the initial contact. And each one was tailored to each victim. The UNSUB did not pick these women at random.

These attacks had been meticulously planned and executed, and they ran on a timeline.

Their focus was going to be on victim number one, Jamie Sanders, today. She was the first, and there was something about her that spoke to the UNSUB, something that triggered him into killing her, into stalking her for a little over a week before snatching her and killing her.

Trevor stood up from the chair he was sitting in and stretched. If he thought his back ached after sitting in the shitty chair yesterday afternoon, it was nothing compared to the way his back felt after hunching over his computer all night and falling asleep in it.

He was too old for this shit.

Trevor walked to the door of his office closet and opened it. He needed a break from these screens and needed to check in with the rest of the team and see where they were with every-thing.

He sent a text to Officer Jones to go watch his shit, and left the room, knowing he would be there soon. The man was reliable.

After opening the door to his closet, he was assaulted with the noise from the precinct. He didn't realize how much his walls muffled the sounds of the other officers going about their day. He almost felt isolated and in a world of his own.

Making his way to the conference room, he couldn't help the pit that grew in his stomach.

Millie.

She was obviously being targeted by the UNSUB as his next victim. Which felt like he was straying from the MO a little.

Well, he definitely was.

His text to her was taunting and threatening.

Probably because he knew he couldn't draw her away. She was too situationally aware to fall for unknown numbers.

The room on the other side of the conference room door sounded silent. Trevor frowned. He was pretty sure they had agreed to stay all night.

He pushed open the door and shook his head. The rest of the team slept, scattered around the room. They, like him, must have succumbed to their bodies' biological urge to need sleep to function.

Trevor tried to shut the door as quietly as he could behind him, but the sound of him entering the room stirred Thomas from his sleep.

"Sorry," Trevor whispered.

Thomas shook his head. "Don't worry about it. I am pretty sure we all fell asleep two hours ago." He stood from his chair and stretched. Trevor's back hurt from sitting in his chair all night, but Thomas was a much larger man than he was, and also older. He was certain he was in a lot of pain as well.

"Did you guys make any progress last night before you all crashed?" Trevor asked.

Thomas nodded. "We have the beginnings of a profile, but I think we needed a couple of hours to recharge our brains in order to finish it."

Trevor nodded. "Beginnings of a profile on day two. That's significant progress."

"Well, we are on the time of a man who has already selected his next victim. We need to work quickly and efficiently."

Thomas's phone dinged, and he looked at it, his frown deepened. "Fuck. Just what we need right now."

"The Blooming Butcher?" Trevor pulled out a chair and sat down.

"Unfortunately."

"Send me the number so I can add it to the file," Trevor said.

"Already done."

"Same old shit?"

"Asking me what I thought of his handywork. If I'm ready to play his game."

"Fuck," Trevor said. "I hate it when they say what they do is a fucking game."

"But this isn't completely unexpected, either. Not with this one. Leaving a signature, taunting us through the language of flowers. We always knew this was going to be a game."

"All very true, but still. Not still, not what I want to hear." Trevor opened his tablet and found the number Thomas had sent to him. He opened the file he was tracking all the different numbers their mystery killer had been using.

He never used the same number twice. He was really adept at spoofing numbers. And it was almost always a florist or a greenhouse.

"Another florist?" Thomas asked.

"Greenhouse. We can't let this get out to the press. That he's only spoofing numbers associated with florists and greenhouses. Along with the flower left at the scene as communication..."

"They'll fucking run with the name some asshole true crime podcaster gave him." Logan was awake and stretching.

"Exactly," Trevor agreed.

"If he kills again, and leaves another flower, that will be enough for the press. They'll find the name that one podcaster gave him, and that's it," Matthew spoke up from where he was sitting up in his chair.

"And then it will only stroke his ego and give him exactly what he wants," Millie spoke softly from where she was sitting.

"Infamy," Trevor finished.

"Exactly."

"We'll try our best to keep things out of the press. But you know those vultures," Thomas said.

"Are you going to respond?" Logan asked.

Thomas shook his head. "Fuck no. Why would I give this asshole the attention he wants? I'll keep receiving the messages and documenting them. I won't give him the satisfaction of a response."

Everyone nodded.

"So, the plan today is to go talk to Jamie's family, correct?" Logan asked.

"That is correct. She is victim number one, and learning more about her life and what it was like, we may be able to figure out the trigger. The thing that set our UNSUB off and had him kill," Thomas explained.

"And why the two-week window," Millie added.

"The two-week window is so precise, there is definitely meaning to it. He has not deviated from it. Not at all," Matthew said.

"I wonder if it has to do with how long it takes him to lure his victims out. Maybe it wasn't always meant to be two weeks, but that just was what worked for Jamie, and he used the same tactics with the others?" Trevor said.

Matthew shook his head. "I don't think so. That's an enormous risk to take with the next victim. It's not guaranteed each woman will fall for his schtick at the exact same time. The fact that each victim is killed exactly two weeks apart means something."

"I'm going to agree with Matty on this one," Thomas spoke up. "The two weeks are part of his signature, and that is significant."

"You mentioned you had the workings of a profile. What do you have so far?" Trevor asked.

Millie turned on her tablet and clicked through a few things. "He's a Predator. He'll present himself as friendly and helpful, but that is part of the ruse to lure in his victim. He's going to be someone people describe as toxic, constantly using people for his own gain. Chronically unemployed. Can't hold a job because once he's gotten everything he can out of people, he moves on. I wouldn't be surprised if he frequented bars and might have a bit of an alcohol problem. When it comes to his crimes, he's sadistic. The overkill on the postmortem stab wounds demonstrates that. The text messages show the UNSUB is trying to gain the victim's trust and confidence. Having the victims meet somewhere else is a sign that he is luring them to a second location, somewhere he's most comfortable. And I would bet money on the fact that he is keeping some kind of trophy of each kill."

"Was there any sign of sexual activity, consensual or otherwise, on the victims? Typically, these guys get off on this, and there's usually a sexual side to the crime." Trevor was frantically taking notes of what Millie had been saying. The profile made sense.

"There was no evidence that he had sex with the women, consensual or otherwise, but we can't rule out that he masturbated at the crime scene," Thomas explained.

"My money is on he did." Logan didn't even look up from where he was typing on his tablet.

"I'm one to agree," Matthew stated.

Trevor made a note about the possibility of masturbation at the crime scene. "Now, to figure out what the trigger is. Are we thinking INCEL taking out his frustration at not getting a date?"

Millie shook her head. "Not quite. We're thinking someone burned this guy real bad, and he can't hurt her. So, instead, he's taking it out on women who are acting like surrogates."

"And the two weeks have to do with something significant in their relationship," Logan added.

"Like it's the length of courtship?" Trevor suggested.

"Exactly," Thomas agreed.

"So, I know the plan is to talk to the victims' families, but are we going right away?" Trevor asked.

"We are taking an hour, and everyone is going to go back to their rooms to shower and change. We'll meet back up here and decide who will head out to talk to Jamie's family, and who will be here combing through every last-minute detail of those text exchanges between her and the UNSUB to find any clues," Thomas explained.

"Easy, I'll go question the family," Millie said. "I can take either Matty or Logan with me."

"I'll go with her," Matthew said.

"Then I'll stay here and comb through the texts," Logan piped up.

"And I'll continue on the road of trying to trace this fucker digitally," Trevor added.

"Are you any closer?" Thomas asked.

Trevor shook his head. "No. With every brick wall I run into, I find five more behind it."

"Well, keep up the work. You're good at what you do, you can solve this problem." Thomas always knew the right things to say to encourage his team.

There was a knock on the door of the conference room.

"Yes?" Thomas answered.

The door opened, and Officer Jones stepped inside holding an enormous bouquet of multicolored roses.

Everyone in the room stopped and stared. Flowers. Fuck. This was something new from the mystery killer.

"Um, sorry to interrupt," Officer Jones said. "I was on my way to watch your computers, and these were delivered for Millie? I believe that's you, Agent Driscoll?"

Millie walked slowly to the flowers. Trevor's heart rate increased. Either the mystery killer had moved to focus on Millie, or their UNSUB was escalating already.

Millie took the flowers from Officer Jones, who quickly dipped back out of the room.

There was a card. She pulled it out, and everyone else in the room waited with bated breath.

Trevor stood and walked over to her, taking the flowers from her hands so she could open the envelope.

Millie opened the envelope, and she visibly relaxed, a smile spreading across her face.

Trevor instantly knew why. "Metallica Guy?"

"Sebastian, yes."

"You need to tell him not to send flowers anymore. Just about gave us all heart attacks," Trevor joked.

Millie laughed. "I'll pass that along."

"Alright, we've already assigned roles for the morning. Let's go clean up." Thomas's tone left no room for argument.

As the group dispersed to head back to their motel, which they hadn't been to since they checked in, Trevor looked over at

Millie, who was still looking at the card from Sebastian, with a wistful smile on her face.

Looking at her, Trevor made a choice. He would support Millie in this endeavor. She may say she just wanted to get laid, but the look on her face reading the card spoke differently.

This was probably going to mean something more than she expected. She was going to fall hard, and either this relationship was going to be successful like Matty's was, or it was going to fail. But either way, Trevor knew he would be by her side. Even if it pained his heart

Chapter Eight

MILLIE

October 6

Millie ran her hand over the crown of her head, smoothing down her hair. It was still wet from her quick shower. Not wanting to take the time to blow-dry her long locks, she pulled them back into a ponytail.

She and Matthew were on the way to talk to Jamie's family. Well, at least her husband. Jamie had two young adult children and two teens. She wasn't sure if the adult children were around and would even want to talk to her. Jamie's husband was dropping everything to be home to talk with them.

"Anything to catch the bastard who did this," were his words when they talked on the phone this morning.

Talking to the families was Millie's least favorite part, but it was what she was strongest at. Each member of the team had something they were better at than the others. Matthew was great at analyzing crime scenes, Logan and Thomas were amazing at interrogations, especially together, and she was great at talking to the families and reading between the lines.

Her phone chimed, and her heart rate increased.

Fucking UNSUB. Ever since he'd texted her all her messages were now Schrödinger's message: from the UNSUB or friend? No one knows until you actually answer it.

She liked it better when the answer was always friend.

Millie pulled out her phone and looked at it, immediately relaxing.

"Sebastian." She watched Matthew relax with the information. Between the UNSUB texting her, and the mystery killer texting Thomas, pretty soon no one's phone would be safe from scrutiny.

Sebastian - Did you get my flowers? I assumed you were at the police precinct, but now I'm wondering if I sent them to the wrong place.

Millie - I got them. I should have messaged you to let you know, but it's been a busy morning.

Sebastian - No need to apologize. I know you're busy. I wanted to let you know I'm thinking of you, so I thought flowers. Were they too much? Because now I'm second-guessing the flowers.

Millie smiled down at the message. Sebastian voicing his insecurities was adorable. It endeared him more to her.

Fuck.

Trevor was right. She was getting warm, fuzzy feelings about this man.

This wasn't good.

It was supposed to be a wham bam thank you ma'am sort of situation. And now, feelings were creeping in.

This was not good at all.

Millie - Flowers were definitely not too much. I loved them.

What was she doing?! She should not be encouraging this nonsense!

*Sebastian - *smiley face emoji* I'm glad. Are we still on for tonight?*

Millie - As of right now, I'll say yes. But depending on work, we may need to postpone.

Sebastian - I understand. Let me know.

Sebastian - Or, rather, I'll check back in with you later.

Millie blushed. He really needed to stop being so fucking fantastic if she was going to quash these feelings she was developing.

Millie - are you trying to get into my pants?

Sebastian - Well, yeah. But most of all, I'm trying to get into your heart...

Millie - You're going to need to try a little harder for that.

*Sebastian - *gif of John Cusak holding a boom box over his head.**

Sebastian - Willing to give it all I've got.

Her mouth twisted into a wide grin.

"You're looking particularly happy over there." Matthew's voice broke her out of her revelry. She had honestly forgotten she was in the car with him.

She cleared her throat. "Um, it's nothing."

"That look is not nothing. Texting with the giver of the flowers?"

Millie smiled before she could stop herself. Quickly, she schooled her features into a more neutral position. "Yes, what of it?"

Matthew laughed. "You don't have to do that. Play tough. It's okay to have feelings."

"I'm not playing tough. We're here on a case. I met a guy who will help me relieve some tension. It's really not a big deal."

"Does he know that?" Matthew asked.

"Know what?"

"That you're only in it for the sex?"

Millie shrugged. "I'm pretty sure he does. We talked about it a little last night. Why?"

"Well, flowers to the workplace don't scream no strings to me."

Millie felt her stomach drop. Shit. Was Sebastian catching these feelings, too? "They don't? What if I wanted the dude to work for me a little bit?"

Matthew laughed. "Multi-colored roses are a pretty high-end flower to give to someone who is a sure thing. I think this guy is looking for something a little more than a one-night stand."

"Well, maybe I don't want more than a one-night stand," Millie said.

Matthew glanced at her quickly before turning his gaze back to the road. "Well, from the smile you had while reading your messages, I never would have guessed that."

"I've gone on one date with him. There's no way I can feel anything more than lust for him at this point in time."

"Funny, I seem to recall saying something pretty similar back this summer when we were in Iowa."

"You and Rebecca are different." Millie wasn't sure exactly how they were different, but she felt they were, and she was going to stand by that assertion. Basically, she was grasping at straws, and she was woman enough to admit that, even just to herself.

Matthew laughed. "If you say so."

They drove in silence for a little while longer. "But, say, hypothetically, if we weren't different. How did you know Rebecca was going to be something more?"

Matthew said nothing for a minute, and then he shrugged. "I don't know. I just knew. We had this connection. And being around her felt natural."

"You're no help."

"How do you feel around this guy?"

Millie shrugged. "I don't know. Comfortable? Like I can be myself and he won't judge me? I've been on so many dates in the last few years that end almost immediately after the guy figures out what I do for a job. Sebastian wanted to know more. And that felt...nice. But I don't know. I've never been in love, so I don't know if I could even recognize the feeling."

"You don't have to be in love. I wasn't even in love with Rebecca after one night. But that feeling of belonging? That's a big deal. His accepting you for who you are? Huge deal. Do you want my advice?"

"Yes, please."

"Be open to the possibility that this could be something more. Don't close yourself off to it."

"Is that what you did? Open yourself up to the possibility?"

Matthew shrugged. "I guess so. I definitely didn't close myself off. But I wasn't completely opposed to the idea either."

"What gave you the push to finally commit to something more with her? To be in love?"

"You don't know? Rebecca hasn't told you?"

Millie shrugged. "It's not something that's ever really come up."

"I got the blessing from her dead husband's spirit."

Silence filled the car. "You're joking, right?"

Matthew shook his head. "Not at all. The music box in her bedroom that her husband had custom made for her played at a very crucial moment. And that is what sealed the deal for me. Having his approval."

"Matty. You're a man of science. You don't honestly believe the spirit of a dead man gave you a sign that you could date his wife, do you?"

"Of course I do. He gave the same sign to Rebecca when she asked him if it was okay for her to be moving on. And he visited

Benji in his dreams and told him it was okay to love me and want me to be his stepfather."

"There are probably more logical—"

"No." Matthew's voice was firm and brokered no arguments. "There isn't. Some things can't be explained away by science. You have to have faith."

Millie looked over at Matthew and scrutinized him. He didn't seem to be bullshitting her. He truly believed everything he was saying. Every logical part of her told her what he believed was impossible, but she loved her friend enough to know when to shut the hell up.

"Oh, and Millie?"

"Yeah?"

"Be careful. We're here to catch a serial killer whose demographics are pretty similar to Sebastian's. And we're all concerned. Don't take that to mean we don't trust you. Take that as we care for you and your safety."

They drove the rest of the way in silence, Millie turning over his advice in her head. She supposed it was easy enough advice, being open to more. She could do that. She didn't need to think this would be some great love story for her, but she could be open to maybe a little more than probably super-hot sex with an incredibly hot man. Maybe they could see each other while she was in town for the case?

That could be nice.

Before she could contemplate more about the status of her love life, they were pulling up in front of Jamie's home. Or, well, it was her former home.

The house was a classic pueblo-style home, typical of historic neighborhoods in New Mexico. The stone had a pinkish tint. There were three stairs leading up to an ornate door, and off the right of the door there was an archway with a wrought-iron gate that led to a beautiful garden.

"I don't want to do this." Millie's voice was almost a whisper.

"I know, but we have to. It's the only way to catch the bastard who killed her and those other women." And who targeted you next were words that were left unsaid but still hung heavy in the car, anyway.

Millie took a deep breath and steeled herself. She could do this. Talking to the family was what she did best. She could look this widower in the eye and figure out what he was hiding between the lines. Maybe he knew who she was texting and didn't think anything of it.

"Let's do this." Millie pulled the door handle and pushed the door to the car open. Stepping into the warm air was shocking at first after being in the air-conditioned car. Plus, having traveled from DC, where fall was firmly in place, being back in summer weather was shocking to her system.

Matthew followed her lead, walking behind her as she started up the stone walkway to the front door. As they neared the house, she could see through the wrought-iron fence to get a better view of the garden. It was slightly overgrown, obviously not having been tended to in months, but she could tell that someone had lovingly tended that garden at some point. Most likely, it was Jamie.

Looking away from the garden with an ache in her chest, Millie turned her attention back to the door. The red door had intricate carvings on it. It was beautiful and fit with the style of the home. What didn't fit, however, was the doorbell, which looked to be one that was also connected to some sort of security camera system.

Matthew pushed the bell, and a jaunty tune played.

They didn't have to wait long for the door to be answered.

A tall, thin man with thinning hair answered the door. He was dressed in a dress shirt that was unbuttoned at the collar, and the sleeves were rolled up to the elbow. He was wearing dress pants but was barefoot.

Millie and Matthew held up their FBI badges so he could clearly see them. "I'm Special Agent Driscoll, and this is Special Agent Grant. We're with the Behavioral Analysis Unit with the FBI. We talked this morning about discussing Jamie and the days leading up to her disappearance?"

Mr. Sanders nodded. "Yes, I remember. Please come in."

They followed Mr. Sanders into the house, closing the door behind them. They walked into a living room that was decorated with care. The furniture wasn't quite antique, but it complemented the historical aspect of the home. The room contained a number of actual antiques, and there were family photos scattered everywhere.

Tears pricked the backs of her eyes. She closed them and took a deep breath. She didn't understand why this case was affecting her the way it was, but she needed to pull it together.

"Please have a seat." Mr. Sanders led them to one of the couches in the main living room. She and Matthew took a seat. Mr. Sanders sat in a chair opposite them.

"I'm not sure how much help I'll be. I told the police everything I could remember about the day she went missing, but it wasn't much."

"Mr. Sanders," Millie started.

"Please call me Steve."

"Steve," Millie started again. "Our job is to ask you questions and help you try to remember things you may think you have forgotten. We aren't interested in just the day she went missing, but the two weeks leading up to her disappearance. Do you think you could help us with that time?"

Steve closed his eyes. Millie could see him moving his lips. It looked like he was counting. He opened his eyes again, and this time there was a look of firm determination in them. "Yes. I think I could. It wasn't that long ago, and I feel pretty confident in my memory of the time."

Millie gave him a soft smile. "Good. That's promising." She glanced over at Matthew, who had his phone out on the table, already recording their conversation, and his tablet in his lap, ready to take notes. She turned back to Steve.

"We have additional evidence that the UNSUB, the um, Unknown Subject, the suspect, had been in contact with Jamie prior to her disappearance."

Steve sat up straighter in his chair. "What do you mean? How was he in contact with her?"

"Via text message," Millie explained. "Do you remember Jamie texting with anyone new during this time?"

Scott closed his eyes gain. Millie could see his eyes moving back and forth under his eyelids, as if he were thinking really hard. Trying to recall things. "She was helping a couple of new clients that week. They were a lot needier than the people she typically worked for."

"What did she do?" Millie asked.

"She was a freelance social media manager for local small businesses. She was amazing at her job and highly sought after," Steve explained.

"Tell me about the new clients," Millie encouraged.

Steve leaned forward in his chair, resting his elbows on his knees. "There were three of them. One was a woman who owns a pet grooming shop, Pet's Best Friend. She was struggling to bring in business and was hoping Jamie could fix that with her social media posts. She texted so much to the point Jamie would refuse to answer right away."

"What's her name?" Millie asked.

"Alyssa St. George."

Millie nodded. "Who else?"

"Um, Callie Turner from the new candy shop, Callie's Candy. She wasn't as bad as St. George, but still, she sent a lot of messages."

Millie was getting nervous. This conversation had started out promising, but now, two out of three of the new clients were women. "Who was the third?"

"Bobby Tucker. He's a local artist. He was trying to establish a business. He was very needy. Texting her at all hours."

"Was she annoyed by it?" Millie asked.

Steve shook his head. "Not really. She seemed to really enjoy doing things for him. Jamie was really creative, and while he was really needy, he gave her a lot of leeway on what to do. She was very excited about what they were doing together."

"Did they ever meet in person?" Millie asked.

Steve's eyes welled up, and he took a deep breath, letting it out shakily. "Um, she was supposed to meet up with him the day she, um, disappeared. I don't know whether she ever made it to their meeting. We said goodbye that morning before I left for work, and that was the last time I saw her."

They talked a while longer before Millie leaned forward and placed her hand on his arm. "I'm so sorry. But thank you so much for taking the time to meet up."

"Do you think anything I've told you will help?" Steve wiped the tear that found its way rolling down his cheek.

Millie nodded. "Absolutely. You have been an immense help."

"Good. I hope you catch the fucking bastard." His voice rang with sorrow and anger. "I'm sorry for my harsh language."

"Don't apologize. You've experienced a significant loss, and we are going to do everything in our power to catch the person who did this."

Millie and Matthew stood up from the couch, Matthew tucking away his devices.

"If you think of anything else, even if it feels unrelated or silly, don't hesitate to reach out, because odds are it is probably helpful, so please reach out," Matthew said.

Steve nodded while he stood. "I'll do that. Thank you so much for coming here. After not hearing from the police for a while, I was losing hope that we would ever find the person who destroyed my family. So, your team coming to town has renewed my faith."

Millie gave him a tight smile. "We are going to do our best to bring some justice for your family."

Matthew put his hand behind Millie's back and led her to the door. Thank God for his disdain for social interactions and niceties. He was always the one to lead them out of an interview. There was a reason he preferred the crime scenes. Fewer people.

They said their goodbyes and walked back to the car. Millie climbed in and closed the door behind her. Looking out her window, she stared at the house one more time, taking in the formerly well cared for garden. Her heart broke for the kids who lost their mother.

She pulled out her phone and hit the first contact before holding the phone up to her ear.

"Yeah?" Trevor answered.

"I need you to run the name Bobby Tucker and let me know what you find."

Chapter Nine

TREVOR

October 6

"Fuck. Yes!" Trevor fist-pumped and almost tipped himself out of his chair.

The second he hung up with Millie, he ran the name she gave him. And there he was. Not a fucking alias. There he was.

Bobby Tucker. Thirty-nine years old. Newly arrived in Calico Rock within the last year. Self-employed. And here was the kicker. His number matched the business number listed for his art shop, which was used to text Jamie during those last two weeks of her life.

When Trevor had run the numbers, he had assumed whoever it was had spoofed the business's number. But apparently, the asshole used his own number.

The number wasn't the same as the ones used to text the other victims or Millie, but that was pretty common in cases like this. When killers killed again, they perfected their MO and made improvements. Tried to cover their tracks a little bit more.

But here he was. He was real.

Trevor picked up his phone and dialed Millie.

"Driscoll."

"I've got him."

There was silence on the other end of the phone. "What?"

"I've. Got. Him."

"I'm coming to your closet."

The line cut off, and Trevor set his phone on the desk. Millie was on her way. He knew she wouldn't be able to resist the lead.

The door to his closet office opened, letting Millie, who was out of breath, in. She must have rushed to get to his office closet so soon.

"What do you mean by you've got him?"

Trevor smiled at her. "Well. I mean exactly that. You gave me a name, and I found the guy." He gestured to the screen of the computer that was sitting directly in front of him on the desk.

Millie walked over to him and leaned over his shoulder. Trevor inhaled the soft lavender and vanilla scent of her and closed his eyes. Back at the academy, when they were both incredibly stressed out, they did some research into aromatherapy. While he didn't completely buy into it, Millie did. Once she learned combining vanilla and lavender was supposed to soothe both mind and body, she bought all the candles, and she mixed her own body wash. Whenever they traveled for a case, she used only her special lavender and vanilla wash to calm herself.

It was her signature scent, and whenever he got a whiff, it did things to him. It was both comforting and erotic. He pushed the erotic part from his mind and focused on the comforting part.

Millie took a second to read the screen and turned to him with a wide smile. "This is fucking amazing."

"I know."

"He's just right there."

"He is."

"This is too easy."

"That is a possibility."

"I'm right though, right? Why didn't the locals catch this? The texts are right here. Let's meet up. From this guy's business phone number and everything."

Trevor shrugged. "It could be a lot of things. The texts weren't even part of the original statements from anybody. The detectives probably didn't think to look. Did the husband say he mentioned it to them?"

Millie leaned back and shook her head in the negative. "No. Since the texts were about her business, and not just some random man texting her, it didn't even cross his mind to tell the police about them. They didn't feel relevant."

"So, that would explain why these texts weren't in the original report."

Millie turned around and hopped onto a clear spot on the desk. She crossed one leg over her other knee and folded her arms. "Are all the numbers other than the one that messaged me the same?"

Trevor shook his head. "No. Only the first one is tied to Bobby. The other three are spoofed from other local businesses."

"Which businesses?"

Trevor pulled his chair closer to the desk, putting his hand on the mouse and clicking through the screens until he got to his document for the case.

"Okay, so Jamie was from this guy Bobby Trevor's art business. Sharon Cruise received text messages from the Pet's Best Friend. Laura Hutchins' texts came from Callie's Candy. And Sarah Bigelow's came from the local Walmart. And yours from the local elementary school."

"Shut. Up." Millie jumped down from the desk and returned to her place over his shoulder.

"What's wrong?"

"So, Steve, Jamie's husband, told us she was working with three new clients in the weeks leading up to her death. And you just named all three."

Trevor looked up at Millie to see if she was joking. She was not. She was completely serious. "What are the odds this Bobby guy knew Jamie was working with these businesses?"

"From what her husband was saying, Jamie was good at her job and was well sought after for her social media marketing. I'm guessing the odds were really fucking good her clients knew who they were."

He pushed his chair away from his desk and folded his arms over his chest. "So, theory."

Millie turned so she was leaning against the desk directly in front of him. She mimicked his posture. "What's your theory?"

"So, this Bobby guy, he starts working with Jamie on social media marketing for his art business. Something triggers him, and he kills her. That unlocks something in him, and he likes it. So, he wants to recreate his experience with Jamie to get the same satisfaction. But it would look really weird if his number popped up on this new woman's phone, so he spoofs the number. When he's trying to decide which number to spoof, he remembers Jamie was working with these other people at the same time he was, so he uses their numbers."

"When texting from a business, would it come up as that business on caller ID?" Millie asked.

"Not while texting, usually only when the call comes from them."

"Who did Sharon, Laura, and Sarah think they were texting with?"

Trevor reached around Millie to pick up his tablet from the desk. He unlocked it and pulled up the document with the text records. "Sharon thought she was texting with a dog groomer."

"Are you for real right now?" Millie's voice was full of disbelief.

"I am completely for real." He turned so Millie could see the screen, and then he read. **"Pet's Best Friend: Hi, is this Sharon Cruise?**

Sharon: Yes? Who is this?

Pet's Best Friend: This is Alyssa St. George from Pet's Best Friend. I wanted to let you know we have an amazing offer for you.

Sharon: Really? I've been trying to get an appointment with you for ages.

Pet's Best Friend: Well, we have an opening for little Gus in two weeks! And we'll even give you our full-service treatment for half off!

Sharon: That's wonderful! When? Pet's Best Friend: September second, but if you come in the day before, we can fill out all the paperwork without Gus there, so you don't have to worry about it."

"He impersonated the dog groomer?" Millie was flabbergasted.

"Apparently."

"But there were more messages between them in the two weeks between this initial contact and his killing her. What did they talk about?"

Trevor scrolled through the rest of the messages. "Mostly about Gus."

"This is so strange."

"Not really. It's very typical with this type of offender to impersonate someone to gain the victim's trust," Trevor explained. "So, he impersonated Alyssa St. George and gained Sharon's trust. That way, when it came time to meet, she didn't even hesitate to meet him."

"I think we can firmly say the UNSUB is a predator," Millie said.

"Yeah, it's pretty obvious now."

Millie brought her hand up to her chin and looked at Trevor. "What was his ruse with the candy store?"

Trevor flipped to the conversation with Laura and the Callie's Candy owner. "She contacted her with some fun coupons for some candy for her kids' birthday treats. Her youngest's birthday was coming up, so she was texting back and forth, trying to plan what the treats would be. The last message was arranging a meetup to look at the treats and make an initial payment."

Millie's eyebrows drew together, and she brought her bottom lip between her teeth. After a minute, she spoke. "Has anyone looked at the security footage around these businesses? The art shop, the dog groomer, or Callie's Candy?"

Trevor shook his head. "No, why would they have? I'm pretty sure they only looked for footage around dumpsites."

"Can you get the footage from those places?"

Trevor looked at her, raising his eyebrow. "Who do you think you're talking to?"

"How long will it take to find it?"

Trevor shrugged. "A while. We don't know the exact time the women were taken, we just know they were taken. And I haven't even looked to see how many cameras are around there. It's going to be a long job. Especially if we're going to be checking the Walmart for Sarah."

"So, this is going to be a late night?"

"I mean, it's mid-morning now, so...yes. I don't see this being done until at best tonight, realistically tomorrow. And that's even if anything was caught on camera. Remember, the UNSUB is a fucking tech genius, so he probably knows where all the cameras are, and we won't even see anything."

"But we're still going to be looking."

"Oh, absolutely we're going to be looking."

Millie pulled out her phone and began typing on it.

"What are you doing?" Trevor asked.

"Texting Sebastian and canceling our date."

Trevor frowned. "You don't need to cancel your date. I've got this."

Millie shook her head. "I don't think I'll be good company right now. My mind is going to be solely on the case."

Trevor ducked his head to hide his smile. He should not be this happy to go through endless hours of CCTV footage. Honestly, typically he would just do this alone with some energy drinks and candy to keep him awake. Maybe he would put on a podcast or something. He's never done this with someone else in the room.

"You really don't need to stick around and watch the footage slowly roll by. You can go work on other parts of the cases."

"Do you not want me here?" Millie's face fell.

"No," Trevor rushed to fix it. "I'm not saying that at all. I would love for you to hang out in here with me, but I'm worried you'll be bored."

Millie flashed him her biggest smile. "You're my best friend. I could never be bored with you."

The comment went straight to his heart. Fuck, he loved this woman. "I'm going to remind you of that statement in about four hours when we have seen the same storefront over and over and over again."

"If I say the phrase I'm bored once, I'll owe you a round of beers at Elephant & Castle when we get back home."

"Done." Trevor held out his hand, and Millie took it, shaking on the deal. "I'm going to bet by dinnertime you're going to crack."

"The challenge is on, Ford. The challenge is on."

"How many cameras did you say you found?" Millie asked, spinning from side to side in the chair she had wheeled into his closet office. Honestly, Trevor was slightly jealous of her chair. It was better than his, and he was tempted to ask her if she would trade.

"Um, about five per block," Trevor answered. "And we are doing a two-block radius, so…"

"A lot. You've found a lot of cameras," Millie finished.

"Yes, a lot. But we are scrolling through them at an increased speed, so that will save us some time."

Millie threw her head back against the back of the chair.

Trevor paused the video he was watching and looked at her. She was going to crack. He just knew it. She had that look. The 'I'd rather be anywhere but here' look. Her eyes were rolled back, and she was staring at the ceiling. Her body was slumped in the seat, and her mouth looked like it was poised to let out an exasperated sigh.

Trevor wouldn't blame Millie if she were bored. They had been at this for hours. It took a while to locate all the different cameras near all the different places they were looking for. And then they had to issue the warrants for the footage. Then, wait for the footage to arrive.

In that time, Trevor and Millie filled the rest of the team in on what they had learned and their theories, and the team agreed.

While they were going through the footage, Matthew and Logan headed out to Pet's Best Friend and Callie's Candy to see if they could find any evidence of the women being taken from those locations. They were going to check in with each other when they returned. If they found any evidence of the women being taken from those locations, it would significantly help Trevor narrow down his search of the CCTV footage.

Although he held little stock in finding anything of significance on these tapes. The guy they were dealing with was not an idiot. He made plans upon plans.

Trevor looked at Millie again. True to her word, she stuck around with him. But she was fading fast. He quirked his mouth into half a smile, just as Millie turned her seat and her head to look at him.

"Stop it." Her voice was annoyed.

"Stop what?"

"Stop willing me to lose our fucking bet."

Trevor shrugged his shoulders and smiled a genuine smile. "I'm doing no such thing."

"You are. You are staring at me and smiling, and you are begging for me to lose. And I'm not going to. I'm having a great time."

"Careful there, Driscoll. You're sounding just a smidge sarcastic," Trevor teased.

"I'm not. I'm genuinely excited to be here. Look at my eyes."

Trevor leaned forward in his seat and made a big show of looking into Millie's ice-blue eyes. "Yeah, no, all I'm seeing is boredom."

Millie reached over and half-heartedly smacked him. "Shut up. I'm not...that word. I'm really enjoying our time together. When was the last time we could just hang out in a room together?"

Trevor turned back to look at the computer screen. "Um, all the time. It's basically our job."

"No, it's not. This is not our job. This is quality time with my best friend." Millie made big gestures with her arms, sweeping them around to show the room.

"If that's how you want to look at it so you're not tempted to complain about being bored, go ahead. I'm going to continue to look at this as my least favorite part of my job."

"The needle in the haystack." Millie nodded her head up and down, with a very sage look on her face.

"Yes. The needle in the fucking haystack."

The room transitioned back into silence while Trevor watched the footage from one of the cameras on the same block as Pet's Best Friend. So far, he hadn't noticed Sharon or her car.

When they had gone back through the statements, they learned her car had been found in the downtown area, where Pet's Best Friend was located, so they knew she had disappeared from that area, but they didn't know why she was there.

Knowing she drove into the area helped and gave Trevor something to look for. Especially knowing which direction she lived and would have probably driven from.

There was a soft knock on the door to the office closet, and both Millie and Trevor's heads turned to look at the door.

"Yeah?" Trevor called out.

The door opened, and instead of a member of the team, Metallica Man, Sebastian stuck his head into the room. His gaze caught on Millie, and his face broke into a wide smile.

"Hey," he said.

Millie sat up quickly, fixing her posture until it was less slouchy, quickly smoothing her hair down on the top of her head. "Hey. What are you doing here?"

Sebastian opened the door all the way, and leaned in the doorjamb, crossing one ankle over the other, his hands in the pockets of his black jeans. "I know you canceled our date, but I wanted to see you, anyway. I got the idea of coming down here and surprising you. I hope that's okay?"

Trevor watched as Millie blushed and ducked her head, a smile on her face, and his stomach plummeted. So much for uninterrupted time with his best friend.

Chapter Ten

SEBASTIAN

October 6

Pride swelled in Sebastian's chest when Millie ducked her head at his question. He had definitely made the right call in coming here.

When Millie had texted to cancel the date, he was disappointed. He had been looking forward to spending more time with her. And not just because they had floated the idea of sex happening tonight. No, he genuinely enjoyed spending time with her. And having all day to think about her, he began wondering what they could do tonight. How much more would he learn?

About an hour ago, he decided, fuck it. He wanted to see her. He was going to surprise her with dinner at the station.

What he didn't expect was finding her in a small room alone with another man.

Jealousy surged through him.

"Um, yeah, no, it's fine. I just wasn't expecting you, is all." Millie responded, bringing her gaze up to meet his.

Sebastian's chest tightened. And other things as well. Yeah, he made the right call in coming here. Seeing her confirmed everything he was feeling.

He was falling for this woman.

He twisted his mouth into a smirk. "Well, you not expecting it is the whole point of a surprise."

The man who was sitting at the desk in front of a slew of computers made a noise. It sounded like a scoff.

Millie turned her attention from Sebastian to the man sitting next to her before turning back to Sebastian. "This is my best friend and fellow team member, Trevor. Trevor, this is Sebastian."

Trevor clicked on something and turned in his chair to look at him. "We've met."

Sebastian began to frown, but stopped. He wasn't expecting the reaction from someone who Millie considered her best friend to be so cold. But he could work with this. He could win over the best friend. "Yeah, we did, but that was as a random dude on the sidewalk. This is as a potential paramour for your best friend. It's like we're meeting for the first time."

Trevor's gaze locked with Sebastian's, and Sebastian held it. Trevor narrowed his eyes, scrutinizing him. Sebastian tried to channel everything he was feeling into his gaze, trying to telegraph to Trevor that he really did like Millie, and that he had nothing to worry about.

Trevor was the first to break the gaze, pushing himself away from the desk and standing from his seat. "Hey Millie, I'm going to go check in with Thomas and see if Matthew and Logan have checked in."

Sebastian looked down, hiding his smile.

He won.

"Yeah, okay, but you don't need to leave," Millie said.

"Nah, I need to stretch, and you don't need an audience for your date. I'll be back in about half an hour." Trevor moved past Millie, resting his hand on her shoulder. Then he moved to the door.

Sebastian held his ground for a minute, not moving out of the way. All he did was stand up to his full height, his hand wrapping around the strap of the messenger bag he had slung across his chest.

The two men stood toe to toe, neither willing to budge. Their gazes locked.

Sebastian narrowed his eyes. This man had feelings for Millie, and it made him wonder if Millie knew. She had to know right? She was good at her job, and her job was reading people.

Trevor broke his gaze and pushed past Sebastian, leaving the room.

Sebastian turned until Trevor's back retreated down the hall. He breathed a sigh of relief. He was glad the man could read the room. He didn't want to spend his limited time with Millie while her jealous friend watched.

No, he wanted Millie all to himself.

Chapter Eleven

MILLIE

October 6

Millie watched the posturing of the two men in front of her and sighed.

Men.

She didn't know why she expected anything different from Trevor. Of course he would scrutinize Sebastian, it was his job to read people. But she had hoped that since Trevor was her best friend, and Sebastian was the man she was dating (seeing?), he would meet Sebastian as more of a friend, and not as an FBI profiler.

Nope. That was asking too much, obviously.

"I'm sorry," Millie said when Trevor left the room.

Sebastian turned back to her and flashed her a kind smile. "You don't need to apologize. I wouldn't expect anything less from your best friend. Isn't it their job to be skeptical of the new guy you're dating?"

Millie shrugged. "I guess. If we're talking about stereotypical tropes. I've personally never experienced that."

"Ouch. Trevor just typically loves whoever you're dating? Should I be worried that he seems to think I'm an asshole?"

Millie shook her head. "No, not that. It's just I haven't really had very many dates in the last few years that have progressed to where they're meeting my best friend, or anyone really. Remember, I told you most men don't like my job."

Sebastian moved into the room and sat in Trevor's abandoned chair. "Well, they're all idiots. Because your job is fucking amazing. I mean, look at this. You are sitting in here on a Tuesday night, in this wonderful...closet?"

Millie laughed. "They told Trevor it was an extra office."

Sebastian looked around, taking in the small space. "This is definitely a closet."

"Oh, yeah, it most definitely is."

"So, are you allowed to talk about what you're doing, or is it top secret?" Sebastian leaned back in the chair, crossing his ankle over his knee.

Millie couldn't resist admiring how good he looked. His long hair was down and looked freshly washed and blow-dried. He was of course wearing his eyeliner, and his beard looked freshly trimmed. In addition to his black jeans, he was wearing a black t-shirt with a long-sleeve plaid flannel shirt worn unbuttoned over it.

"We're going through CCTV footage," Millie said.

Sebastian nodded. "Sounds scintillating."

Millie laughed. "Most of this job involves high-energy tasks like this. Aren't you jealous?"

He shook his head. "Nah. I'm good. I'll stick with construction. At least I'm not stuck in a small closet all day staring at a screen."

"This has been a very boring day, that's for sure. And I'm not even really looking at the screens. I'm just here for moral support!"

Sebastian smiled at her. "That is very generous of you. Because I can think of several things I would rather do than sit in this closet and look at hours of footage featuring," he leaned in to look closer at the screen. "Is that Pet's Best Friend?"

"Yep."

"Well, at least you get to look at lots of footage of adorable animals."

"Definitely a perk of this job. Cute animal footage."

"Find anything yet?" Sebastian leaned further into the computer screen, looking at the image frozen there.

"That, I'm not at liberty to say." Millie turned her seat so she was also looking at the computer screen.

"Knew this job of yours came with classified information you couldn't tell me." Sebastian turned his gaze toward her and smiled.

Millie returned the smile. "Well, if details of the case get out, it makes our job harder. There are certain things only the UNSUB would know."

"Makes sense. When I watch shows like CSI, the detectives can solve the case in a matter of days. Is that true?"

Millie shrugged. "Honestly, it depends really on the case. Most of the time, though, no. We can't solve things in days. Take, for instance, what we're doing now. Trevor and I decided this morning we would go through the CCTV footage of certain parts of Calico Rock. Sounds easy enough, right? We just got permission to go through the footage an hour ago."

"You've been only going through the footage for an hour and you already looked like you wanted to be anywhere but here?"

"Yes, and don't you dare let that secret out to Trevor. If he asks, I'm having the time of my life and there's nowhere else I would rather be. We have a bet, and I need to win it."

Sebastian laughed. "Your secret's safe with me." He mimed zipping his lips.

Fuck, he was adorable.

"Oh!" He pulled his bag off and moved it in front of him. "I brought you dinner. I wasn't sure whether you would have time to eat. Your text made it sound like you were in for a long night, and maybe you would skip a meal. Since you're not from here, I thought I would give you a little taste of another local favorite."

Sebastian pulled two wrapped sandwiches out of his bag.

"Wow, those are huge."

"They make them smaller, but this way you'll be able to enjoy it for dinner and maybe a late-night meal or for lunch tomorrow. And now that I think about it, I'm hoping there is somewhere to store the rest of your sandwich."

"There's a fridge here."

"Good. Now, I didn't know what kind of sandwich you liked, so I chose two I enjoy, and they're the most popular on the menu. The guy Sal, his sandwich shop has been in his family for generations. They have a deal with a few local farms, so the meat and all of their toppings are fresh. So, which would you like, turkey and Swiss with all the fixings, or all the Italian meats with oil and vinegar?" Sebastian held up both sandwiches, one in each hand, and moved them up and down, making them dance to a tune only he could hear.

Millie looked between the sandwiches, and honestly couldn't decide which one sounded better. "Um, I don't know, they both sound good."

"Easy." Sebastian sat both sandwiches on the desk and unwrapped them. They were already sliced in half, so he picked up half of each sandwich and swapped them. "Now you can try both."

Well, that was it. She couldn't help it now. Whatever nebulous feelings she had for this man had now just notched over to full-on feelings.

She liked him, she really liked him.

"Thank you," she said, finding her voice. "This whole thing is very thoughtful, because you're right, I wouldn't have eaten anything."

"My mom was a single mom. She worked multiple jobs, and taking care of herself was always pretty low on the list," Sebastian explained. "You remind me of her a lot. Hardworking, strong, badass. Which is why when you sent that text, I knew you would be pulling all-nighter, and neglecting yourself, just like her."

"I'm going to take the comparison to your mom as a compliment."

"Believe me, it's the highest compliment I can give."

"Maybe someday I'll be able to meet her?" Millie cringed. Where the hell did that come from? Apparently, her brain was speed-running this relationship. Is this how Rebecca felt when she met Matthew? She would have to message her later and ask how long it took to get from first date to thinking about moving to DC.

"Unfortunately, my mother passed away several years ago. But I wish you could meet. She would love you. She always told me she hoped I would find a nice woman who could like me for who I was, who wouldn't want to change me. And who could take care of herself."

Millie cocked her head to one side. "We have known each other for a little over twenty-four hours. How can you be so sure I'm anything like that?"

Sebastian shrugged. "Call it a gut instinct."

"I'm sorry for canceling our date. Our real one, that is."

"You don't need to apologize. You're in Calico Rock for work, so naturally, work is going to take precedence, especially when your job is as important as yours is. And I still get to see you, so the night's not a total loss."

"Yeah, but there were implications about what tonight would bring. You're not disappointed?"

Sebastian shook his head. "No. You want to know why?"

Millie nodded.

Sebastian rolled his chair toward Millie until they were right in front of each other. Sebastian moved his hands down to her knees, parting them so he could roll himself so he was between her legs. He moved his hand slowly up her thighs, up her arms, until they rested on her shoulders, pulling her body forward as he himself leaned in. He brought his mouth to her ear, whispering. "You're all I thought about last night. I can't get you out of my head. You're intoxicating. The anticipation of us actually being together is fucking hot as hell, and when we can finally fuck, it's going to be glorious."

Millie wished she could clench her legs together, because his words went straight to her core. He was so fucking hot, and she was so worked up from months of no action that she was ready to climb into his lap right now and fuck the consequences.

Sebastian moved back enough so that he could meet her gaze. He smirked. "I can tell my words are affecting you."

Millie nodded.

"Do you like dirty talk?"

"Based on how I'm feeling right now, apparently I do."

"Maybe later we can have a little fun via our phones. If you know what I mean."

Millie barely held back a moan. Of course, she knew what he meant. And she was really hoping she could find her way to her motel later tonight. And fuck, she wished she had packed something with her to help her along when they talked.

Sebastian let out a small huff of a laugh, his warm breath ghosting across her cheek. And then he leaned forward, capturing her lips with his.

The kiss lit her whole body aflame. She brought her arms up, encircling his shoulders, pulling him closer to her, while opening her mouth, letting him gain entrance. Their tongues battled for dominance as he stood up from his seat, stepping fulling between her spread legs, pressing his body to hers.

Through the thin fabric of her dress pants, she could feel him hard against her center. Almost involuntarily, she shifted herself, rubbing against him. She pulled away, letting out a moan as pleasure shot through her.

Sebastian ran kisses down her cheek, down her neck, stopping where her neck and shoulder met, nibbling just a little.

"Fuck," Millie breathed out.

Sebastian answered by pressing his length against her again.

"We need to stop," she breathed out, not meaning a single word. Stopping was the last thing she wanted to do right now. In fact, what she really wanted to do was for the two of them to have less clothes on. Much less clothes. Screw the fact that this closet didn't lock. She didn't want to stop. The idea of someone walking in right now was actually kind of hot.

Sebastian pulled back. His lips swollen, and his hair thoroughly mussed. He pushed his length into her center one more time, and they both bit back a moan of pleasure. "If you insist."

"Oh, as much as I don't want to, I have to insist. Trevor could be back at any time, and I really, really don't want him walking in on us."

"Why? He'll be jealous?"

"No. Why would he be jealous?"

Sebastian shrugged. "You're an attractive woman, he has eyes."

"He and I are just friends. We don't see each other like that. He is the first person I talk to about my dates. He encourages me to go out and makes fun of me when my dates fail. He even has a stupid nickname for me. He's definitely not jealous. If he walked in, I would be utterly embarrassed. That's why we need to stop."

This time, Sebastian pulled back fully and gave her a smile. "Fine. We'll stop. On one condition."

"Consent doesn't need conditions, but I'll play along. What is your condition?"

"What is your nickname that Trevor gave you?"

Millie shook her head, pushing him far enough away from her so she could stand up. "Nope, not telling you that. It's embarrassing."

"Well, now you've basically guaranteed that I want to know. More than anything."

Millie sighed, running a hand through her hair trying to smooth it out. "Fine. He calls me Millisecond Millie."

Sebastian smirked. "Because it only takes you a millisecond to—"

"No," Millie interrupted. "No. Nothing like that. No, because it only takes a millisecond after someone learns what I do for a job for them to make an excuse to leave the date."

"Losers. All of them. The more I learn about your job, the more I want to be with you. Except maybe for this part." He gestured toward the computers. "This part makes me feel sorry for you and want to whisk you away to do something way more fun."

"Yeah, this part really sucks."

"What is your favorite part?"

Millie didn't even have to think about it. "As painful as it is, talking with the victims' families. Knowing that I'm going to bring them the closure they need. That is honestly the best part of the job."

Sebastian gave her a small smile. "You're a better person than I am. I don't know whether I could handle talking to them. Looking at the sadness in their eyes? That would break my heart right along with theirs. I don't know how you can do it."

Millie shrugged. "It has taken a lot of practice. A lot of work. But I think I'm naturally a people person, and that has really helped."

"Total opposite of me. I'm a total introvert. My asking you out is probably the most daring thing I've ever done. And I've completely second-guessed myself every step of the way."

"Hearing that really surprises me. Nothing about you screams introvert. You come across as very extroverted. Very confident."

Sebastian laughed. "Well, maybe I should get into acting, because I feel the exact opposite of that. I took a huge risk with the sandwich thing, not like me at all."

"Well, you fooled me. You're coming across as very confident. And everything you're doing is working for me. Like, really working."

"Then I'll keep doing what I'm doing. Whatever that is."

"Just keep being yourself. I like you."

Sebastian gave her a crooked smile. "I like you, too, and all I've ever done is show you who I really am."

Silence fell between them, their gazes locked on one another.

Sebastian cleared his throat. "We should eat these sandwiches before you have to get to work and I have to leave."

After they finished their sandwiches, Millie walked Sebastian to the door of the precinct, and they had shared a chaste kiss goodbye with the promise that they would reconnect later that night. Millie would make sure of it.

Then she went to where the refrigerator was and stored the rest of her sandwich. She had eaten half of each half, wanting to try both, and she had zero regrets. She still had leftover sandwiches, and she got to eat two different and very delicious sandwiches. Overall, the whole situation was a win.

She used the restroom and splashed some water on her face before returning to the closet office, finding Trevor had already returned.

"You're back," Trevor said, not bothering to turn around and watch her walk in.

"Yeah, did you think I wouldn't be?"

"Honestly, yeah. I thought you would take the opportunity to find something else to work on. Somewhere else to be. A more interesting task."

"Nothing is more interesting than this." Millie cringed when the words came out of her mouth. Not even she believed that bullshit.

Trevor started laughing. And he didn't stop. He actually held his fucking sides while he laughed.

Millie wasn't amused. "You can stop anytime."

Trevor shook his head. "Nope. Did you hear yourself? Nothing else is more interesting than this? Just admit you're bored, declare me the winner of the bet, and then you can go hang out with Logan and Matthew as they go through crime scene photos."

Millie frowned. "Ugh, somehow that sounds even worse than this. And you know how much I hate to lose, so I'm not giving in that easily. Did you find anything while I was gone?"

"I just got back. I took some time to get myself dinner after checking in with the rest of the team."

"Did they find anything?"

Trevor shook his head. "No. At least, nothing obvious. They took a lot of pictures, and they're back here zooming in and going over everything with a fine-toothed comb. They're hoping maybe I can find something in all of this footage. If I find something, they're going to go back out and look more once I have a more specific area."

Millie nodded. "Makes sense. Why work harder when they can work smarter?"

"Exactly."

Millie wheeled her chair back over next to the desk, right next to Trevor, so she could see what he was seeing. She couldn't help the blush that rose on her cheeks remembering what had just transpired in this room.

"So, nothing yet?" She just needed to keep her mind on work. That's all she needed to do.

Trevor shook his head. "Not yet. I think I'm going to move out further away from the store. I doubt she made it to the store. Someone would have come forward saying they saw her."

"That's a good point. And so far, we've had no eyewitnesses come forward."

"Yep. Maybe we should have Thomas add that to what he says at the press conference. Ask if there are any eyewitnesses on the days the women went missing to please come forward."

Millie nodded. "Yeah, make sure they emphasize that they may not have seen them actually get taken, but if they saw them at all, that could help us figure out where they were taken by building a timeline."

Trevor clicked out of the video he was watching and opened up a new one. "This camera is about a block west from Pet's Best Friend. That's the direction Sharon would have been driving from. Maybe we'll catch her car, or her walking from where she had parked her car."

"Fingers crossed."

Trevor pressed play on the video and then sped the tape up. He leaned back in his chair, keeping his gaze on the computer screen. "Did you have a nice date with Sebastian?"

Millie leaned back in her chair, mimicking his posture, keeping her gaze on the computer. "Yeah, it was good. He brought me these amazing sandwiches. I'll have to tell the rest of the team about it. It's a local deli, been in the family for generations, and the sandwiches were probably the best I've ever eaten."

"Really? Definitely don't keep that information to yourself. We all love sandwiches, and we all especially love places we can bring back here to consume while we work."

"You know what the best part of our last major case was?" Millie asked.

"Rebecca's parents cooking us every meal?" Trevor guessed.

"Yes. It was so nice not having to worry about where our next meal was going to come from. And not have to eat fast food the whole time we were there."

"Yeah, it's too bad Guillermo turned out to be a serial killer. His cooking was fucking amazing."

The two friends let silence fall between them, but Millie was happy to note there wasn't anything awkward about it. Maybe meeting and talking to Sebastian had eased whatever had been bothering Trevor about him. Seeing how much he cared for her already.

Millie closed her eyes. She was exhausted. They hadn't talked about it yet, but she was sure tonight they were going to be able to go back to the motel and get some actual sleep, in shifts.

She opened her eyes and stared at the screen some more. It was all the same, just cars and people moving past speedily. She was about to close her eyes again when something on the screen caught her attention. It had skipped.

"Wait." She sat up straighter in her chair.

"Yeah, I saw it, too." Trevor stopped the video and backed it up.

Playing it at normal speed, they watched the cars and people move past the camera, and then, sure enough, there it was again. The video glitched out and skipped.

"Play it again," Millie said, leaning forward in her chair, locking her gaze on the timestamp in the bottom right corner of the screen.

Trevor did as she asked, backing the video up. When he started it up again, she watched the seconds click by in sequential order until the glitch happened and there was a significant skip.

"Five minutes," she whispered. "There are five minutes missing from this tape."

Someone had altered the video.

Chapter Twelve

TREVOR

October 6

"Motherfucker!" Trevor slammed his hands on the desk and pushed himself away. The chair wheeled back as far as it could go, and he stood up.

"Calm down," Millie said from her seat next to him, her gaze still locked on the computer screen.

"Calm down? How do you expect me to calm down when this asshole is constantly at least five steps ahead of us? We need to look into the people who found the bodies? Sorry, deleted. The victims had been getting text messages from someone leading up to their disappearances? Spoofed numbers. Hey, let's check the footage on the CCTV cameras. Oh wait, nope, the fucker has already gotten there, too."

Trevor couldn't remember the last time he had been so frustrated at a case. It seemed as if everything was working against him. Them. The team.

"You need to take a deep breath. I don't think I've ever seen you Hulk out like this before. I'm worried you're going to smash one of these computers, and they are not ours to smash."

Trevor tried to take a deep breath, but it was not working. He could still feel himself boiling. "I don't understand. How did he know we were going to look through these videos?"

"Maybe he knew he got caught on camera and erased these weeks ago." Millie was trying to be the voice of reason, and he admired her for that. His brain just didn't want to accept that. Because...

"It's just too damn convenient," Trevor said out loud.

"What is?"

"The fact that the exact moments we need were cut, and not only were they cut, they were cut sloppily. Like he wanted us to know he had done it. He's taunting us, Millie."

Millie frowned. He could tell she was trying to choose her words wisely. He was aware of how he sounded. He sounded fucking crazy. But he knew what he was talking about. He wasn't being paranoid.

"Trevor—"

"No. Stop."

"Do you really believe the UNSUB is taunting us? Or does it just feel that way since we have hit brick wall after brick wall on this case? Is he really one step ahead of us, or was he just a really fucking good planner and we're just slowly uncovering each of his little breadcrumbs?"

He stopped his pacing and looked over at Millie. She was looking at him with her no-nonsense look, and he just...stopped. She was right. Of course, she was right. She was always right.

"Fine."

"That's it. I give this whole monologue, offering very logical explanations for your frustrations, and I get 'fine'?" Millie threw her hands up in mock frustration.

Trevor couldn't help but let a smile slip onto his face. "You're amazing, Millie. I don't know what I would ever do without you." He kept his tone even, faking a monotone.

Millie beamed at him. "Smash computers and form a tin hat wearing group of crime-conspiracy nut jobs?"

Trevor scoffed. "That's taking it a bit far, don't you think?"

She deepened her voice and brought her eyebrows down in a scowl. "He's watching us and deleting files in real time."

"I didn't say that. Exactly."

"It's the spirit of what you were saying."

He thought back to what he had ranted. "You're right."

"Is it my birthday? Because you have been saying my favorite phrase over and over again."

"Fuck off."

"Nope. Say it again, Trev. Tell me I'm right."

"You're basically guaranteeing I never say that phrase again."

"Nah, you'll forget you made this statement, and you'll use it again, and you'll fuel my ego. It's how I gain my power."

"By being right?"

"By being told I was right. There's a difference."

This time, Trevor let out a full laugh. "Of course there is."

"There is. And someday, maybe, you, too, will know the high of being told you're right."

"Fuck off." There was no bite to his words, only good humor.

"I guess we should probably tell the rest of the team that we have been foiled again."

"Yes, and even though this one is edited, we still need to go through the rest of the videos. Not only to confirm that they're all edited, but to see how much was spliced out."

"You're right." As he moved back to the desk, he grabbed the chair he had thrown behind him and wheeled it closer to the desk before taking a seat. "This video was missing a solid five minutes. That means that there was a five-minute window during which something was caught on camera that the UNSUB didn't want us to see."

"And we have an exact time to look into finding eyewitnesses."

"Along with a general location."

"She didn't make it to Pet's Best Friend."

Trevor shook his head. "She did not. He must have grabbed her on her way there."

"I'm going to make a note of the location of this camera and take it to Matthew and Logan. They can start asking around." Millie took a piece of paper and made a note of the corner the camera was located and stood up from her seat and left the room without another word.

Trevor turned back to his computer and trimmed the video where it glitched and saved it to a separate file. He then typed up a detailed report of what they found in the video.

Everything about the job had to look toward a court case. They needed to document everything. When they caught the guy, they needed to make sure there were no loopholes that would get the case thrown out or certain evidence inadmissible in court. Dotting all the I's and crossing all the T's was essential.

And mind-numbing at times.

Once he had typed up the report on the video, he picked up his phone and glanced at it. Without second-guessing himself, he dialed the first number in his phone.

"Hola, *mijo*!" his mother's vibrant voice came through the phone.

"Hola, *mami*." Trevor always felt better when he talked to his mom. "How are things back in DC?"

His mom laughed. "You've been gone a day!"

"Yeah, but you know how I get when I'm gone."

"Homesick. It's good here. Was a little colder than yesterday."

"That sounds nice. It feels like summer here still," Trevor answered. "I already miss the colder weather."

"Hopefully, you'll solve the case quickly and be able to come home. But I know the weather isn't what you wanted to talk to me about. Why did you call?"

Trevor sighed. He loved his mom for this exact reason: she could see through his bullshit almost immediately. "So, since we got here, Millie has started dating someone."

There was silence on the other end of the line. For a second, Trevor thought that maybe the call had been disconnected. But then he heard his mom sigh, and he braced himself for a lecture from his mom. But that's not what he got. "Are you okay?"

He let out his breath slowly through his teeth. "I'm fine. You know, happy for her."

His mom clicked her tongue. "Mijo, if you're telling her you're happy for her with that tone, then she's not buying it. I don't buy it."

"I'm pretty sure I'm selling it. I met the guy tonight. He seems...okay."

"You are really not selling it. Also, you've been in town for a day. How did she even meet someone so quickly?"

"She met him on the street yesterday. He was just walking by and, boom. Date."

"Are you going to let this affect the case? Your jealousy?"

"No. But I thought I was over her. I don't know what happened. We've been happily platonic for a decade, and now, she goes on one date with a guy and I'm suddenly falling back on old feelings. It's bananas."

"Do you want to date her?"

"No, she's my best friend. That's all."

"Then maybe this jealousy you're feeling has nothing to do with romance, but with the fact that you will no longer be the number one man in her life. That you'll be replaced."

Trevor thought about what his mom had just said. Maybe that's why he's been feeling the way he was. For as long as he could remember, both he and Millie had both been single. It had always been him and her against the world. Now, if she's serious about this guy, then it would drastically change their dynamic. If she had a boyfriend, he would be the last one on the team not paired off.

He would be alone.

That explained why he was suddenly jealous of Sebastian. It wasn't that he wanted to date Millie, he just didn't want to lose her.

"I think you're right, *Mami*. I don't want my relationship with Millie to change. And if she gets into a serious relationship with someone, nothing will be the same."

"Yes. And I know that change isn't something that you handle well, *mijo*. But you can't stop Millie from finding someone who she will be happy with just because you want to keep her to yourself. If you truly love her, you will let her go and find happiness where she can."

"I know. It's just hard. It's been the two of us for the last ten years."

"And you will still be the two of you, but different. Just because she finds love with someone else doesn't mean she'll stop being your best friend."

"But what if the guy she is seeing doesn't like the fact that her best friend is a man?" Trevor thought back to earlier that night when Sebastian refused to move when he was trying to leave the room. The look in his eyes screamed he wasn't okay with Trevor.

"Well," his mom started. "If he's not okay with you, then hopefully Millie will take that as a sign that maybe he's not the man for her. A good partner accepts all of your friends. I hope that when you find someone, they would be okay with your best friend being Millie, and if she wasn't, you would realize that she may not be right for you."

In his heart, he knew his mom was right. But his brain couldn't help but wonder if Millie would really sacrifice a romantic relationship for him. She had been single for so long. She lamented it constantly and said often she was desperate for companionship. Now that she had found it, would she sacrifice it for him?

"I can hear you thinking, you've always been a loud thinker," his mom chimed in. "She would choose you. You know that."

"But—"

"She would choose you."

"Thanks, mom. You're always good at calming me down, talking me out of a spiral and knocking some sense into me."

"You're welcome. Now, go catch a serial killer so you can come home. You owe me a dinner."

"Will do. *Te Amo.*"

"*Te amo, mijo.*"

Trevor hung up his phone and turned back to his computer. He had more footage to go through.

"Sorry I was gone so long," Millie threw open the door to the office closet, and Trevor jumped. "Matthew and Logan wanted to virtually walk the area since it's getting dark, and while they did that, Thomas and I came up with a game plan on trying to find any eyewitnesses. There are a lot of shops on that street, and many of them have large windows on their storefronts. It's likely someone working that day might have seen something."

Trevor perked up at that news. "That's great! Finally, some good news. You can't delete someone's memory like you can these videos."

"Not yet anyway. My bet is we're a decade out from being to do the zappy thing from "Men in Black"."

Trevor turned away from the computer and raised his eyebrow. "Really? A decade?"

Millie shrugged. "Why not? Either we get the zappy tech from Men in Black or AI will take over the world Terminator style. It honestly could go either way at this point. But I'm hoping for zappy memory erasers rather than robot overlords." She held up her hand with her fingers crossed.

Trevor shook his head. "You're ridiculous."

"I'm realistic."

"I wish I had a zappy memory eraser thing right now so I could forget this conversation."

"You're grumpy, which means you're tired and hungry. So, it's a good thing that I'm here to tell you we have been summarily dismissed from the premises, and Thomas said if he walks into this room and sees us in ten minutes, he will be displeased."

Trevor looked back at his computer, which had another video queued up and ready to go through.

Since Millie had left to tell the rest of the team about the missing footage, he had gone through the rest of the cameras that they had pulled from around Pet's Best Friend and found one more camera where the footage had been spliced, and that was from the next camera further west than the first. That meant that was the direction they should focus on.

His plan had been to look at the footage near Callie's Candy, but the idea of being able to go to bed and get some sleep was a lot more appealing.

"How long are they giving us?" Trevor asked as he shut down most of the computers. He kept the one running his program tracking the hack on the police station files up.

"Since we can't really question anyone or go look at any crime scenes since it's dark and getting late, Thomas is giving us the night. He told us to return at six, refreshed and ready to go."

Trevor's spirits rose. A full night's sleep sounded fantastic right about now. "Perfect. Now I just need to find some food."

"I have some sandwich left over in the fridge. You can have some if you want."

Trevor's spirits sank just a little with the reminder of Millie's previous date. But he was starving, and she had made that sandwich sound really appealing. "Are you sure? You basically said the sandwich was the best thing you've eaten. You really talked it up. And you want to share it with me?"

Millie shrugged. "Well, I really like you, and I really need you to try this sandwich to back me up. Logan is very skeptical. He is pretty sold that some sandwich shop from his hometown in Minnesota has the best sandwiches."

Trevor had gone home with Logan and his husband, Josh, once. It was to celebrate Logan's fortieth birthday. He and Matthew had been the only members of the team able to attend. Logan's parents had his favorite sandwich shop catered in.

"I mean, those were some pretty fucking amazing sandwiches. I may have to side with Logan on this one."

Millie threw up her hands in exasperation. "You haven't even tried this New Mexico sandwich!"

"Millie. I don't think you understand just how amazing these Minnesota sandwiches were. They were perfection. I don't think anything can beat them."

"Is everything in this room set for you to go home for the night?" Millie asked.

"Yes."

Millie reached over and grabbed his hand and began pulling him toward the door.

Trevor laughed, letting her pull him along. She marched him to the kitchen and threw open the fridge. Setting the sandwich on the counter, she let go of his hand to unwrap it. "Pick your poison. Turkey or Italian?"

Trevor looked at the sandwiches and had to admit they looked pretty amazing. "Italian. That's what I had in Minnesota. So, it's a fair comparison."

Millie handed him the Italian sandwich.

Trevor lifted it to his mouth and took a bite.

It was good. But not as good as the Minnesota sandwich. Which, to be fair, may have something to do with the freshness, but he wasn't quite sure if that was it.

He looked up at Millie and was about to tell her that, but she was looking at him with such expectation that he lost his resolve to tell the truth. He decided to fib a little. For the good of their friendship.

Or at least that's what he told himself is why he said what he said.

Swallowing the sandwich, he smiled. "This is amazing."

"Right?"

"Best sandwich ever."

"For real?"

"For real."

"And you'll tell Logan that tomorrow? That this sandwich beats his stupid Minnesota sandwich?"

Trevor smiled at her. "Yes, I can defend this sandwich's honor against Logan and his claims."

Millie squealed in delight and ran over to him, throwing her arms around his shoulders, pulling him into a hug. "Thank you!"

Trevor was surprised at the reaction, but didn't hesitate to wrap his arms around her, returning the hug, careful not to get the sandwich on her clothes.

"You're welcome."

And as he stood in the kitchen of the police precinct, holding his best friend in his arms, Trevor had to wonder if maybe he and his mom had it wrong about his feelings after all.

Chapter Thirteen

MILLIE

October 7

Millie wiped the condensation from the mirror and looked at her reflection. She still looked fucking exhausted. The dark circles under her eyes stood out starkly against her pale skin. She was a good girl, and tried to get some sleep when she got back to her motel.

She and Sebastian had FaceTimed, but he took one look at her and decided they would keep things PG for now. So instead of hot virtual sex, they spent an hour chatting to each other while they each lay in their respective beds.

They talked about everything and nothing. It was lovely.

And it did nothing to discourage her feelings for him.

If anything, she was falling harder for him.

After they hung up, her exhausted body collapsed into a deep, dreamless sleep. But when her alarm went off at five so she could get up with enough time to shower, she felt like she hadn't slept at all.

The worst part of this job was the lack of sleep she got when they were on a case.

She stared at her reflection and debated whether she was going to use the motel's dinky hair dryer to dry her hair. She shook her head. Of course, she wasn't going to. She pulled her long black hair over her shoulder and began braiding it. She then took that braid and wrapped it into a bun at the back of her head.

Easy and professional-looking and took less time than using that sad excuse for a hair dryer.

Walking back into her room, Millie looked at her blazer and debated grabbing it. She was already wearing a black long-sleeved dress shirt. She looked at her phone and pulled up the weather app. It was going to be another scorcher. Too hot for the blazer. She would just leave it. No point in bringing it if she wasn't going to wear it.

Closing the weather app, she pulled up her messaging app and opened up the thread between her and Sebastian. She opened up the camera and snapped a selfie and sent it to him.

Millie - Good morning.

She set her phone down, not expecting a reply, it was early. But her phone dinged almost immediately.

Sebastian - Good morning, beautiful.

Millie - You're up early.

Sebastian - I'm already at work, sweetheart. Construction needs to start before the sun in this heat.

Millie - Didn't even think about you being at work. Hopefully, I'm not interrupting anything.

Sebastian - You're not. It's a slow morning. We're waiting for some materials to be delivered. They're late. As usual.

Millie - Well, I hope you have a good day, and make sure you stay hydrated.

Sebastian - Yes, dear. I hope you have a more exciting day than you did yesterday.

Millie - I'm moving out of the closet and going to go question some people.

Sebastian - Good luck. I'll check in later. Maybe we can see each other somehow tonight.

Millie - I would like that.

*Sebastian - *Kissing Face Emoji**

*Millie - *Kissing Face Emoji**

Millie held her phone to her chest and took a deep breath before letting it out. She was going to make sure they could see each other tonight, and she was going to bring him back here, to her room and they were going to fuck, because holy shit, she was ready to have him fulfill all those promises he's been spouting.

Sebastian was right. This foreplay was amazing, but he had spent all this time working her up, and she had not had time to release any of the tension that had been building up, and she was feeling a little desperate.

No, tonight was the night. She and Sebastian were going to have sex, and get it out of her system, and once they did that, she could re-evaluate her feelings. Because maybe she was mistaking lust for something more.

That had to be it.

She had just met him two days before. It was impossible to feel anything more than lust at this point. Scientifically speaking.

But Matthew and Rebecca, the voice in the back of her head whispered, and she immediately shook it out. Matthew and Rebecca were an anomaly.

There was no such thing as love at first sight.

Statistically, if people fall in love immediately, their relationships are bound to fail in the long run.

Not that she was saying Matthew and Rebecca were destined to fail. The two of them were perfect for each other, and they were very logical about their relationship, and they were both at the same stage of their lives and ready to settle down.

But she and Sebastian?

They were destined to be a fling while she was here on this case. They were not a long-term thing.

They weren't.

At least that's what Millie was telling herself.

Sebastian just ticked all the boxes she needed right now.

He was also a unicorn who didn't run screaming from her when she told him what her job was, and he listened to her when she talked, and opened up and talked about himself...

And suddenly, Millie wondered what the odds of him being willing to move to Washington, DC, would be. He worked in construction, which was a job he could do anywhere. He said he didn't have any other ties here in Calico Rock...

Millie shook her head. It wasn't good for her. And it didn't do well to think about it.

With one last look at her blazer, still thinking it would be better to do without, Millie left her motel room, ready to meet up with the rest of the team to drive over to the precinct.

"Remind me what we know about Bobby Tucker?" Millie asked as she climbed into the black SUV and fastened her seatbelt.

She and Thomas were on their way to question Bobby casually, at his place of business. It was business hours, and he was the last known contact with Jamie. It was their best lead.

"He owns his own art shop, and he had hired Jamie to do his social media marketing. He had just asked to meet up when she disappeared."

"That's it?"

"From what Trevor could find, he's a thirty-nine-year-old man, and he's fairly new to town. He has no ties to Calico Rock other than his shop."

"Where did he move from?"

"Virginia. And he has no criminal record that we can find."

Millie hummed. "So, if we ran his DNA..."

"It would come back with nothing."

Millie bit back a sigh. She knew they were going into this with almost nothing, but she still didn't have to be happy about it.

It wasn't a long drive from the police precinct to the art shop. They were both in the downtown area, where Trevor was scouting all the CCTV video. They probably could have walked the distance. However, in this heat, they probably would have melted.

Pulling into an empty spot, Thomas put a sign on the dash informing any parking meter maids that their car was a federal vehicle and they didn't need to feed the meter, therefore don't waste their time with tickets.

They snagged a spot right in front of the art gallery, which was a little bigger than Millie had imagined an art gallery in a town the size of Calico Rock would be.

The storefront had one of those old-fashioned window display areas, and in it there were some faux cacti and some fabric the color of the desert sands of New Mexico. Hanging on the board was a large painting of red rock formations against the setting sun.

Millie let out a low whistle. She had to hand it to him...this man was talented.

She and Thomas exchanged a look before Thomas gestured for her to enter first. She pulled open the door, and cool air immediately blasted her. If anything, they were going to be very comfortable during their session this morning.

The art gallery was full of paintings similar to the one in the display window. Lots of paintings of the landscapes of New Mexico. And every single one of them was beautiful.

While she hoped this was their man and they could fuck off out of this town and back home to DC where the weather made sense, she also hoped he wasn't the man they wanted and she could come back to this art shop and buy a painting from him.

Did she have any attachment to New Mexico? No.

Could she admire the beauty of the landscape? Absolutely.

The man in question came out from the back of the gallery with the chime of the door. He was about six feet tall and bulky. His arms had muscles that were reminiscent of a Marvel movie star. He had a shaved head, but he wasn't bald. Dark fuzz covered the dome of his head. He was wearing a plain gray shirt that looked like it was slightly too small to hold all his muscles, and his face was whatever the male version of resting bitch face was. This man looked like he belonged in an MMA ring, not in an art gallery.

"Can I help you?" he asked as he approached.

Thomas and Millie both whipped out their badges as if they had rehearsed this move.

"I'm Special Agent Fleming, and this is Special Agent Driscoll. We're with the Behavioral Analysis Unit with the FBI, and we were wondering if we could ask you a few questions?"

The man screwed up his face. "Me?"

"Are you Bobby Tucker?" Millie asked.

The man nodded.

"Then yes, we would like to ask you a few questions."

Bobby gestured for them to follow him through the gallery until they came to the back room, where he housed an office. "Please come in and take a seat. I would offer you something to drink, but I mostly keep energy drinks around in case I'm working in my studio late."

"That's okay, you don't need to offer us anything. We're fine." Thomas was adopting his role as good cop. That was what he always did in interrogations. An older Black man with a gentle voice was pretty soothing to most criminals. Thomas would lure them in with his unassuming old-man vibes, and then whoever was in the room with him, typically Logan, would swoop in and catch them off guard. It worked ninety percent of the time. People sometimes said he reminded them of James Earl Jones in "Field of Dreams".

Millie wasn't great at being bad cop, but apparently today was the day she was going to have to be at least a little okay at it.

Bobby raised his eyebrow and looked between the two of them. "You'll have to excuse me, but I keep racking my brain about why the FBI would be here wanting to question me. And I keep coming up blank. Is this something to do with my art?"

"Kind of," Millie started. "What can you tell me about your relationship with Jamie Sanders?"

"Jamie Sanders? You mean the woman who was murdered a couple of months ago? Found out in a park? That Jamie Sanders?"

Thomas nodded. "Yes. That Jamie Sanders."

Bobby shook his head. "I hired her to do my social media work. She was the best person in town, came highly recommended by everyone here. And she was doing a great job for the few weeks we worked together. I had no problems with her. But that's it. That is the extent of our relationship."

"From what her husband told us, you were a bit excessive with your texting, texting all day and night. You were what he described as a difficult client." Thomas kept his voice calm and even, his face held a genial expression.

Bobby looked confused. "What? No, I barely messaged her. I sent her an email with what I wanted, and then she did it. She even went above and beyond what I asked for. I was very happy with my business with her. I never texted her. Especially not incessantly."

"Our records show that you texted Mrs. Sanders several times a day over the course of the two weeks you worked together." Millie made a show of pulling out her tablet and scrolling through to the files of the text messages. She opened up the exchange between Tucker and Sanders before laying the tablet on the desk, facing him so he could read what was on the screen.

Bobby looked down at the tablet, his mouth open and floundering, trying to find words to say. "I didn't send these. I didn't send any of these."

"That's your number, isn't it?" Millie gestured down at the tablet to the number prominently displayed.

"It is, but—"

"Did Mrs. Sanders meet all the expectations sent through these messages?" Millie interrupted.

"She did, yes. But I thought she was just going above and beyond what I asked. Look, I'm new in town, and I wanted my business to be successful. I asked the lady at Pet's Best Friend who had done her social media. She told me she was using Jamie Sanders. I looked her up and contacted her through her website. We emailed back and forth a couple of times to hammer out the details, and after I sent my initial payment, that was it. I didn't contact her again. I figured if I needed her to do more for me, I would. When she started posting more, I just assumed I was getting some new customer bonus in order to try to retain my business. That's it. I don't even have her phone number. Look."

Bobby pulled his phone from his pocket and slid it across to Millie and Thomas. Thomas picked it up and looked at Bobby questioningly.

"The code is 5687. My birthday," Bobby said, gesturing at the phone.

Thomas entered the code and pulled up his messaging app. Scrolling through a little, he stopped and turned the phone back to face Bobby. "How do you explain this?"

Bobby's mouth dropped open. Millie peeked over the phone, and even though she was reading upside down, she could see what was there. Message thread between Bobby and Jamie. The same one they pulled from her phone records.

Damning evidence against Bobby.

"This is impossible. I never texted her. We only messaged—" He stopped right there, shutting his mouth tight, his eyes widening, knowing he had made a grave error.

Millie leaned forward on the desk, folding her arms under her. "You only messaged where?"

Bobby shook his head. "I think we're done here."

Millie felt her stomach drop. Damn. So close, yet so far.

Thomas nodded. "That's fine. But make sure you stick around town, Bobby. It wouldn't look good if you skipped town."

"I don't want to see you back here unless you have a fucking warrant." Bobby kept his tone genial, which was good for him.

"Oh, don't worry. Next time we see you, we'll be questioning you in a much more formal manner." Millie also kept her tone genial, saying everything with a smile on her face.

"And I'll make sure I have my lawyer present." Bobby also had a smile on his face when he answered.

Millie and Thomas stood from the chairs they were seated in, and saw themselves out of the office. Millie could hear Bobby on the phone with someone, probably his lawyer. While she was glad people were cognizant of their rights, it always slowed things down when they did. She much preferred an ignorant suspect who loved to chat. Things went a lot faster and easier that way.

But at least this trip wasn't a complete bust. They now had evidence that he had messaged Jamie on his phone. It was right there. He could deny it all he wanted, but the messages were there. They also had a hint that he talked to her by other means. They just had to figure out what those other means were.

Warm air blasted Millie as she stepped out of the air-conditioned building, and she groaned. It shouldn't be this hot in October. It was unnatural.

She pulled out her phone and dialed Trevor.

"Ford."

"Hey, we need you to do something for us."

"What do you need?"

"When we were talking to Bobby, he slipped and mentioned that he and Jamie messaged each other, but he insisted it wasn't via text message, but by some other means. I need you to find those other means."

"On it."

The line disconnected, and Millie pocketed her phone. This bastard had something to do with the murder of these women, and Millie was determined to figure out what it was.

Chapter Fourteen

TREVOR

October 7

Trevor hung up with Millie and immediately got to work trying to figure out how Bobby and Jamie had been communicating. If it wasn't through text messaging, how?

He pulled up her social media and, using the passwords her husband had provided, he could get onto her computer. Jamie's husband had come to the station that morning and dropped off her computer and planner, hoping that maybe they would help. Trevor couldn't believe it was still in the possession of her family. The detectives down here were proving more and more incompetent. It was fucking frustrating.

Trevor plugged in the password to her Instagram and clicked into her DMs.

BINGO.

There they were. Messages between Jamie and Bobby.

Keeping the Instagram DMs open on one screen, he opened up the transcripts of the text messages between the two of them. If two different people sent the messages, he should be able to tell the difference.

With the two side by side, he began by comparing time-stamps.

He frowned.

The Instagram DMs were what started first. That was how Bobby initiated contact with Jamie. The two talked about business for two solid days strictly on Instagram before the text messages on the phone started. But the strange part was, there was no communication between the two to start communicating via text.

None.

It just...happened.

And Jamie didn't even question it. Or if she did, those messages weren't in the transcripts that they had. Which Trevor didn't even question at this point. The UNSUB was technologically ahead of them, so he could have easily deleted them to cover his tracks.

Scanning back and forth between the screens, Trevor read each message. Sometimes a text message was sent simultaneously with an Instagram DM, and they were on completely different topics. Which could mean two things: the two modes of messaging were done by two different people, and the UNSUB wasn't monitoring the DMs. Which felt like a very amateur move for someone who had been one step ahead of them the entire time.

But it was his first time. Maybe he learned from any mistakes and perfected them between victims?

Trevor continued scrolling and then stopped. He re-read the DM several times before he picked up his phone and dialed.

"Driscoll."

"Bobby and Jamie were having an affair."

"What?"

"That artist, Bobby, and Jamie were having an affair," he repeated.

"How did we not know this?"

"Because they communicated via Instagram DMs. And the UNSUB didn't know about it either because he wasn't monitoring the DMs, so it wasn't even mentioned in the text messages."

"Wait, so you're saying that the UNSUB communicated with Jamie via text message and Bobby communicated with her via Instagram, and she didn't know they were different people?"

"I'm not saying she didn't know. The texts and DMs sometimes came in simultaneously, and about completely different things. She may have suspected, or maybe she thought Bobby was covering his tracks."

"So, he was texting her random shit on the phone to cover up their hanky panky. Her husband might have looked at her text messages, but he probably wouldn't have looked at her DMs. Had the two met up in person? Was this like a physical affair? Or just a sexting affair?"

Trevor scrolled a little further. "Oh, they totally met up at least once. A couple of days before she died."

"Do you think the UNSUB knew this? Remind me of what the text said that lured her out."

Trevor scrolled down to the message sent the day she died. "He said, 'Hey, I think we should go over this campaign in person. Can you meet me at my shop?' And she replied, 'Sure' and used a little winky face emoji."

"She probably thought he was using coded language," Millie muttered.

"She absolutely did, because they were boinking each other in his little back room at his shop."

"No wonder the weasel got all cagey when I started asking questions. They were fucking, so of course that just makes him look even more suspicious. Are you certain the two communications were written by two different people?"

"I mean, they were either written by two different people, or this Bobby guy was a fucking genius at covering his tracks. Because, like I said, there are overlapping messages, and the tones are different. I'll have to look at them deeper to prove it definitively, but on the surface level, my gut is saying these are written by two different men."

"Your gut is typically not wrong, so we're going to go with that." Millie sighed. "Fuck, now we have to go back in there and question him about his affair. He is such a fucking douche canoe."

"Do you think he knows something?"

"I don't know, he was so sketchy and twitchy. I don't know if it's because he knows something, or if he thought we knew about their affair. But I need to go back in there and talk to him to see if he knows more than what he's giving us."

"Why don't you give him the day? Let him stew a bit. Go back tomorrow, see if he squeals like a pig."

"Good idea. What are you going to work on?"

"Going to comb through the other victims' social media messages and compare them to their texts. Maybe I can find somewhere else where the asshole made a mistake."

"Good luck. We're walking over to talk to Alyssa St. George, the owner of Pet's Best Friend. We'll let you know if we learn anything of note."

"Thanks. And I'll do the same for you."

They hung up, and Trevor turned back to his computer monitors. The messages between Jamie and both real and fake Bobby were still up. He sat back, folding his arms across his chest, and let his eyes focus on the screens.

There had to be something between these messages that would be a clue, other than the fact that text Bobby obviously didn't know what Instagram Bobby was talking to Jamie about. Mostly, did Jamie know she was talking to two different people?

The language between the two was eerily similar. The UNSUB obviously had enough access to Bobby to mimic his speech. Eerily accurate impersonation. This guy either was a genius, or he was feeding shit into an AI program.

Exiting out of the messages between Jamie and Bobby, Trevor pulled up the texts exchanged between Sharon and the owner of Pet's Best Friend. Then, he pulled up Sharon's social media. She was very active across several platforms. He started rooting around looking for any interactions between her and St. George.

There was a soft knock on the door, breaking his concentration.

"Yeah."

The door opened, and he turned to see who it was, freezing when he recognized the man.

"Oh," Sebastian stopped short of entering the room. "Millie isn't here?"

Trevor shook his head. "She's in the field."

"Shit. I was hoping to surprise her with breakfast." He half-heartedly held up a nondescript white paper sack.

Trevor tried to school his face into something neutral even though he was annoyed by this man's interruption. "She didn't even come here this morning. And even if she did, we get early starts. She's been out for a couple hours now."

"Noted. Is it okay if I..." Sebastian used the bag to gesture at the desk next to Trevor's monitors.

Trevor shrugged, turning back to the computers, trying to ignore the other man.

He felt Sebastian move to set the bag down on the desk, and out of the corner of his eye, he caught him pulling out his cell phone and aiming it at the desk.

"What the fuck do you think you're doing?" Trevor leaped from his seat and stood in front of the other man, blocking his view.

"Taking a picture of the bag and texting it to Millie."

"This is an active investigation. You can't be taking pictures in here."

"Fuck. I didn't know."

"Just text her you left her something. I'll make sure she gets it. Now, get out."

"Jealous much?" Sebastian muttered under his breath as he turned to leave, just loud enough for Trevor to overhear.

"Excuse me?"

Sebastian turned around, his darkly lined eyes narrowed. "You heard what I said."

"Yeah, I did. And I don't think I'm the person in this room who is jealous."

Sebastian scoffed. "You think I'm jealous of you?"

"Yeah, I do. And I think you knew Millie wouldn't be here this morning, and the only reason you came here this morning was to mark your territory."

If he wasn't looking for it, Trevor would have missed the slight change in Sebastian's demeanor as Trevor's words hit their mark.

"You can't be further from the truth. You're jealous because you've finally realized Millie doesn't want a fucking geek like you. She wants a real man who can give her what she needs."

"And is that you? A man who is cosplaying the fucking Winter Soldier at his angstiest."

"Wow, an insult only a fucking nerd would make. Surprise."

Trevor took five steps, closing the gap between the two of them, not allowing the slight height difference between the two of them to intimidate him. "Millie is my best friend and has been for the last decade. She's special, and she obviously has found something she likes about you. If you fucking hurt her..."

"You'll what?" Sebastian lowered his head, locking his gaze with Trevor. "You'll kick my ass? Maybe I should report you to your superior. Threatening a civilian."

"Go ahead. Report me. You'll get the same fucking talk from him. He thinks of Millie as a daughter."

Sebastian let out a soft laugh, shaking his head. He took a step back. "Watch your back. Millie may be your best friend now, but I don't think she will be for long."

"What's that supposed to mean?"

"Don't worry about it." Sebastian nodded his head toward Trevor's computers. "Good luck with your search." Without another word, Sebastian turned and walked out of the door, slamming it behind him.

Trevor stood locked in place staring at the closed door, an uneasy feeling creeping its way through his chest.

Chapter Fifteen

MILLIE

October 7

"I'm sorry, what did you say?" Millie walked out of the dog groomer, holding a hand to her ear to hear what the person on the other line was saying.

"Can you get away tonight? I want to cook you dinner." Sebastian was saying on the other line.

"I can try. What time?"

"Whenever you can. I want to see you."

"Yeah, I can text you when I know more about my schedule tonight."

"Cool. I brought you breakfast this morning. Dropped it in that closet you were working in."

Millie smiled to herself. This man was something else. She couldn't remember the last time someone had made sure she was well fed on a case. "That's really sweet of you. Hopefully, it's something that can keep?"

"Pastries from my favorite bakery. I didn't know what you would like, so I brought you some of my favorites." Millie caught a tone in his voice that didn't seem quite right.

"I look forward to eating them. Hey, is everything okay? You sound a little off."

Sebastian sighed on the other end of the line. "I mean, I didn't want to make a big deal about it, but when I dropped off the breakfast, your friend threatened me."

Millie frowned. "Threatened you?"

"Yeah. All I did was drop off breakfast, and he got all pissed off. I really don't understand what happened. He was pretty upset."

"You probably caught him off guard. He more than likely wasn't expecting you. Sometimes he reacts viscerally. You two probably had a little misunderstanding."

"Are you just going to take his side?"

"I'm not taking anyone's side."

"I'm really upset about this. You said he's your best friend, fine, but I thought we were going to have something. But if you're going to side with him all the time..."

"Look," Millie interrupted. "I'll talk to him, find out what happened, and I'll tell him to be little more polite next time."

"Whatever. Text me when you can come over, and I'll start making dinner. I'll text you my address." Without waiting for a reply, the call disconnected.

Millie stared down at her phone for a second, perplexed. Immediately, she opened up her phone app and pressed Rebecca's number.

"You're lucky I'm on lunch right now, Driscoll, calling me in the middle of the school day like this."

"Shit, I didn't even look at the time. I'm sorry."

"Don't apologize, I was just giving you a hard time. What's up?"

"Sebastian went to drop off breakfast for me this morning and, apparently, Trevor threatened him."

"Threatened him as in," Rebecca deepens her voice, "if you break her heart, I break you?"

"Honestly? Maybe? Sebastian was a little vague about exactly how he was threatened. He just said he was threatened."

"I don't know Trevor that well, but I can't imagine him saying something too scary."

"I know. And then Sebastian got really pissy and accused me of taking Trevor's side over his."

"And you said, I don't have time for you throwing a tantrum and broke things off?"

"I told him I would talk to Trev, and we have a dinner date tonight at his house." Millie's words came out in a rush, and she cringed as she heard them.

"Millie!"

"I know!"

"You cannot be so horny that you're going to sabotage your relationship with Trevor and throw out all of your dignity."

"I'm not throwing out my dignity."

"You are. And you're letting that man manipulate you."

"He's not manipulating me. I think I would know if he were."

"I'm not trained like you are in reading people's intentions, but I'm pretty sure that man just got you to sell out your best friend in order to go to his house for dinner and sex."

Millie frowned. Was that what happened? She thought back to the conversation. "Okay, maybe a little bit of manipulation, but not a lot."

"Millie!"

"I really like him, okay? And we're still in early days. Maybe after I go over to his house for dinner, and all this sexual tension is finally resolved, whatever there is between us will be dead and I can move on, dignity intact."

"And if you still feel strongly about him after you resolve your sexual tension?"

"Then I will talk to him about how he can't just manipulate me to get what he wants. We'll set boundaries. I'm nearly forty, I can set boundaries."

"Okay. I just don't want to see you hurt."

"I'm not going to get hurt."

"How's the case on your end? When I talked to Matty before I went into school this morning, he sounded frustrated."

"Yeah, it's not going great. Turns out the UNSUB is some sort of fucking genius." The door to the groomer opened, and Thomas walked out, looking at his phone. "Hey, Thomas is here. I gotta go."

"Talk to Trevor. Get his side of the story before you believe everything Sebastian said. And text me letting me know you are okay."

"Will do. Talk later."

"Later."

Millie hung up with Rebecca and pocketed her phone before turning to Thomas. "What do you have?"

"Trevor has gone through the social media messages of the other three vics, and none of them had extensive contact with the businesses the UNSUB spoofed. Just basic entering contests or asking about availability."

"And St. George confirmed she wasn't the one who sent Sharon the message about having an opening for the dog?"

"Correct. The day Sharon disappeared, St. George found her dog, Gus, running down the sidewalk, leash attached, but didn't know who he belonged to until she saw the story on the news that night. Otherwise, she never personally talked to Sharon."

"At least the dog made it out okay."

"There's always a bright side."

Millie's phone dinged with an incoming message. She glanced down at her phone and froze.

"What's wrong?" Thomas stepped closer to her, trying to see what she was seeing.

She turned her phone toward him.

UNKNOWN - *Even though you look exhausted today, you're looking really sexy.*

Thomas looked up from the phone and immediately glanced around. "The fucker is spying on us."

Millie looked around, too. The sun was blinding and re-flected off the windows of the other buildings, making it very difficult to see anything. He could be anywhere.

"This is Special Agent Fleming. The UNSUB made contact with Special Agent Driscoll again about two minutes ago. He has eyes on her. We are standing on the sidewalk outside of Pet's Best Friend. You need to send officers to canvas the area."

He didn't wait for a reply before hanging up and redialing. "Ford. He sent another message to Driscoll. I need you to trace it now. He has eyes on her."

Millie raised her hand to shield her eyes from the sun, but it didn't help. Where was this man spying on her from?

She glanced down at her phone. She can try to draw him out.

MILLIE - *It seems pretty unfair that you can see me and I can't see you. Where are you?*

UNKNOWN - *Tsk Tsk Agent Driscoll. You think I'm an amateur? You have to try better than that.*

MILLIE - *But obviously you're nearby. You can see that I look like shit this morning.*

UNKNOWN - *I believe I said you look tired, yet sexy.*

MILLIE - My mistake. So, are you? Nearby?

UNKNOWN - I have eyes on you, if that's what you mean. That's what Agent Fleming said, right? That I have eyes on you?

Millie looked up from her phone and looked frantically around. He was not only close enough to see her, he could also hear them.

In the distance, she could hear the approaching sirens of the backup Thomas had requested. She needed to keep him talking. Maybe that would be a clue as to where he was.

TREVOR - Keep texting him. Get him to continue responding. The more he texts, the easier it will be to triangulate his actual position.

Millie smiled. She had to hand it to her friend to be on the same page she was.

MILLIE - On it. BTW, we need to talk soon about this morning.

TREVOR - I agree.

Millie switched back to the conversation with the UNSUB.

MILLIE - It seems pretty unfair that you have eyes on me and you're giving me all of these compliments, but I have no idea what you look like.

UNKNOWN - Let's just say I'm your type.

MILLIE - How do you even know what my type is?

UNKNOWN - Thirty-eight years old, professional woman, your type is the type of man other women like you are attracted to: whoever will give you the time of day. Tell me, Agent Driscoll, is your biological clock ticking like fucking crazy?

It was as if a boulder had hit her right in the chest. Fuck. The audacity of this motherfucker.

MILLIE - My biological clock is just fine, you fucking asshole.

UNKNOWN - Seems like I have struck a nerve, Agent Driscoll.

MILLIE - You've struck nothing. You're really veering from your MO here, jerkface. Maybe I'm the one who touched a nerve.

UNKNOWN - Have I really though? Or are you simply missing key information?

MILLIE - What do you mean?

UNKNOWN - I mean. Think about it a little more, Agent Driscoll. You're smart. Look at the victims.

MILLIE - Tell me more.

UNDELIVERED

"FUCK!" Millie screamed at her phone. The UNSUB dropped the number. The communication was over. The only thing she could hope for at this point was that Trevor got what he needed.

"Come on," Thomas spoke next to her. "Let's head back to the precinct. See what they've found there."

Millie merely nodded and followed Thomas back to the vehicle, not taking her eyes off of the streets. He was out there somewhere. But as Thomas ushered her into the passenger side of the car, she couldn't think about him watching her, she could only think about what he had told her. That she and the victims had something in common.

But what?

The drive to the precinct was quick, and before Millie knew it, she and Thomas were hopping out of the car and rushing in.

"Please tell me you could get something?" Thomas addressed Trevor the second he breached the conference room door.

Trevor was standing holding a tablet, his dark hair mussed, his dress shirt unbuttoned at the collar and untucked from his slacks. "The fucker has state-of-the-art technology. He was bouncing his signal off every tower from here to Vegas, it seemed like. I was just starting to bypass whatever he was using to pinpoint it to the area, but then you stopped texting him."

"Not my fault. The last text I sent bounced back as undeliverable. He must have ditched the number." Millie ran her hands across the top of her head before dropping them in frustration. She had her hair up in what would now be considered a messy bun, and she didn't get the satisfaction of running her hands through her hair.

"I had thought he was just using a burner, but he may be using a program on his computer to spoof the numbers and bounce them. This is some high-tech hacker shit."

"Add that to the profile. This guy is not just tech savvy, he's a fucking professional," Matthew said.

"Was he taunting you?" Logan asked.

Millie shook her head. "No. Not really? He was flirting in a weird, insulting way? What really stood out to me was that he gave me a clue about the victims."

"What do you mean?" Logan leaned forward in the chair he was seated in, resting his elbows on the table in front of him.

"So, I kind of taunted him back, you know? Pointed out that he was really veering from his MO. And then he said," she pulled out her phone to make sure she was going to quote him accurately. "Have I really though? Or are you simply missing key information?"

"What the fuck is that supposed to mean?" Matthew threw his hands up in exasperation.

"It means the asshole manipulated the fucking text messages," Trevor practically growled.

"He can do that?" Logan asked.

"Yeah, he can."

"Is that something you can fix?" Thomas asked.

"Of course." Trevor closed his eyes and took a deep breath. "If you need me, I'll be in my closet, trying to undo something else this fucker did to manipulate the investigation."

Trevor stormed out of the room, and Millie's eyes followed him. While she knew she needed to stay and debrief with the rest of the team, she also needed to talk to Trevor about the morning and his interaction with Sebastian, so she followed him out. "I'll be right back," she tossed out over her shoulder as she pushed through the door.

She made it to the closet in time to follow Trevor in before the door had even had a chance to close.

"Your breakfast is on the table," Trevor said, his gaze on the computer as he sat down

"Thanks, but I also want to talk about what happened this morning."

Trevor paused and turned slightly in his chair. "You mean when Sebastian came in here to drop off your breakfast and insulted me?"

"What?"

"Yeah, he came in here and called me a nerd and said some shit about how you wouldn't be my best friend for long before storming out of here."

Millie frowned. Sebastian had definitely left that part out. But it lent some context to the stuff Sebastian had told her. "I'm sorry he insulted you, but maybe he did it because you threatened him."

It was Trevor's turn to frown, drawing his brow down. "I didn't threaten him."

"Sebastian called me while I was at Pet's Best Friend. He told me you threatened him. He was pretty upset."

He shook his head. "I never...Look, he came in here and told me he wanted to surprise you with breakfast, but he was disappointed you weren't here. He set the bag down, and he went to take a picture of the desk, and I stopped him since there is a lot of sensitive information on the screens of the computer, but I never threatened him, not really. If anyone was threatening anyone, it was him."

"I told him I wouldn't be here. He knew that. When he called, he told me he wanted to make sure I had food for later. You must have misheard him. And maybe you're stressed out about everything with the case, but I need you to not threaten him again, please."

"I didn't mishear him. And I didn't threaten him. I don't know why you're not believing me, and why you're taking his side over mine."

"There aren't sides."

Trevor scoffed. "It sure as hell feels like there are. I'm having to defend myself to you. We've been friends for a decade, and you've known this man for like two minutes. And here you are, not even listening to what I have to say, and just blindly believing him."

"I'm not blindly believing him. I'm just saying there is no reason for him to lie to me about something like this."

"There's no reason I would lie to you about this!" Trevor shouted.

"Yes, there is! You're jealous that I've found someone!"

Her words echoed off the walls of the small closet, and Millie immediately regretted them as she watched Trevor's face fall.

"I think you should leave."

"Trev, I'm sorry—"

"Go, Millie. I need to work, and I don't want to say anything that will hurt this friendship. What I will say is I'm not jealous. I was actually very happy you found someone. You deserve to be happy. But that's all I will say. Now, go. I need to work."

Trevor punctuated his sentence by turning around and facing his computer.

Millie knew better than to say anything else. She knew his moods, and if she said anything else, he would say something he would probably regret, and she didn't want it directed at her. Because whatever he would say would definitely break her heart, and she was already feeling a lot of feelings. Instead, she turned and left the closet. And as the door closed behind her, she leaned her back against the door and slid to the ground. And that's when she let her tears flow freely.

Chapter Sixteen

SEBASTIAN

October 7

Sebastian smiled down at his phone. Millie had just messaged him that she was on her way over for dinner. Setting the phone down on his counter, he walked toward the freezer. He pulled out a frozen lasagna and some garlic bread and walked it over to set on his stove. Reading the back of the box, he chose a number in between the two oven temperatures and set the oven to it.

As he waited for the oven to preheat, he walked through his apartment picking up some of his clutter, whistling while he worked.

It had been a while since he had brought a girl to his apartment, and it made him a little giddy. He really liked Millie, and he couldn't wait to spend this time alone with her. True, she was only in town for a short time, but he was going to make that time count.

He was already plotting out which takeout to bring her tomorrow. And which meals to bring her. Part of his seduction scheme was to make Calico Rock so appealing to her she would consider staying past the case closing. Step one was the food. Show her all the best local restaurants. Calico Rock may be a small town, but there was a growing local food scene. And she already knew about most of the businesses on the square. True, this was no Washington, D.C., but he knew she could be happy here.

Perhaps he was getting a little ahead of himself. He could only hope that she felt the same way he did about her. It was a good sign that she took his side in the argument between him and Trevor this morning.

Sebastian didn't know what it was about him, but he just didn't like him. He rubbed him the wrong way. The way he was gatekeeping Millie from him. Questioning his motives. The behavioral analyst thing was attractive on Millie, but it was annoying on Trevor.

Sebastian paused his cleaning when he got to a photo of his mom. She'd been gone for almost four months now, and he still had big feelings about it.

Then the oven beeped, signaling it was preheated and ready. Sebastian walked over to the oven and put the lasagna and garlic bread in.

Now he just needed to wait for his date to arrive.

Chapter Seventeen

MILLIE

October 7

Millie pulled the car up to the curb in front of the apartment building Sebastian had texted her the address to earlier. She knew her way around the city well enough now to know the pool where Victim Number Three, Laura, had been found, was right up the road, so he wasn't lying the day they met. He lived very close.

Before getting out of the car, she smoothed down her shirt, making sure she didn't have any wrinkles. She would have liked to have gone back to the motel to freshen up before meeting him, but she didn't have time.

After her argument with Trevor, she had set herself up in the conference room with Matthew and Logan, the three of them going through the victimology trying to piece together something that would connect the four victims together. They were getting really close, but they decided to take a break, and that's when she excused herself, ducking into the bathroom real quick to fix her hair and touch up her lip gloss.

Normally before a date, she would talk to Trevor and get a pep talk, but they were currently not speaking. Which, even though it had only been a couple of hours, felt...wrong. Just wrong. She would make sure to make up with him when she got back. They had never fought like this before, and she really regretted some things she had said to him. And she knew if she called Rebecca, she would say the same things she was currently thinking.

Millie shook her head, ridding it of thoughts of Trevor. Going into a date with someone else was not the time to be thinking about another man. She was going to walk in there, and she would not be Special Agent Driscoll, she would just be Millie. She would give Sebastian her complete attention and not think about the crime scene just down the road and the person who reported finding the body, who could possibly have also been the UNSUB.

"Stop it," she whispered. "Turn your brain off for one fucking night. If Matthew could do it, you certainly can."

Taking one more deep breath and letting it out slowly, she opened the door to the car and made her way to Sebastian's apartment.

The apartment complex differed from the ones in DC, but was very similar to the kind you would find in her hometown of Sunset Harbor, California. Back east, the doors to the apartments were typically inside buildings. Here, as in California, all the doors opened out to the outside. The landscaping of the complex consisted of a lot of brown rocks and cacti. The building itself was tan-painted concrete that definitely needed a facelift. Sebastian's apartment was set back from the road a bit. His green door was one of the few that didn't have some sort of adornment on it. Both of his neighbors had wreaths. The only personalization on the outside of the apartment was a rough brown mat that simply said, welcome.

Millie took a deep breath, raised her hand, and knocked. It didn't take more than thirty seconds before it opened and Sebastian's smiling face greeted her. The second she saw him, she instantly relaxed.

"Hey." He grinned down at her.

"Hey."

"Come on in." He stepped out of the way, letting her walk past him into the apartment.

As she walked into the apartment, she could smell dinner. "It smells delightful in here. What's for dinner? I can already tell it's something with garlic."

Sebastian chuckled. "Lasagna and garlic bread. I hope that's okay."

"Absolutely. You made a lasagna from scratch?"

"No, there's a lady who does freezer meals in town. I order from her a couple of times a month and stock the freezer. When I invited you for dinner, I had to check the freezer and make sure I still had something in there. I lucked out and there was this lasagna."

"Wow. I need to look into the area around where I live and see if there's anyone out there who does that. I would love to just stock up my freezer and not have to worry about dinner."

"Washington, D.C., is much bigger than Calico Rock. I can almost guarantee there is someone out there who does this."

"Good point."

"Please come in and have a seat." He gestured toward the small brown loveseat sitting in the main living area of the apartment. "There is still some time before dinner will be ready."

Millie walked over to the couch and took a seat. It was not as comfortable as it looked. With as plush as it looked, she really thought it would be softer. "Did you go into work today?"

Sebastian sat next to her on the couch, their thighs touching, his arm flung over the back. Millie's cheeks warmed, and certain parts of her anatomy clenched in anticipation.

"I did. I went in early this morning, before the sun really came up. We wanted to get our work done before it really got too hot."

"And you spent the rest of the day here?"

"Yeah, I had to clean and get things ready for you."

"You didn't need to put that much effort in."

"Gotta impress my girl. I heard women really like men who have their shit together."

Millie laughed. "You heard right."

"Well, points for me. Do I get bonus points for knowing how to do my own laundry?"

She pretended to think about it. "Mmm, I think laundry gets you five bonus points."

Sebastian leaned really close to her, his mouth right to her ear. "And how many points for knowing how to get a woman off?"

She shivered, and her breath quickened. "I think you're going to have to prove that by demonstration in order to earn any points."

His tongue snaked out and dipped into her ear before he gave her earlobe a little nip. "I'll be glad to give you a demonstration."

Millie shivered. "Yes, please."

Sebastian chuckled, the vibrations tickling her ear. He moved forward, placing a kiss on her neck underneath her ear, and moved down the column of her neck, moving his body closer to hers.

Millie's body was on fire, synapses firing everywhere. It had been way too long since she had last been touched this way. She turned until she was facing him, and he shifted to press her back into the couch, his weight settling nicely on top of her. She opened her legs, and he settled himself between her thighs.

She moaned as his hardness pressed against her center in just the right spot. She could feel him smirk against her skin as he gently nipped at her pulse point, while also pressing into her again, more firmly. She moaned again.

Sebastian brought his hand down, running it up the length of her leg, before coming up to her blouse-covered breast. He gave her a soft squeeze through the fabric of the shirt before expertly unbuttoning enough buttons to expose her breasts. Pulling down the cup of her bra, he brought his hand back to her breast, massaging it and lightly pinching her nipple, moving his mouth to finally capture hers in a kiss.

As their tongues battled for dominance, they moved against each other is passionate desperation, both chasing release. It didn't take long for Millie to reach her peak. She pulled away from Sebastian's mouth, threw her head back and cried out.

As she came back down, she opened her eyes, locking her gaze with his. He gave her a self-satisfied smirk, and she just shook her head.

Almost simultaneously, they both reached for the buttons of each other's pants, and somewhere in the background the timer for the oven went off, forgotten.

Chapter Eighteen

TREVOR

October 7

Trevor rubbed his hands down his face before glancing at the clock on his computer again. It was nine o'clock. Millie had left hours ago to go to the bastard Sebastian's house for dinner. She still wasn't back yet. Which meant only one thing. She had sex with him.

Trevor tamped down the jealousy rising in his throat. Well, he wasn't sure if it was jealousy or betrayal. He still couldn't believe the fight that he and Millie had earlier. They never fought, or if they did, they immediately made up. But they hadn't. She hadn't even apologized for the hurtful shit she had slung at him. He didn't think it was his place to apologize in this case. He had brought up legitimate concerns, and she accused him of the same fucking thing Sebastian had. Had even used the same language. Which meant she had only talked to Sebastian before him.

Something inside his brain niggled at the thought of Sebastian. His gut was telling him there was something seriously wrong with that man. But if he brought it up to anyone, they would just tell him he was jealous, or whatever. But he wasn't.

Seriously.

He wasn't.

He was simply looking out for his best friend. It had nothing to do with the unrequited feelings he had learned to shove deep down inside himself.

Really.

It was something else.

Trevor didn't like to judge people by the way they looked. His line of work cured him of that habit. When the most unassuming person could easily turn out to be a cold-blooded killer and the roughest-looking person could be the nicest, most charitable person, you learned quickly not to judge by looks alone. So, it wasn't Sebastian's 'bad boy' look that made Trevor do a double take. It wasn't something else. Something deeper.

Everything about him seemed superficial. He brought Millie food, but it never really felt like he was doing it because he cared about her. It was like he was buttering her up, trying to gain her trust.

Which, fair. He was attracted to her. He wanted her in his bed, so of course he was going to do things to make her want to sleep with him. But it didn't feel like he was only after that.

He had picked a fight with Trevor this morning, and then immediately warped the story to Millie.

He was manipulative, and he wasn't afraid of showing that side to Trevor.

When Trevor confronted him about his motives for coming to the closet, he could see something in his eyes shutter. He was controlling his emotions, and things happened so fast that Trevor didn't have time to analyze it in the moment, but the more he thought about it, the more he knew there was something there.

He needed to bring it up to the team, without it seeming like he was jealous.

Trevor was pretty certain he was the only person other than Millie to have met Sebastian in person. Maybe instead of him bringing it up to the team, he somehow got someone else from the team to meet Sebastian? The more profilers to have eyes on him, the better, probably.

Satisfied he had solved the Sebastian problem, at least for now, he turned his attention back to the computer.

All afternoon and evening he had been going back through the text messages to see what he could find. Officer Jones had brought him some food when it became evident he wasn't going to take a break to eat. The rookie was a pretty cool guy. They chatted a little about tech stuff before he left him alone again.

Trevor was hoping he could figure out if he could connect any of the text messages to an online messaging feature. He was pretty certain that's how the UNSUB was messaging Millie this afternoon. It was a quick and easy way to spoof numbers and cover up his tracks.

Trevor knew he had sophisticated programs, and he was a talented hacker. It was the only way he was able to stay five steps ahead of them. How else he could hack into the police database, spoof numbers, keep them on their toes?

The UNSUB had told Millie that she had something in common with the other victims. That he wasn't deviating from his MO, Trevor had assumed he had been manipulating the texts, but what if that wasn't it? That wasn't new information, Trevor knew that. And he knew that once he could recover anything the fucker had deleted or hidden, he would probably find the taunting, the manipulation.

But what if that isn't what he meant?

They all assumed that choosing Millie as his probable next victim was moving in a different direction. The other four victims were married, and they had children. Millie was neither of those things. The UNSUB still insisted he wasn't deviating from the MO.

Trevor opened up the texts between Millie and the UNSUB again.

UNKNOWN - I mean. Think about it a little more, Agent Driscoll. You're smart. Look at the victims.

'Look at the victims.' Trevor rolled that phrase around in his mind a few times. What specifically about the victims though?

He pulled up the document with the information about the victims. What should he be looking for?

They were all women between the ages of thirty-six and fifty-two. They were all married. All four were moms. So far, the only thing Millie had in common with them was their ages. She fell into the age bracket.

She fell into the age bracket.

Trevor sat up straighter in his chair. Were they looking too deep into the victimology? Was age the most significant factor to the unsub when he chose a victim? That couldn't be it. There had to be more. What was he missing?

He lined up the images of all four women across the screen.

That's when he saw it.

The women were all in the same age range, sure. However, how had they not seen this before?

All four victims had dark hair. The eye colors weren't all the same, but that didn't seem to matter. Their physical appearances were similar enough. He pulled up a picture of Millie and added it to the lineup.

Dark hair, right age range, light eyes like Sharon.

Fuck.

She fit the victim profile.

She wasn't married or a mom, but that's what the UNSUB was taunting her about. Her lack of motherhood.

He needed to find the missing text messages. He wondered if, once they found all the missing pieces if suddenly the case would open up to them, suddenly make sense?

Trevor shook his head. That would be too easy. There was no way the UNSUB would lead them to the answer. He had to know Trevor would find the texts, and it wasn't that large of a leap to figure out that all the women looked alike. This was a man who was always two steps ahead of them at all times. He wouldn't give away his game in one text to Millie.

They were still missing something, and it had to be something significant.

He picked up his phone and hit the first number.

"Fleming."

"We're missing something in the victimology."

"I know. Logan, Matthew, and I are on it. How's the text retrieval going?"

"A work in progress."

"Keep at it, and I will let you know what we come up with in the victimology."

"Sounds good. Have you heard anything from Millie?"

Silence fell on the other side of the line. "Trevor..."

"Never mind."

"She's going to be okay. You have to trust her."

"I trust her. It's him I don't trust."

"The feeling is mutual. But we have to focus on the case. It's our priority. We need to trust Millie and her instincts, whether we like it or not. If she doesn't show up to work in the morning, then we worry."

"Focusing on the case."

He hung up with Thomas and turned back to his computer. Sighing, he bent down to pick his water up off the floor. He didn't enjoy having an open container of liquid anywhere near the electronic equipment. Tempting too many fates for his comfort.

As he brought the cup up to his mouth to take a drink, an alarm went off on one of the screens. He jerked at the sound, causing his water to splash all over his chest, but he didn't care. Quickly setting the cup back on the floor, he sat back up so quickly the blood rushed to his head, causing him to be dizzy for a second. It took another second for him to find the screen that was beeping.

It was the one trying to find inconsistencies with Victim Number Three, Laura's, text messages. Rolling his chair closer to the desk, he put his hand on his mouse and stopped the beep. It was an alert that the program he was using had found something.

On the screen, he had pulled up the text history of Laura and the supposed candy shoppe. In black were all the messages they had access to before he realized the UNSUB had manipulated the messages somehow. In red were the things that the computer found.

Trevor's eyes widened. There were dozens of found messages. Dozens of messages passed between the UNSUB and Laura, beginning almost a week after Jamie disappeared, and escalating in frequency as the dates led up to the day she disappeared. He leaned forward in his seat, moving closer to the screens.

His eyes scanned the communication and then froze.

"Holy shit."

Chapter Nineteen

MILLIE

October 7

The ring of her phone roused Millie from the light sleep she had fallen into. She tried to sit up, but the arm around her tightened, pulling her closer into his body.

"Ignore it," Sebastian whispered in her ear, giving it a little nip.

"I can't. It's work."

Sebastian trailed his mouth down the column of her neck, running one of his hands up the side of her body before bringing it around and giving her breast a squeeze. "You deserve a night off. We haven't even had dinner yet."

Millie let out a breathy moan, pushing her body back against his, feeling his hardness against her bare ass. "Whose fault is that?"

"I'm not sorry." He nipped the spot between her neck and shoulder. "Are you?"

She answered with another moan as the hand on her breast moved between her legs, finding her wet, and ready.

He moved away from her long enough to open his bed side drawer to grab a condom and don it, and then he was back around her, lifting her leg to drape over his before pushing into her.

And then all thoughts about the phone that kept ringing were far from her mind.

Later, Millie was wide awake as Sebastian was sprawled out on his back, snoring. Quietly, she pulled back the covers and stood from the bed. Her first stop was the bathroom to clean up. Her second was to walk around the apartment and try to find all the pieces of her clothes, dressing herself. Then she found her phone.

Five missed calls.

Three from Thomas, one from Matthew, and one from Logan.

Zero from Trevor, and something in her chest ached at the thought he was still mad enough at her he wasn't one of the ones to call her. He was usually the first one to call her.

They didn't leave voicemails, which meant it wasn't an emergency, but they also called her five times.

She sat down on the couch and dialed Thomas.

"Fleming."

"Hey, what'd I miss?"

"She lives."

"Thomas."

"We just sent Trevor to track your phone. You're a target, Millie. You need to answer your damn phone."

"I was...busy." Millie cringed. She knew the men knew what she was doing. What she didn't need, though, was for people to tease her about it. She was not helping the situation.

Luckily, she was on the phone with Thomas and not Logan. "Get back here. Trevor found something."

Millie sat up straight. "He figured out the text messages?"

"Yes."

She stood up and rushed to where her shoes were by the door, slipping her feet into them. She glanced back toward the bedroom where Sebastian was sleeping and decided she would just text him when she got back to the precinct, apologizing.

Slipping out the door, she turned her attention back to Thomas. "What did he find?"

She made it back to her car, and as she started it, her phone switched over to the Bluetooth. "Trevor discovered that communication between the UNSUB and the victims began via text about a week before they went missing, and the texts were very similar to the ones you received."

A chill ran down Millie's back, and she struggled to breathe. "I started receiving texts almost a week post Sarah was discovered."

"You did."

"He really isn't deviating from his MO when it comes to me."

"He's not."

"Did Trevor recover all the text messages?"

"Just for victims three and four."

Laura and Sarah.

"I'm five minutes out."

"See you soon."

The line disconnected, and Millie's mind reeled. Honestly, she wasn't scared of the UNSUB. She knew the team and how they worked, and she knew they would never get to where the UNSUB got close to her. They would catch him before that point.

Matthew got caught and almost killed, the voice in her head supplied, and she tried to shake the thought free. Matthew's being kidnapped and nearly killed back in May was an anomaly. They always went out with a partner.

Unless you're out fucking a love interest, like Matthew was. Like you are now.

"Shut up," she muttered to herself in the quiet car.

Maybe she shouldn't have gone off alone to meet Sebastian. Anything could happen to her between his apartment and the precinct.

Of course, Guillermo took Matthew from the hotel where the entire team was staying, with Rebecca and Benji just on the other side of the door.

"Stop catastrophizing the situation, Millie. You're safe. You're allowed to have a social life. No one is going to kidnap you."

Her little pep talk ended as she pulled into the precinct's lot. Turning the car off, she stared at the nondescript building. She knew she needed to go in there and work on the case, but also, she would need to be in the same room as Trevor, who she owed a huge apology.

Who would know she just had sex with a man he didn't trust.

Maybe she could avoid Trevor for the rest of the night. They could start fresh in the morning.

Who was she kidding? They were a small team. There was no avoiding him. And if she did, everyone else would wonder what she was doing and why, and she really didn't want to bring everyone else in on her issues.

Taking a deep breath, she let it out slowly before deciding to put on her big girl panties and just get it over with.

She hated this.

Pushing open the door, she closed it behind her. As she walked up to the precinct, she smoothed down her hair with shaky hands.

She should have taken the time to shower. She was positive she smelled of sex.

Amazing sex.

Millie pulled her phone out to check the time. After midnight in D.C., much too late to call Rebecca to decompose the situation. That would have to wait until the morning.

Usually, she would also talk to Trevor, but that wasn't an option. The hurt crept back in, and she rubbed her chest.

Instead, she quickly typed out a text to Sebastian before shoving her phone back in her pocket. She felt slightly guilty leaving while he was sleeping, but she was sure he would understand.

Between Trevor and Sebastian, she was experiencing emotional whiplash. She was experiencing a level of happiness with Sebastian she hadn't felt in a long time, while at the same time, a level of heartbreak with Trevor she wasn't quite sure she wanted to acknowledge.

Pulling open the door, she shook her head. Focus on the case.

Millie pulled open the door to the precinct and smiled at the woman who buzzed her back into the bullpen. Things were pretty quiet. Small towns at night didn't tend to create busy overnight police work. The handful of officers were sitting at their desks working on paperwork. Winding her way through the maze of desks, it wasn't long before she was at the conference room. Looking through the window, she tensed up. They were all in there. Her eyes immediately sought Trevor.

His dark hair was mussed as if he had been running his hand through it constantly, sticking straight up in places. There were dark circles under his eyes, and she knew he hadn't been sleeping. He had been giving his all to this case, and she was, what? Finding the next great love of her life?

He brought his head around and his gaze locked with hers. He seemed to physically relax when he saw her. Obviously, her not answering her phone was worrying him, even though he didn't call.

He didn't call, but he still cared.

There was still hope for their friendship after all.

Right then, she decided they wouldn't talk about her date with Sebastian. She would talk about her relationship with Sebastian with Rebecca, and she would fix her friendship with Trevor by keeping the two men separate.

Yes, this could work.

She put her hand on the handle of the room and pulled the door open.

She could have her cake and eat it, too.

What could possibly go wrong?

Chapter Twenty

TREVOR

October 7

Trevor watched as Millie entered the conference room. He had been anxious when they couldn't get ahold of her. It wasn't like her to ignore her phone while they were on a case.

She usually wasn't getting laid while they were on a case.

Trevor shook his head, banishing those thoughts. He needed to keep his shit together, focus on the case, and not what was going on with Millie and Sebastian. If he wanted to salvage his friendship with Millie, he had to just ignore the niggling voice in the back of his head.

The one that told him the reason she didn't answer the phone was malicious.

The one that said she must have been hurt somewhere in order to not answer her phone, to prioritize the case.

But no. Apparently, her priorities were not where they should be on this case. He wracked his brain, and he knew when they were in Iowa, Matthew never let his new relationship with Rebecca hinder his work on the case. The only time he didn't answer his phone, and they thought he'd flaked out, he had been banged on the head with a bar and dragged to the basement of the killer.

So, forgive him if he thought the same thing had happened to Millie, since that was his baseline.

Trevor cleared his throat and focused back on the task at hand. Now that Millie was there, they could do the briefing. "About an hour ago, I was able to unscramble the messages between the UNSUB and both victims three and four, Laura and Sarah. I'm still working on the messages with victims one and two, Jamie and Sharon."

He pressed a button on his tablet and brought up the string of texts he recovered. "This is the string between the UNSUB and Laura. As you can see, the stuff in black is what we knew. The text chain between Laura and what she assumed to be Callie's Candy. All in the few days leading up to her disappearance. Very mundane. She won a contest, and it's time to pick up the prize. These started just a few days prior to her disappearance."

Trevor pushed another button on his tablet, and the words in red were highlighted. "These messages in read? These were what I recovered tonight."

Dozens of messages popped up. All of them seemingly between Laura and Callie, the candy shop owner. All about a week before her disappearance.

"We need to question Laura's husband. And the other husbands. If he was messaging the women prior to them getting their messages that lured them to the second location, they may have mentioned something."

"He plays at being the person they think they're meeting for weeks." Logan said.

"You're right," Millie spoke up. "All of those messages, he's pretending to be the candy lady."

"He's building these relationships between himself and the victim, gaining their trust," Trevor explained.

"And once he feels like he has their trust, he can lure them to a second location," Thomas finished. "I think I have enough to give a profile. Everyone, go back to the hotel, get a few hours of sleep. We're going to start bright and early tomorrow morning with a press conference."

Trevor wiped the sleep out of his eyes before resuming his stance at the front of the briefing room. Thomas was at the podium looking freshly washed and rested. He stood to his right, legs slightly spread, his hands clasped in front of him. To his right, stood Logan, also in the same stance. Millie and Matthew were to Thomas' left. In front of them, most of Calico Rock's officers sat, waiting to take notes on what Thomas was going to report.

"Good morning," Thomas spoke into the microphone. "I'm Special Agent Fleming. I'm a behavioral analyst with the FBI. We are here in Calico Rock to assist in the investigation into the murder of four women over the course of the last two months. I come before you to ask for your help. The man who is committing these murders is still out there amongst you. We need your help in bringing him in.

"The man we are looking for is a predator, but he'll present himself as friendly, helpful, however, this is part of his ruse to lure in his victim. He's going to be someone those closest to him would describe as toxic, someone constantly using people for his own gain. Our suspect will be chronically unemployed, can't hold a job because once he's gotten everything he can out of people, he moves on. He might frequent bars and might have an alcohol problem. He uses text messages to gain the victim's trust only to lure them to a second location, somewhere he's most comfortable. He is possibly keeping trophies, but we're not sure about that one yet. But there is one thing, someone burned this guy bad, and he is using the victims as surrogates, and the time frame, two weeks, is significant to whatever relationship burned him.

"Do you have any questions?"

A hand near the back of the room raised. Thomas gestured at him to speak. "What about his altering the investigation records?"

Thomas motioned behind him at Trevor, and they swapped positions so Trevor was now at the microphone. "So, what we're finding is the suspect is very technologically advanced. He can hack into any system and alter records, even text messages. He impersonated local businesses to lure the victims to him. However, he'll be working at a job that masks his abilities. Think blue-collar or minimum-wage jobs."

"Can we do anything to keep him out? What's stopping him from reading our records right now?"

"I have installed a state-of-the-art firewall, which should keep him out. Or at least slow him down. Hopefully, we can catch him before he can break into our files."

The office seemed satisfied with Trevor's answers and sat back in his seat.

Trevor looked out at the faces of the other officers. "Any other questions?"

No other hands went up.

"Then, thank you for your time, and let's work together to catch this asshole."

The sound of chairs scraping against the tiled floor echoed through the room as the officers began to leave the room.

Trevor moved to leave with them, heading back to his closet office to do some more work on trying to see if he could trace where the UNSUB was sending the messages.

Before he could get more than a few steps, a hand touched his arm, stopping him. He knew without turning around who it was.

Millie.

"Can we talk?" Her voice was quiet, timid, not at all like her.

He turned around and saw her for the first time this morning. Really looked at her. She had her hair pulled up in a bun on the back of her head, and there were dark circles under her eyes. Instead of putting up a fight, even if he truly didn't mean it, he threw her a bone and simply nodded his head.

She gave him a wane smile and turned and led him through the crowd to the side door, which led into a small hallway. A few feet down, they were at the door of his make-shift office. He had no idea that hallway led from the briefing room. They stepped inside and shut the door behind them.

"I'm sorry," Millie blurted. "I'm sorry I was so angry at you and said the things I said. I hate the way things are between us."

Trevor gave her a small smile. "Apology accepted. I also hate how things were between us. If I had seen you alone earlier, I would have apologized first. For the record, I'm sorry. You know I'm happy you've found someone, but you also know that I worry about you. I can't help it."

"I worry about you, too. Have you gotten any sleep since we've been here?"

He nodded. "Yeah, last night I went and got a solid five hours. Since I had that break in the case, I rewarded myself with some quality sleep at the shitty motel."

Millie laughed. "That motel *is* pretty shitty."

With that laugh, it was as if a weight had been lifted off of Trevor's chest. Things between them felt almost normal. "What's on the agenda today?"

"We need to talk to Laura's husband. It's the interview I'm dreading the most. I don't know why. There's something about her death that is really affecting me."

"I'll go with you." Trevor didn't even think before he spoke. He didn't even want to go to the interviews, he didn't even have time to go to the interviews, but the thought of Millie having to go, well not alone, but with someone she wasn't as close to really bothered him.

"Are you sure? Don't you have things you need to get done here? I was going to go with Thomas."

"I can pause things here for a couple hours and go with you. Unless you really want to go with Thomas."

"No, I want to go with you." Millie almost yelled before he could finish his sentence.

Trevor bit back a smile and nodded. "Okay, then it's settled. We'll go together."

Things were feeling normal between them for the first time in days. There was no weird tension, just two friends knowing what each other needed.

And then the door to the closet opened up, and Sebastian stuck his head in, and Trevor knew that this was the new normal, and he better not fuck this moment up, or else he would probably lose Millie forever.

Chapter Twenty-One

SEBASTIAN

October 8

"Am I interrupting?" Sebastian pushed his way into the closet. He hadn't even bothered knocking. He didn't want to give the two a chance to stop doing whatever it was they were doing before he caught them.

He was pleasantly surprised that they were only talking. And talking about work at that. Maybe he was wrong about the relationship between the two of them. Perhaps they were simply just friends, as they claimed.

Well, they may have been just friends, but there was definitely a one-sided, unrequited sort of love going on with Trevor. But Millie didn't reciprocate. No, as soon as he walked in, Millie's eyes were on him. Her mouth spread into a wide, genuine smile.

No, Millie was his. And he was a lucky fucking bastard.

"You're not." Millie made her way around Trevor toward him as he fully stepped into the room. When she got to him, she wrapped her arms around his neck and pulled him down into a kiss.

Sebastian smiled into it, wrapping his arms around her waist and pulling her to his body, pressing against her so she could feel his physical reaction to the kiss. He knew the second she could feel it as she gasped and pulled him closer to her.

He reached behind his back and grasped the doorknob, pulling it open, and moving the two of them out of the closet and away from their audience. As much as he wanted to make Trevor jealous, he didn't want an audience during his very rare alone time with Millie.

Once the door shut behind them, he pushed her against the wall and moved his hands down her body, until they were on the backs of her thighs. He easily lifted her until her legs wrapped around his waist. He immediately pushed against her. She was wearing thin slacks, and even though he was wearing jeans, her heat radiated against his achingly hard cock. He pushed against her, and she let out a deep sigh, dropping her head to his shoulder.

"If you were wearing a skirt, we could totally fuck right now." He moved his mouth to place open-mouthed kisses along her neck.

"While that sounds amazing, I am working right now," she panted into his ear.

He let out a chuckle. "You're right. This will be enough of a tease to keep us both wanting through the day. Can you come by tonight?"

"Maybe. I'll let you know."

"I missed waking up with you in my arms this morning."

"I'm sorry. We had a break—"

"You don't need to apologize. I understand. I just wanted to share how I felt. I don't ever want you to feel guilty about your job. If this is going to work out long term, we have to have a little bit of give and take."

Millie brought her head up from his shoulder and locked her gaze with his. "Work this out long term? I thought this was supposed to be a fling?"

He shrugged. "I mean, I think we started off that way. Wanting to work off some of this sexual tension between us, but I don't know about you, but I definitely feel something...more. You know what I'm talking about?"

Sebastian couldn't read what was going through Millie's mind. Her eyes were on his, but almost blank. He really wished he had her superpower. Did he ruin everything with his confession?

"Yeah," she said after what seemed to be an eternity, "I do feel it. I was hoping it wasn't just me. The fact that you feel the same way is relieving."

Sebastian broke into a huge smile. "So, we both agree, not a fling?"

"Not a fling, but..."

"But...?"

"What happens when we leave? How will that work?"

Sebastian shrugged again. "We'll figure that out when it happens."

He leaned forward and placed a soft kiss on her lips. When he pulled back, Millie was smiling, and it reached her eyes, causing them to almost sparkle. Fuck, he loved her ice-blue eyes.

"Okay. I'll set aside my Type A, must plan everything, personality for a little bit, and accept that we will plan something later." She pushed forward and gave him another kiss.

Yeah, he was a lucky bastard. He, the weird kid in school, and now the man who got double takes when walking around in public because of how he looked, got the hot girl. And she liked him back. Really liked him. For once, fate was granting him fortune, and he was walking on cloud fucking nine.

Chapter Twenty-Two

MILLIE

October 8

The house they pulled up to was a cute little ranch, set back from the road. Millie looked out her window at the array of desert plants the Hutchins family used to landscape their front yard. Succulents lined the walkway, and a couple of tall cacti stood near the front door. A couple of small tricycles and a scooter also littered the well-landscaped yard.

Millie jumped when she felt a warm hand settle on hers. She glanced over to see Trevor looking at her with concern clear on his face.

"Are you okay?"

She nodded. "Yeah. I'll be fine."

"You can wait here. I can go talk to them. Or I can call Matthew and Logan. I'm sure they would be happy to come here and relieve us."

Millie shook her head. "I can do this. This is my job."

Trevor squeezed her hand before moving to undo his seatbelt. He opened his car door and stepped out, shutting it behind him, leaving her alone in the car to gather her thoughts.

She closed her eyes and took a deep breath. There was nothing different talking to Laura's husband than any other surviving family member of a victim. She didn't know why this particular victim was affecting her so much. Back when she first started at the BAU, victims would occasionally get to her. But she wasn't green anymore. She's been doing this job for more than a decade. Talking to families was her specialty.

Opening her eyes, she gripped the door handle and pushed it open, stepping into the warmth of the morning, once again regretting her choice of packing only her thicker slacks and jackets. She really should have thought about bringing her summer suits.

Moving around the car, she met Trevor on the walkway up to the house. Pausing only to nod at Trevor, she marched her way up to the door, determined not to be dissuaded.

The door was yellow with a variety of succulents painted in a group at the center top. The house screamed happy. And Millie's stomach twisted with the thought of the children who lost their mother. Was the inside as happy as the outside implied? Probably not.

She rang the bell and took a step back, aligning herself with Trevor, who had made his way up the path. It took a few minutes, but the door swung open, revealing a man with mussed hair and wearing sweats and an old t-shirt. Dark circles deeply rimmed his dark eyes, and he wore a scraggly beard.

"Can I help you?" He asked, his voice gravelly.

"I'm Special Agent Driscoll and this is Special Agent Ford. We're with the FBI. I believe you were expecting us this morning?"

The man stood a little straighter, lifting a hand to smooth back his hair. "Um, yeah. I'm sorry. It's been a little bit of a rough morning, and I forgot all about you coming. Please come in. And don't judge me."

He opened the door wider, allowing Millie and Trevor to step inside. Toys littered the house everywhere. There were piles of mostly folded laundry on the couch and coffee table that faced a TV, which was currently playing some children's show with a blue dog and an orange dog. Sitting on the floor in front of the TV was a little girl dressed in a princess dress nightgown, her hair pulled into a low ponytail. She didn't even look away from the screen when they walked in.

Millie's heart broke even further.

Laura's husband gestured for them to keep following him until they were in the dining room. "Please have a seat. I hope you don't mind, it's not the most comfortable, but I don't want Lucy hearing anything."

Millie pulled out a wooden chair, and Trevor pulled one out next to her. "Mr. Hutchens, —"

"Brad, please," Laura's husband interrupted. "Please call me Brad."

"Brad," Millie started over, "we are currently investigating your wife's murder. During this investigation, we have come across some text messages that appear to be between Laura and her murderer. Do you recall anything strange in the weeks leading up to Laura's disappearance?"

"Strange how?"

"Did Laura seem...off?" Trevor asked. "Like she was hiding something?"

Brad shook his head. "No. Everything seemed normal. I mean, as normal as possible. School had just started again, and we were both working full-time outside of the home. She was exhausted, but the normal amount of exhausted of a mom of two who worked full time and volunteered."

"Where did she volunteer?" Millie asked.

"She was on the board of our local library. So, she would help plan events for the library."

"Did you spend a lot of time together before she disappeared?" Trevor asked.

"Of course. Any time we weren't at work, we were together."

"Or when she was volunteering." Trevor interjected.

"Yes, then, too. But that was a once-a-month commitment."

"She didn't mention any strange text messages?" Millie asked.

"Only the messages from the candy shoppe."

Millie sat up straighter. "Messages, plural?"

"Yeah. She and Callie, the owner of the candy shoppe, were talking on and off for a couple weeks. Laura had reached out about treats for Lucy's birthday party. They were ironing out the details. And then the morning she disappeared, Laura called and told me she had won some sort of free package or something, so she was going to go check it out on her lunch break. That was the last we talked." Brad's voice cracked.

Millie and Trevor exchanged a look.

"What was that?" Brad pointed between the two of them. "You two shared a look."

Millie bit her lip and widened her eyes at Trevor, hoping he would take this part. She didn't want to be the one to tell him about the fake out.

Trevor turned toward Brad. "We believe that Callie wasn't texting Laura. What we are seeing in the evidence is the killer pretended to be Callie to lure Laura into a safe place to..." he trailed off, letting them fill in the blanks.

Brad closed his eyes, bringing his fist up to his mouth. Millie's chest tightened, and she had to force her arms down, suppressing the urge to hug the man in front of her.

"We didn't know. We thought it was real. We didn't know."

"That was the intent." Trevor's voice was gentle. "The killer wanted you to think it was real. The fact that you weren't aware you were being tricked means the killer did his job correctly."

"But how did he manage to do it?"

"He's very skilled in technology." Trevor kept the answer simple.

"Did you or your wife come into contact with anyone new in the last few months? Anyone who would have seemed to be overly attentive? Maybe nicer than they should be for being a complete stranger?"

Brad closed his eyes, and Millie could see his lips moving as he tried to remember something. She could see the desperation in his mannerisms. He wanted to find something she could tell. He stiffened, and his eyes shot open.

"There was this one guy back in August. We were at the pool. It was a weeknight, after we both got off work, and we thought it would be fun to go swimming as a family because it was ungodly hot. We were struggling with all the stuff we had to bring, plus the girls, and this man stopped to help us. He was really nice, and he ended up paying to go in so he could help us carry our stuff. He stuck around for a few minutes talking to Laura, but then he left. I didn't think anything more about it."

Millie sat forward in her seat, leaning on her forearms on the table in front of her. "Do you remember anything about this man? What he looked like, a name?"

Brad shook his head. "My memory is already pretty shit, but ever since Laura...I'm sorry. We never got his name. I know that. And I want to say he had dark hair? I don't know. I'm so sorry."

Millie reached her hand across the table and rested it on Brad's. "Don't be sorry. You've already been an immense help."

"I have?" He sounded skeptical.

"Yeah. Because of you, we know that you were approached by a man a few weeks before Laura died, in the place where they found her. You've created a connection. Something for us to follow up on. We can now look through any camera footage and try to find that interaction. Do you remember the exact day you went to the pool?"

Brad shook his head. "I don't. Laura was our family calendar. She was better at remembering days and dates than I am. I know it was the last week of August, and it was a weekday. Beyond that..."

"I can work with that," Trevor reassured him. "And if you happen to remember anything, the exact date, what the man looked like — call us." He slid his card across the table to Brad, who picked it up and looked at it.

"Yeah, I'll do that. I'm sorry I'm not more help right now."

"Like I said, don't apologize. Sometimes these conversations are triggers. In a few hours, or a few days, you'll probably remember something. When you do, call us. Well, call Trevor. Whatever you remember, it will help him narrow down which footage he needs to look through." Millie tilted her head toward Trevor, smiling.

Brad nodded. "I'll do that. The second I remember something, I'll call you."

Millie and Trevor pushed back from the table standing. "We'll get out of your hair so you can get back to your morning."

"Thank you. I'm working from home right now. Anna is in school right now, and Lucy doesn't want to go to day care since..."

"Understood." Millie pushed in her chair and made her way to the door, walking past Lucy, who was still sitting in front of the television watching the same show.

As she walked through the room, her gaze caught on the family pictures that lined the wall. Laura's smiling face drew her attention. She was too young. Her kids were too young. Millie clenched her fists. This bastard had to pay for what he did to this family. To all the families. Squaring her shoulders, she walked out the door with determination.

Once the door closed behind them, Trevor turned toward Millie. "Approached the last week of August at the pool. If it's our UNSUB, he was in the middle of stalking Sharon. Which means..."

"That he was already picking out his next target." Millie finished. "Yeah, I was already thinking about that."

"He meticulously planned out each kill. He stalked the women, lured them out, and brutally murdered them as they put up a fight."

"The fucker was organized and sadistic."

"And we know with this type of killer, he must have kept trophies of each kill, but what did he keep? No one has said anything has been taken."

Millie bit her lip. Trevor was right. Nothing was reported missing from the women. And then it hit her. "What if he's not taking physical trophies? He's techy, right? What if he's instead doing something digital?"

Trevor turned to face her. "Like pictures?"

"Yeah, or maybe, as sick as it sounds, video?"

"No, that makes sense. And he probably rewatches the videos to get off later."

"But what is the two-week window?"

"I don't know, but we need to figure it out, because we have less than a week until it closes, and he snatches you."

Millie shook her head. "I'm really trying not to think about that."

"You know we won't let him get to you, right?"

"I do. That's why I'm choosing not to think about it right now."

"Probably a good thing."

"Definitely a good thing. Should we head back to the precinct?"

Trevor shook his head. "I think I want to go to the pool again. See if I can spot where the cameras are placed."

His phone pinged with a message, and he fished it out of his pocket. "Motherfucker."

"What's wrong?"

"Thomas just went into my closet to make sure everything was fine, and just as he walked in, he watched as all the work I had done finding the missing text messages disappeared from the screen."

"What? They just disappeared?"

"Shit like that doesn't just disappear. I'm pretty sure the UNSUB fucking hacked into my computers and deleted them."

Millie felt her blood run cold. "But I thought you had state-of-the-art protections?"

"Yeah, I do. But apparently it wasn't enough. Fuck!"

"Will you be able to get it back?"

"I don't know. But..."

"You need to go back to the precinct and get working on it."

"I'm sorry."

"Don't apologize. Let's just go back and get what you lost back."

Chapter Twenty-Three

TREVOR

October 12

"You piece of shit!" Trevor picked up a pencil off the desk just so he could have something to throw across the room in frustration.

He had spent the last three days trying to recover everything that he had found. Not only had the UNSUB deleted all the text messages he had recovered, he had corrupted his entire system. He spent the entirety of Friday simply getting back into his programs. He spent Saturday and Sunday trying to sort out what he still had and what was missing. And he had to hand it to the bastard. He was fucking thorough. The UNSUB fucked up everything. Everything.

Trevor had spent all his time in the closet trying to unfuck the mess the asshole made. Members of the team would bring him food, and Millie had gone to the local Walmart and found him a bedroll and a sleeping bag he had set up in the corner of the room. He slept only when he couldn't keep his eyes open any longer.

What frustrated him the most was that he didn't know how the killer breached his system. He shouldn't have been able to get in. No way.

The door to the room opened, and Thomas walked in. "Any progress?"

"I've managed to get back into the system, and I think I've figured out what was deleted and what we still have. Other than that, we're essentially back to square one. All the work I put in prior to Thursday is either gone or corrupt."

Thomas let out a low whistle. "You think you'll be able to get it back?"

"I'm sure I can get it back. It's just taking a lot longer than I expected it to."

"Any idea how he got in in the first place?"

Trevor turned his head, giving Thomas a look.

The older man chuckled. "I'll take that as a no." He sighed. "I hate to be that person, giving you more work..."

At this, Trevor fully rotated his chair around to face his supervisor. "What do you have?"

Thomas lifted his phone in his right hand, giving it a little shake. "Blooming Butcher."

"Fuck. That asshole sure knows when it's the least convenient for us to pop up. He's been quiet since that text on the sixth asking if we were ready to play his game."

"Yeah, and now he's back in contact. And he has left me more frustrated than I've ever been. Apparently, playing his game means solving fucking word puzzles."

"Word puzzles?"

"Riddles. He sent a riddle to try to solve."

"If you solve it, does it prevent him from killing his next victim, or does it clue you into who and where he is?"

"Unclear."

Trevor reached his hand out. "Let me see."

Thomas handed his phone over, and Trevor swiped to read the message on the phone.

UNKNOWN - *I have a pattern, but no face or name,*
Stories and headlines fuel my dark fame.
Tracks I leave are puzzles for the wise,
Who am I, hidden behind countless lies?

Trevor handed the phone back to Thomas. "Forward the messages to me, as usual. I'll see what I can do as far as seeing where they originated, but I'm going to be honest with you, this is going to be lower on my priority list right now."

"I understand. You need to keep your focus on this case, especially since..."

"Since Millie's countdown to kidnapping is coming up quickly."

"While I wouldn't word it exactly as you did, but exactly that. We're on a time crunch here. And we both know, even if we figure out whatever it is this asshole is trying to tell us, killers like him won't just not kill the person they've already picked out."

Trevor nodded in agreement. "You're not wrong. I'll still try to trace the message, but I have a feeling just like the other ones, it will come up empty."

"I expect nothing less from the asshole. But we have to try."

"We have to try."

"Listen, Trevor, you're getting enough rest, right?"

Trevor ran his hands down his face, his hands catching on the rough growth of a beard coming in. "I'm getting a couple of hours a night."

"You can't put your health on the line—"

"He's going after Millie!" Trevor's voice trembled as he nearly shouted the words.

"Yes. I know. We all know. And we're all working around the clock to make sure Millie is safe. But we are not putting our health on the line. You need proper rest. I know Millie brought you a makeshift bed, but really, I think that you should maybe go to the motel and get a proper night's rest. Set up something on the computers, and one of us will monitor it at all times. I promise we'll do our best to make sure nothing bad happens. Some of us have been trained on how to do what you do. Let us take something off your plate."

Trevor shook his head. "I know you mean well, but the last time I left, everything was erased. I'm not going to take any more chances. Not with the deadline looming. Not when we still don't have any idea of who this guy is and how he's doing what he's doing. It's too risky."

"You not being up at your peak performance is taking a risk. If you don't want to leave, fine. But get someone else in here while you sleep so you can sleep for longer. Then we can humor your superstition, and you can get some sleep."

Trevor thought about what Thomas was saying. The man had a point. He really wasn't operating at his peak level. He was consuming all the caffeine, and he was trying to get the minimum sleep. However, his brain was becoming sluggish. And he knew it was because he wasn't getting enough sleep. He sighed. "Fine. Send in a babysitter. But I'm setting things to have alarms so that the second anything goes wrong, it'll wake me up right away. And I can hopefully stop whatever is going on before it gets worse."

Thomas shook his head. "Not exactly the answer I was hoping for, but I'll take it. I'll send in Logan when he gets back. He and Millie are out in the field right now. Talking to Sarah's family since her case is a little different from the others."

"Yeah. Instead of a local business contacting her, it was the local Walmart. Which baffles me. Once I get the text messages back, I'll see if the killer had contacted her in any other way prior to luring her out with Walmart."

"And if he had picked her out prior to killing Laura, like he had Laura."

"Right. The timeline is muddy at best." Trevor groaned as he ran his hands down his face. "This fucking case."

"This is two in a row now where we've traveled and the UNSUB is frustratingly gumming up the investigation."

"I mean, it's to be expected with these cases, right? That's why we're called in. The cases are too complicated for the local PD. But I honestly feel like these cases have been a little bit extra."

Thomas chuckled. "Definitely been a little bit extra. I'm not going to deny it. I'll send Logan in as soon as he gets back. Matthew and I are going to walk the drop scenes."

"Again?"

"Fucking. Again."

"How many times have you been to the scenes?"

Thomas sighed. "Matthew has been to a difference scene every day. He keeps hoping something will speak to him. That something will stand out."

Trevor shook his head. "He must be really frustrated at this point."

"As you can imagine, he would like to get home to his family. But besides that, he knows he's missing something, but he doesn't know what it is."

"It's the eyewitness." Trevor sat back in his chair. "It's the person who found the bodies. The fact that they were deleted from the report, and no one can seem to remember who they were, it's what's throwing everything off."

"Matthew must have had us all on the ground next to that vestibule dozens of times. There's no way—"

"The jogger could have seen Laura's body lying there."

"Exactly."

"I had the same thought on the first day we were here. The jogger had to have been the UNSUB. Right?"

Thomas nodded. "That is the best guess. What do we have for cameras at or near the pool?"

"The pool has some cameras inside. The manager has sent the footage from the entire summer over to me."

Thomas let out a low whistle. "That is a lot of footage."

"It is, but since I don't know the angles, the cameras are catching, and Brad didn't know exactly which day he and his family encountered that 'Good Samaritan,' I thought it would be prudent to just have all the footage."

"Have you had a chance to start looking through it yet?"

Trevor shook his head. "No. Everything on my computers are completely scrambled. I don't know what the asshole did, or how he did it, but it's making want to throw my fucking computer out the window."

"Probably a good thing you don't have a window."

"Smart ass."

Thomas chuckled. "It's why you love me. I'll get out of your hair. Good luck."

He turned to leave the room, but Trevor stopped him.

"Hey. Message the flower asshole back. Tell him that if he wants to be a Batman villain, pick someone cooler than the fucking Riddler. We're not even going to bother solving the riddle. It's not worth our time."

Thomas nodded. "Good thinking. Let me know where your trace tells you the text was sent. Maybe there's a pattern we can see."

"Will do."

Thomas left the closet, and Trevor closed his eyes and leaned his head back against his chair. He was fading fast, but he wouldn't allow himself to take a nap until he had Logan in here. That way he could get some solid rest instead of the fitful cat naps he was taking.

Opening his eyes, he turned his chair back to his desk and stared at his screens.

What was he missing? How did this asshole best him?

He had peeled back layer after layer after layer. Nevertheless, there was a tangled web of nonsense blocking everything.

He reached for his mouse, when another knock at the door startled him causing him to knock down an open plastic jar of chocolate-covered espresso beans Millie bought him from Callie's Candy when they went to talk to the owner. He'd been popping them by the handful and hadn't bothered to put the lid back on. Now, they crashed to the floor and across his desk, and he could hear every single bean as it bounced on the tile.

"Shit." He shoved back his chair and dropped to the ground. He started gathering up as many espresso beans as he could. It was such a waste. He really loved these things. He pulled his computer tower forward to check behind it for any beans that might have bounced in that direction.

The door opened, and Officer Jones poked his head in. "We're ordering in food from the Chinese place. Want anything?"

Trevor turned his head, answering over his shoulder. "Yeah. Sure. You know my order. Thanks, man."

Officer Jones nodded and turned to leave.

When he was gone, Trevor turned his attention back to his cleanup.

As he peered behind the computer tower, his eyes locked onto something he never even thought to look for when he returned to the closet on Friday.

Stuck inside the back of the computer was the smallest, flattest USB drive he had ever seen.

"Son of a bitch."

Trevor moved so quickly out of the desk that he nearly hit his head on the bottom of the desk.

He leapt up to the computer, espresso beans forgotten, and grabbed his mouse. He quickly clicked through to the file manager and shook his head. The computer showed the USB drive as empty. He wasn't going crazy.

Pulling up a window, he typed some stuff into the commands, and he worked through the backdoor of the computer, and there it was.

It had been buried. This whole time, Trevor wondered how the UNSUB had gotten around his firewall, and why every single time he tried to undo what the UNSUB had done, it would just go back the way it was.

Typing some stuff into the computer, he was able to disconnect the USB drive, and using a tissue, he extracted the device, setting it aside. Hopefully, it would have fingerprints on it.

Looking at his screens, Trevor smiled. Everything he had thought was lost began popping back up.

The son of a bitch must have been in a hurry, using the USB device to put some malware on his computer to basically render it useless, and hide the data rather than completely deleting it.

It was sloppy.

It was the slip they needed.

However, there was one thing that was really bothering Trevor. In order to put the device into the computer, the UNSUB would have had to come into the precinct, into his closet and place it there. Or have someone do it for him.

And Trevor didn't know which one made him the most uneasy. That the UNSUB was able to enter with no one noticing, or there was an accomplice amongst them.

Chapter Twenty-Four

MILLIE

October 12

Millie fell back onto the bed, pushing her hair out of her face, panting. "Wow."

Next to her, Sebastian laughed breathily. "You can say that again."

"Wow."

They both devolved into giggles as Sebastian wrapped his arm around Millie and pulled her into him. She came easily and laid her head on his sweaty chest as they both came down from the high they had just experienced.

Millie had to admit it had been a long time since she was having so much amazing sex. She and Sebastian seemed to click in all the right ways. Physically and emotionally.

After she and Logan had finished talking to Sarah's husband, Logan had been assigned to babysit Trevor while he took a much-needed nap, and Millie used that as an excuse to come see Sebastian.

It was becoming quite a habit. She felt slightly guilty, leaving the team every night for the last three days. However, she also knew their time was limited, and she wanted to take advantage of every second she could with Sebastian.

"We're good together." Sebastian pressed a kiss into her hair. "We should be doing this more."

Millie laughed. "We're already doing it every day, multiple times. I don't know how we could possibly fit in anymore."

"Well, we are missing out on some prime morning times."

"Sebastian..."

"I know. You have to work. But what about when the case is over?"

"I'm sure I can take a couple days off. Lord knows I have plenty of vacation time banked. I can spend a week here, just the two of us. No responsibilities. Well, at least for me, unless you can get time off."

Sebastian shook his head. "I would still have to go to the site, but you know it's flexible. I can get my hours in. And then spend it with you."

"That sounds really lovely. I can explore the area. Maybe take some day trips. Having a vacation will be really nice."

Sebastian cleared his throat before speaking quietly. "What if you move here?"

The question seemed to just hang there in the room with them. Millie stiffened, and Sebastian's arms tightened around her, holding her in place.

"I've done some research. There's an FBI field office in Albuquerque. You can transfer there."

Millie had briefly toyed with the idea of moving here to stay with him, but only ever briefly. "Profilers don't work in field offices. We're stationed in Quantico."

"You don't think they would make an exception?"

Millie shook her head. "No, I don't."

"Does anyone else on your team have a partner? How do their relationships work?"

"Their partners live in DC with them. Rebecca, my best friend, literally just moved from Iowa two months ago so she could be with her fiancé."

"I can't move. My work is here."

"And my work is in DC. You're in construction. Couldn't you find work in DC? Rebecca is a teacher, and she managed to find a job there when she moved."

Sebastian let out a slow sigh. "I really don't want to move somewhere the weather is shit half the year. I don't know why you're automatically shooting down the idea of you moving here. Think about it. We have the best weather. You've already experienced all the amazing food we have here. We're only a day's drive from California, so we can do some weekends away at the beach. Visit your family. Cost of living here is a hell of a lot cheaper than where you are now."

Millie rolled around what he was saying in her mind. Being a day's drive from her family was definitely a perk. Her nieces and nephew were definitely not getting younger. She was missing a lot of the key parts of their lives as she lived over three thousand miles away. There was only so much bonding she could do over FaceTime. "While it sounds amazing, my job—"

"Do you really need to be a dedicated profiler? You're working in the field now. You could do that full time, and just sort of be a part-time profiler."

Millie sat up and looked down at him. "You're asking me to give up the job I trained for, a job I'm really good at, to move here to be with you?"

Sebastian pushed himself into a sitting position, leaning against his headboard. "I mean, all good relationships come with a bit of a sacrifice."

"Yeah, sacrifices like whether the toilet paper roll is over or under, or which part of town do we live in. Not giving up entire careers."

Millie pulled away from Sebastian, wrapping herself in the sheet as she stood from the bed, going in search for the clothes they had strewn around the apartment when she had come over earlier.

Sebastian didn't get out of bed. He stayed where he was. "I don't understand why you're upset."

Millie whipped around, her newly discovered pants in one hand, her other still holding the sheet up around her chest. "If you don't understand why I'm upset," she gesticulated with her pants, tears rushing unbidden to her eyes, "then I don't know if we're as much of a fit as I had hoped we were."

She turned back around, continuing her search for her clothes. She was desperate to get out of the apartment, away from him. All she wanted to do was fall apart somewhere safe, and call Rebecca and tell her everything, and be reassured she wasn't crazy.

Normally she would talk to Trevor about this, but what she really didn't need to hear right now was 'I told you so.'

"Come on," Sebastian called from the bed, where he was still lounging. "I think you're overreacting."

"Well," she called back, "I think you're under-reacting."

"Millie. Come back to bed."

"No."

"You're being stubborn."

"I'm being a realist."

Sebastian came striding out into the living room, not bothering to cover himself up. He leaned against his doorframe and crossed his arms across his chest, a smirk drawn across his face. "Come back to bed."

Millie had found her bra and was in the process of hooking it behind her back. She averted her gaze, not wanting to be tempted by the absolute vision of her not-quite boyfriend, but not quite fling. Honestly, she didn't know what to define what she and Sebastian were.

"No. I think it's best if we take some time and think about what we want out of this, whatever this is."

"Relationship." Confidence dripped out of Sebastian's mouth with every word. "You can say it. I thought we already established this as more than we were expecting. I don't want to put words in your mouth, but I know what I'm feeling. I like you. A lot, and I thought you felt the same way I did. That's why we were talking about the future."

Millie threw her hands up with a sigh. "I like you, I do. But in a 'let's see how long-distance works' sort of way, not in a 'give up a job I love and move across the country' sort of way."

"You just said your best friend gave up her job and moved across the country to be with someone on your team. Maybe you should talk to her about giving up her dream job to move to be with someone she loves."

Millie shook her head with a small laugh. "Okay, I'm starting to think you're only listening to what you want to hear, and not to what I'm saying."

"I'm listening to what you're saying. I've repeated it back to you. I think you're the one who's not listening. You're being stubborn, and you're set in your ways. You've been single too long, you're not ready to compromise with a partner."

Millie grabbed her shirt off the floor and violently shoved her arms through the holes, and started buttoning it up. "I'm leaving."

"You'll be back."

"No. I won't."

"You will." He stopped leaning against the doorway of his room and started walking toward her. "You'll realize that I'm right, and you'll be back. When you're ready to compromise like an adult."

She finished buttoning her shirt, and keeping her gaze on his face, she walked toward him, and pointed her finger right at him. "How come I'm expected to be the one to give up my life? Maybe it's you who has been single too long and doesn't know how to compromise. Call me when you grow the fuck up."

Without waiting for a reply, she spun on her heel, grabbed her bag, which she had dropped on the floor by the door, and walked out.

She didn't slow until she got to her car. And only then did she allow the tears of frustration begin to fall down her face. She allowed herself only five minutes to fall apart, and then, taking a deep breath, she scrubbed her hands down her face, pulling herself together.

Before putting the car into drive, she hit dial on her phone.

"Hey," the friendly voice on the other end answered. "I was just thinking about you. I haven't heard from you for a few days. Are you still in that honeymoon period?"

"He's a fucking selfish asshole."

Rebecca laughed. "Wow, what happened?"

"He wants me to move here. Give up being a profiler."

"He's an asshole."

Millie laughed. "That didn't take long to turn you."

"Look. If there's one thing I've learned about all of you in a short time, is that you all love your jobs. And you especially. You're an amazing profiler, and this is your dream job. I couldn't even imagine asking Matty to quit his job for me."

"What made you decide to quit your job and move to D.C.?"

Rebecca was quiet for a minute. "You're not seriously considering quitting your job and moving to New Mexico, are you?"

Millie scoffed. "Of course not. But when I brought up the idea of him moving to D.C., he acted as though it was the biggest inconvenience in the world."

"Remind me what he does?"

"He works in construction. He told me starting in a new place would be a burden."

"His job field is attractive to transients. Sometimes it pays cash under the table. And he told you that moving to a larger city with more job opportunities was a burden?"

"He also said something about the weather being shit half the year. He seems really insistent on my moving here."

"You guys have only known each other for a week. You don't need to be worried about who is going to move where."

"How long before you and Matty talked about it?"

Rebecca was quiet on the other line. "We talked about long distance a lot during that time during the case. And the most we talked about was for me and Benji coming to visit. We didn't talk about us permanently moving there until well into the summer. And you have to take into consideration that my life had basically imploded at the end of the case. Moving Benji and me out of Cove Creek was a straightforward decision. It was something we were talking about doing before Jaime even died."

"So, what you're saying is your experience was different."

"A little. But also, a week into Matty and my relationship, we hadn't even broached the subject of either of us moving. A week in, we were still trying to figure out what we were to each other. We spent time getting to know each other and establishing baselines."

"He told me I've been single so long I don't know how to compromise."

Rebecca sighed. "Listen, it sounds like feelings were elevated tonight. You both probably said a few things you'll be regretting later. My advice is, take some time to cool off, and then try to talk again. You're in the honeymoon phase of a new relationship. You're still learning who you are to each other. A relationship isn't all sex. You've got to connect on a different level. You guys do talk, right?"

"Of course," Millie rushed to say. "We talk all the time."

Internally, she cringed. They did talk, a little. Not as much as they had on their first date, or before they started sleeping together. Mostly, it was small talk. She really did like him, but was she conflating lust with deeper feelings?

"I can tell from your tone that you're lying right now. So, next piece of advice: next time the two of you are together, talk before you rip each other's clothes off. And if you get to know one another better, maybe it'll be easier to have the conversation about relocating to be together. But honestly, you should bring up long distance, and what that would look like. He says you can't compromise, then compromise. You won't move, not before you can test long distance."

Millie nodded along before she remembered Rebecca couldn't see her. "You're right. You're so full of expert advice. I don't know what I would do without you."

"You would talk to Trevor."

Millie closed her eyes. She was right. Typically, she would have this conversation with Trevor. But things were still awkward between them. And her spending nearly every evening with Sebastian didn't help matters. He had also sequestered himself in his closet, refusing to leave. She stopped by and gave him a bedroll and a sleeping bag, and she brought him some candy after they visited the candy shop, but it wasn't the same between them, and it sucked.

It really sucked.

"Have you talked to him anymore?" Rebecca spoke up after Millie had been silent for a while.

"Not really. I think the case isn't helping. He's so stressed out and functioning on very little sleep. I think things will get better once the case is over, and we can go home. Everything will be better once we are home."

"Except for whatever is happening with Sebastian."

"I don't know. Maybe distance will help things? I think if we're forced to talk rather than just sleep together, maybe it will help our relationship."

"I think that's a great idea. Call him tomorrow and tell him you want to table the relocation talk, but you're willing to keep an open mind."

"Diplomatic."

"Honest."

Millie heard the voice of Benji in the background asking his mom something. "Do you need to go? Does he need you for something?"

"Always, but he was just asking if it was Matty. This is the longest we've been apart since we moved. He's getting a little anxious."

Millie's heart constricted for the little boy. He had lost his father, so of course he would be anxious when his new stepfather was not with them. "I'll let you go. When I get back into the precinct, I'll have Matty call you."

"We talked to him earlier."

"I'll have him call you. I think it would help Benji."

"Okay. Let me know if you need any more advice."

"I will. You're the best."

"Well, I did find the love of my life - twice."

"Sure. Rub it in."

They both laughed, and Millie already felt lighter than she had when she first called Rebecca.

They ended up doing what Rebecca explained was a 'Midwest Goodbye' and talked for a little bit longer. Made tentative plans for a girls' day when Millie returned, and by the time they hung up, Mille felt amazing.

She missed Trevor, and he was always her closest friend, but she was glad she had met Rebecca six months ago. It was nice to have a second best friend.

Taking one more deep breath, she shut off the car and unbuckled her seatbelt. It was time to go in and continue the case. The faster they finished this, the sooner she could go home.

Chapter Twenty-Five

Sebastian

October 12

Sebastian stepped out of the shower and pulled on a pair of boxers. After Millie stormed out of his apartment, he had taken a moment to get clean and gather his thoughts.

It seemed a little uncharacteristic of Millie to get so worked up, but what did he know? They had only really known each other for about a week. They were still learning about each other. And apparently, he just learned Millie had quite the temper.

And it was sort of hot.

Scratch that. Incredibly hot.

When she got upset, his initial reaction was to apologize and try to fix everything. However, the angrier she got, the more fun he seemed to have.

Also, the more turned on he seemed to get.

So, he kept riling her up. He didn't expect her to storm out. Of course, he did say some bullshit about her being chronically single, so that probably had something to do with it.

Oops.

He didn't intend to get that mean. He was having fun. Honestly, he hadn't meant half of it.

Sebastian had brought up moving simply to test the waters. What he didn't expect was for Millie to freak out like she did.

He would need to fix this. He didn't want to lose her over something as stupid as this.

He reached for his phone and pulled up her contact.

Now, the question was: should he call or text?

Call. Definitely call. The tone typically got lost over text. He didn't want his words to be misconstrued and have Millie be even more pissed off at him.

He quickly hit dial, and it rang twice before being sent directly to voicemail. Of course. He should have expected nothing less. His girlfriend was smart, smarter than he was, that's for sure. And she would want to take tonight to cool off. He should have waited to call in the morning.

Oh well, he would leave a message, and hopefully she would listen to it.

"Hey," he spoke after the beep sounded, "I'm sorry for tonight. I didn't mean anything I said. I brought up moving to test the waters. I didn't know it would make you so upset, and things sort of spiraled out from there. Let me make it up to you. Tomorrow night. I'll take you somewhere special. Please call or text me to confirm. Give me another chance. Please."

He hung up and padded over to his couch and sat down, still in his boxers. Pulling up the maps app, he began scrolling through places he could take her. He truly wanted it to be special.

A night for her to remember forever.

Chapter Twenty-Six

TREVOR

October 13

"Ford."

"This is the crime lab. We have the results on the drive you sent us yesterday. We were able to pull a partial print from it. It's a match to the partial we recovered from the victims."

Trevor let out a sigh. "No other prints?"

"Not that we could find. That was the best we could pull."

"And still not in the system?"

"Still not in the system. We'll let you know if anything changes."

"Thank you."

"No problem."

Trevor hung up his phone, setting it to the side on his desk. Leaning forward, he dropped his head into his hands. Of course they would find a partial fingerprint, and it would be the killer's the one person whose fingerprints they haven't been able to identify, because he wasn't in the system.

And if his prints were the only ones on the device, how did it even get in his office in the first place? Did the UNSUB sneak in? Did he have an accomplice? If he had an accomplice, why were their fingerprints not on the drive?

Because they're law enforcement and they know not to touch the fucking drive. The thought entered his mind unbidden, but he had to admit, it was true. There were only two explanations of how it ended up in his computer: either the UNSUB came in while he was out of the office, which meant he knew when he was gone, or there was someone inside.

Honestly, he was hoping for the creepy stalkiness of the UNSUB always knowing whether he was there. He didn't want to think of them having a mole on the inside.

That would be the worst. He didn't think he could handle the betrayal of an inside job.

But...

An inside job would make sense.

If the UNSUB had someone on the inside, the erasure of the files would make so much sense. Maybe the UNSUB was not as tech savvy as he appeared to be. If he had an inside accomplice, the changing of the reports, deleting of the people who found the bodies, could have been done so easily. All it would take was someone with the correct credentials logging in and doing a little doctoring.

At the beginning of the case, everything was so disjointed, it would have been easy for someone to sneak in and take care of it. The UNSUB would have just had to let the accomplice know what to change. Whatever alias he was using when he talked with the police officer after he 'discovered' the body.

It was quite common for a killer to integrate themselves into an investigation. It went along with their need to control the situation. And their egos wouldn't let them just sit out. They needed to see their work through to fruition. The Zodiac Killer notoriously sent letters to the press and police officers to taunt them about the case. BTK sent anonymous packages to the police to taunt them. It was the narcissistic personalities that trended with the people who became serial killers. They needed attention. They thrived on it.

The problem was, being in the police station, the number of suspects of who could be helping the UNSUB was significant. But the people who were in and of this room, other than members of his team were few. Officer Jones and Sebastian.

The door to his office opened, and Millie stepped inside.

"Hey," she greeted, holding up a bag of espresso beans. "Logan mentioned you may have had an accident with your other bag, so I brought you another."

Trevor laughed. "I don't know if giving me another bag is a good idea. I'm just going to pour them into the old container, and then we'll have this problem all over again."

Millie shook her head and held up what she had in her other hand. It was a long, flat, lidded plastic container. "You can pour them in this. It's flat, so you will have a harder time knocking it over with your hand. And with its shape, you can sort of push it against your screens, and away from the edge of the desk. It's short, so it won't block anything."

Trevor smiled widely. He'd missed her. And it was for things like this. She was so fucking thoughtful. "You're amazing."

"You're damn right I am." She walked over to the desk and set the container and the espresso beans down. She turned so she was leaning against the desk with her arms crossed across her chest. "What are you working on?"

"I just got off the phone with the crime lab. They found a match to the print on the USB stick."

Millie brightened, standing a little straighter. "Really?"

"Yeah. Matches the prints found on the victims."

She slumped back against the table. "Fuck."

"Yep."

"We don't have a match for those prints."

"Yep."

Silence fell between them as Millie directed her gaze at the ceiling and bit her bottom lip between her teeth in thought. After a moment, she quickly snapped her gaze back down to Trevor. "Wait. If it has the suspect's prints on it, how did it get into your computer?"

"That is the ten-thousand-dollar question, isn't it?"

"You're not thinking…"

Trevor shrugged. "I don't know. It's the most logical explanation, isn't it?"

Millie shook her head. "I don't like it. My stomach just did this clenching thing. The thought that someone who works here…"

"I've had all these thoughts."

"We're thinking accomplice, right?"

"That's the biggest hope. I really don't think it's the UNSUB. I think the sabotage would be a little bigger if the UNSUB were here in the building."

"So, we're now looking for someone who has connections to the police department."

"Another fucking needle in the haystack. Because the connection can be anything. It can be a relative, a friend, an acquaintance, someone who is blackmailing someone else. The possibilities are endless."

Millie let out a groan. "How is the video search going?"

"Honestly, I haven't really started. I've been spending time trying to get the fucking computer to work again. Since I removed the memory stick, and everything went back to normal, I was going through the text messages again. There has to be something in them that we're missing. There's a reason he didn't want us looking at them."

"Do you think it's Bobby?"

"Do I think what's Bobby?"

"Think about it. The text messages between him and Jamie are pretty damning. It's probably why he wanted them gone."

Trevor did think about it. And she wasn't wrong. When they questioned him, he didn't admit the affair. He was dismissive. He kicked them out of the shop. "I think we need to question Bobby again."

He pulled up the Instagram messages between Bobby and Jamie, the salacious ones on one screen. On the screen right next to it, he pulled up the texts between the two.

Millie turned so she was facing the screens, leaning forward onto her forearms so she could get a good look at the screens.

"You can get a chair," Trevor said, not taking his eyes off the screen.

Millie shook her head. "I'm good. If I move, I'll get distracted."

Silence filled the room as they both took the time to read. Trevor's eyes moved back and forth over the texts. Over and over again. What were they missing?

"I don't know if it's because we've read these so many times over the past week, but I don't know. Were we wrong? Could these have been written by the same person?" Millie gestured between the two screens with her finger.

Trevor ran a hand down his face. "I don't know. But, maybe? I could have sworn they felt different before."

"Same. I thought there was something off between them. Like the language was different, but..."

"But now maybe it's not that far off?"

"Exactly."

Trevor pulled up the text exchange between Sharon and Alyssa St. George, the owner of Pet's Best Friend. They knew for a fact that St. George hadn't been texting with Sharon prior to her death. He scrutinized the text. "These match, I think."

Millie leaned closer, and Trevor could really smell the scent of her soap. He closed his eyes briefly before snapping them back open, shaking himself out of it. She was in a relationship, and things were finally getting back to normal between them. He didn't need to make things weird by sniffing her.

"I think you're right." Millie leaned back before standing up straight, crossing her arms across her chest. "These are very similar. I'm going to bring Bobby in for questioning."

"Do you think he's going to talk?"

"Who the fuck even knows. But if I get him in a room with Matthew, I think we'll get something out of him. At the very least, we could get him to admit at least the affair."

"Getting Matthew in there would be beneficial. He's the best at this."

"He is. And I think he can get Bobby to admit to the affair. And maybe open up more. He has a trustworthy face."

"And he wasn't the one who questioned him before. New face. New tactics."

Millie opened her mouth to say something, but her phone went off interrupting her. She pulled out her phone and looked at it.

"Is that from the killer? The window is closing."

Millie shook her head. "No. It's Sebastian. We're going on a date tonight, and he's been texting me all day, teasing me. It's supposed to be a surprise."

Trevor nodded. "Sounds special. Don't you two normally see each other every night?"

"Yeah, but we got into a fight last night, and he's wanting to make it up to me. He's told me to dress up, and he's taking me out on the town."

"What was your fight about?"

Millie shrugged. "Something stupid. It's no big deal."

Trevor bit his tongue to stop himself from responding. If Millie wanted to tell him, she would. He didn't like the rift in their relationship. In the past, when she was dating someone, he would know everything. But now? He knew nothing. Only that she was seeing him every night.

Millie tucked her phone away into her pocket, turning her attention back to him. Even though he had tried to school his features, her reaction to him proved he was unsuccessful. "Trevor—"

He waved his hand. "Don't worry about it. You don't have to tell me anything you don't want to. I just hope you have someone to talk to about whatever it was."

"I called Rebecca right after it happened."

Trevor tried not to feel jealous about this revelation. He knew this was inevitable. Ever since they had met Rebecca back in May, the two had been growing closer. Apparently, he was being replaced.

"I'm not replacing you," Millie said.

Trevor's gaze snapped up to hers. "I didn't say you were."

"No, but I could tell you're thinking it. And I'm not. In fact, you were the first person I wanted to call, but I was worried about how you were going to react, and I didn't want to fight with you. Things have been...tenuous between us lately, and it's just starting to get better. I didn't want to jeopardize anything between us more."

Trevor gave her a sad smile. "I hate this, whatever is going on between us. I liked being the person you came to to talk about this stuff. And I hate that you don't think you can now."

"Me, too. And I think being here is really messing everything up. I think once we get home, things can sort of even out."

Trevor nodded. "I agree. Getting back on familiar territory."

"Exactly. I'm so sorry, Trevor."

"You don't need to apologize for going to Rebecca. I'm glad you have someone else you can turn to. Did she give you the advice you needed?"

Millie nodded. "Yeah. Talking to her was really helpful. I think she was the one I needed to talk to. I needed advice about long distance."

Trevor's heart constricted. Things must be becoming more serious between Sebastian and Millie if they were arguing about what they were going to do after the case was closed. He honestly was hoping their relationship would fizzle out once they went back to DC.

"Oh," was all he squeezed out.

"Yeah."

Awkward silence filled the room as the two stared at each other. Millie fidgeted with the bottom of her suit jacket, and Trevor distracted himself with clicking around uselessly on his computers.

"Well," Millie finally spoke up. "I'm going to go find Matthew and see about bringing Bobby in for some more questioning."

Trevor nodded. "Good luck. Let me know if he tells you anything new."

"I will. Good luck with whatever you're going to be doing."

"Footage."

"Fun."

"Yep."

Millie moved past him to the door. She stopped, her hand on the handle, before turning around. She looked like she was going to say something else, but thought better of it. Turning back to the door, she opened it, and left.

Trevor returned his full attention to his task. Closing out all the text messages, he pulled up the first of the pool footage.

It was going to be a long afternoon.

Chapter Twenty-Seven

MILLIE

October 13

Millie quickly finished shoving the rest of her sandwich in her face before crumpling the paper it had been wrapped in and throwing it in the nearby wastebasket.

It was shaping up to be one of those days.

After visiting with Trevor in the closet and deciding that interrogating Bobby was the next most logical step, she had immediately gone to find Matthew, who had agreed with her.

The next couple hours had been painstakingly slow as they went about getting a warrant to bring in Bobby for questioning. Their evidence was flimsy at best, but it was all they had to go on. Apparently, a judge agreed with them and drafted the warrant. A couple officers went to serve it, and Millie took that opportunity to quickly eat some lunch. She couldn't remember if she had even had breakfast this morning, which was definitely not a great sign for how the day was going.

And of course, the second she sat down to eat said sandwich, she got word Bobby was ready for them in the interrogation room.

Because of course he was.

Hence, the shoving the food in her face as quickly as possible.

She wiped her hands on her pants and quickly made her way to the interrogation room.

Matthew was waiting for her outside the room. He was standing alone, facing the window, looking in on Bobby. He was wearing his signature button-down shirt and black dress pants, and his shaggy brown hair was messier than normal. This was the longest he's been away from Rebecca and Benji, and she could tell it was taking a toll on him. They really needed to solve this case. Everyone would benefit from being at home.

"Hey," she greeted as she came to a stop next to him.

He turned his head toward her, giving her a small smile. "Hey. Did you get something to eat?"

She nodded. "Yeah. You?"

He shook his head. "No. I used my time to talk to Benji. He's stuck sitting at school while Becks has a meeting. He was bored and texted to see if we could FaceTime. So, I spent my break talking with him. I'll get something when we finish up here."

Millie frowned. "Poor Benji."

"Yeah. He asked when I would be home so he could hang at the Bureau with us again. I told him I didn't know. The look on his face..." He broke off, his voice catching a little, before shaking his head. "Anyway, it will be really nice to wrap this case up. I think I'm going to take some vacation when we get back."

"Oh? Going to take the family somewhere?"

"No, I'm just going to be home with them. They have fall break coming up soon, and if I'm home by then, it'll be nice to just hang out, just the three of us."

Millie gave him a small smile. "Well, should we go in there and see if this asshole is the right asshole?"

Matthew chuckled. "Yes. Let's go see if we can get him to talk. About anything, really. Thomas told me he clammed up pretty quickly the last time you talked to him."

"Yes, well, we were on his territory then. This time he's on ours. We have a little bit of an upper hand now."

"Plus, we have proof he was having an affair with Jamie."

"That, too."

Matthew reached for the handle of the door. "Ready?"

Millie gave him a half-smile. "Let's do it."

Matthew pushed open the door, and they stepped into the room. Bobby was sitting on one side of the metal table. He was looking around the room, and his leg was bouncing up and down. When he noticed they had entered the room, his head whipped toward them and his leg stopped moving.

"What is the meaning of this?" he nearly shouted. "I don't understand why I've been brought in. I told you everything I knew when you invaded my shop."

Matthew and Millie made their way to the table. Millie pulled out her chair and sat down immediately, folding her hands in front of her on the table. Matthew stayed standing, one hand on his chair, the other in his pocket.

"Are you sure you told us everything you knew, Mr. Tucker?"

Bobby looked taken aback. "Y-yes, I'm sure."

Millie dipped her head to hide her smile. They were already tripping him up with one question. This was going to be fucking easy. Schooling her features, she brought her head back up, leveling her gaze at Bobby.

Matthew tilted his head to the side, remaining standing. "Are you sure? You don't sound it. You sound like maybe you're hiding something."

Bobby cleared his throat, his leg starting its bouncing again. "Wh-what would I possibly be hiding? I hired Jamie to do some marketing for my shop. That's it. That was the extent of our relationship. I barely knew her."

"Hmmm," Matthew pulled out his chair, finally taking a seat. Leaving the chair about half a foot away from the table, he leaned back and brought his right ankle up to his left knee, and folded his arms across his chest. "You see, it's funny. We did some digging, and we found some evidence that maybe, just maybe, you may be leaving out some key details about the true nature of your relationship with Mrs. Sanders."

Bobby began shaking his head back and forth rapidly. "No. No. I have told you everything. Whatever it is you think you've found is wrong."

Matthew glanced over at Millie, and she pulled out the transcripts of the Instagram messages between Bobby and Jamie from the folder that had been sitting on the table. She slid them across to Bobby. He stopped fidgeting and looked down at what had been placed in front of them. As soon as he took in what it was, his eyes widened, and his gaze flew up to them.

"Where the fuck did you get these?"

"Where do you think? Your phone records." Matthew didn't change his posture, just kept staring across at him, incredibly cool.

"That's an invasion of privacy."

"You're a person of interest in an active murder investigation. You have no privacy."

Millie watched as Bobby dropped his gaze back to the transcript and brought his hand up to his forehead, rubbing it back and forth, his leg still bouncing, only this time with more frequency. After a few minutes, he brought his gaze back up, but instead of focusing his attention on Matthew, he focused on her.

"This isn't what it looks like."

Millie put her arms on the table and leaned forward, locking her gaze with his. "You mean you weren't having an affair with Jamie Sanders?"

"No, I mean, yes. I was having an affair with her. But I didn't kill her."

"Why should we believe you? You haven't told the truth once since we met you."

Bobby opened and closed his mouth a few times, no sound coming out. Millie smirked, and this time she didn't hide it. This was the most uncomfortable he had been since they had come into the room. Gone was the cocky confidence at his art shop.

He stopped fidgeting and placed his hands flat on the table in front of him, leaning in, keeping his gaze locked on Millie's, completely disregarding Matthew. Interesting.

"Look. Things between Jamie and me started off perfectly professional. And during one of our meetings, things just sort of...clicked between us. She and her husband were having a bit of a rough patch. But it was never really serious between us. Just sex."

Matthew moved so both his feet were on the floor, leaning forward until his forearms were on the table. He leaned until his chest was resting against the table. Millie loved to see him work. He was fantastic at reading people, so usually he stayed out of the room and observed. However, when he interrogated someone, he was top tier.

"Mr. Tucker, would you say her being committed to her husband was upsetting?"

Bobby shook his head. "No. It was a little thrilling, actually. Sneaking around made me feel like a teenager again."

"Did she try to end things?"

Bobby shook his head again. "No. We were going strong. Until she..."

"Why two separate chats?" Millie gestured toward the transcripts in front of him.

Bobby shrugged. "I think it was because it felt more clandestine. She was coming to see me a lot, and we needed a cover. Just in case her husband checked her phone. Have you looked into him? I bet he could be a jealous bastard. He probably found out about our affair and went off the rails."

"Did Jamie say anything that would cause you to draw those conclusions?" Matthew asked.

Bobby shrugged. "Did Jamie say anything? She, um, may have hinted a few times that some of their disagreements got out of hand."

If Millie wasn't looking for it, she would have missed it. Not only did he repeat the question, he ran his hand through his hair as he was answering. The shift in Matthew's posture next to her indicated he had caught it, too. It was very subtle, but Bobby was lying.

"What sort of things did Jamie tell you?" Millie was careful to keep her tone as neutral as possible. She didn't want to give away that they had caught on. Not yet.

"What did she tell me? Just uh, sometimes when they were arguing, her husband would throw things. Not exactly at her, but toward her? And he would grab her sometimes. She was scared he would find out about us, and that it would cause him to hurt her worse than normal."

Millie cringed internally. His language was falling apart now. It wouldn't take long before he completely crumbled. "Very eloquent."

"Look," Bobby slammed his hand down on the table, the boom against the metal echoing through the room, causing everyone to jump in their seats slightly. "I'm under a lot of pressure right now, and I'm not exactly focusing on perfect language, you stuck-up bitch."

Millie sat back in her seat a little and eyed Bobby. It didn't take a whole lot to drive him off the rails.

Matthew didn't even flinch at Bobby's outburst. He simply continued his questioning, unbothered. "I think you're projecting your own actions onto Mr. Sanders in order to draw the attention from you to him."

Bobby scoffed. "Why would you think that?" His voice had risen nearly an octave higher than it had been at the beginning of the interrogation.

Matthew smirked. "Your voice is higher than it was before. You can't stop fidgeting to save your life. That knee of yours is going to drill a hole in our floor before too long. And your language is deteriorating. You're lying to us."

"Fuck you!"

"That's not a denial."

Bobby's face was growing redder, and as Matthew stated, that knee of his was not stopping anytime soon. "Why would I lie about this?"

Millie shrugged. "I don't know. Maybe it has something to do with your temper, which can erupt on a dime. It didn't take that long to get you to call me a bitch. Did you call Jamie a bitch as you stabbed her over, and over, and over again?"

Bobby shoved himself away from the table, the legs of his chair scraping against the concrete of the floor, causing both Millie and Matthew to cringe. "I didn't kill her!"

"Then why are you lying?"

"Because you think I killed her!"

"You're not really helping your case if you're going to lie to us." Matthew had gotten to his feet as soon as Bobby had leapt to his. He remained on his side of the table, but he had adjusted to the side so he could move around it and subdue Bobby if he needed to.

Millie stayed in her seat, but moved her chair out slightly. Sitting back in her seat, she continued the questioning. "But you did yell at her? Abuse her? Everything you've accused her husband of doing?"

"No!" Bobby started pacing the room, like he was a tiger trapped in a cage at the zoo. "I loved her! I loved her, okay. And she loved me. She was going to leave her husband for me. She told me."

"You two had been sleeping together for a few weeks at best, and she was going to leave her husband for you?" Matthew sounded skeptical.

"Yeah. When you know, you know, right? She and her husband had married young, and things between them were fizzling out now that their nest was emptying. With her job doing graphic design, she's very artistic, and we hit it off. She really was going to tell her husband about us and how she was leaving him."

"When was this?" Millie asked.

"We talked about it the day before she went missing. I swear, I would never hurt her. Ever. Please, you have to believe me." Bobby's voice cracked as he stopped his pacing and tried to plead his case.

Millie pushed back from the table and stood. "You know? I think that's the first truthful thing out of your mouth all day."

Millie followed Matthew out of the interrogation room. As the door closed behind them, she relaxed for the first time in an hour. They really got nowhere with Bobby. He was sticking with his story, but the more he told it, the less she believed it.

He was either really fucking nervous, or he was lying.

She leaned against the wall as Matthew came to a stop in front of her. "So, what do you think?"

"I think he's our best suspect right now, and we should proceed as if everything he said is a lie. They're going to take his prints, and we'll run them. We'll see if they're a match. Just in case they're not, we'll print Mr. Sanders. Maybe Bobby wasn't a liar. Maybe he was telling us the truth, and we made him nervous. Since we don't have any better leads, we'll have to go with what we have."

Millie nodded. Her phone buzzed, and she pulled it out. Sebastian.

"The killer?" Matthew asked, nodding at her phone. "Because if it is, that will exonerate Bobby right now."

She shook her head. "Sebastian. He's been texting me all day. Lots of apologies, lots of hints about where he's going to take me tonight."

Matthew hummed, bringing his gaze to the floor while he rocked back on his heels.

"What?"

Matthew shrugged. "Nothing."

"Don't nothing me, Grant. I know an avoidance posture when I see it. What's going on?"

He shrugged again. "I don't know. There's just something about this guy I'm not vibing with."

"You haven't even met him."

"I know. Which is why I haven't said anything. But I don't know. I want to be supportive, because you seem happy, but my Spidey Sense is tingling, if you know what I mean."

Millie tried to run her hand through her hair before remembering she had pulled it up into a ponytail that morning, and she didn't get very far. She dropped her hand to her side. "You're starting to sound like Trevor."

Matthew brought his gaze back up to hers. "I'm really surprised that you didn't drop the guy the second Trevor told you he didn't like him."

"Why would I do that? Not everyone I date has to be approved of by Trevor."

"No, but I know if one of you told me the person I was dating had bad vibes, I would seriously consider what they're saying. We're all in the business of reading people."

"Sebastian said Trevor is jealous because he secretly wants to date me, and you know? He's not wrong. Trevor has always sort of carried a torch for me, and we've always sort of gone with it. But the second I find someone I could see myself seriously dating, he digs the feelings back up like he can tell me not to date someone else."

"I don't think that's what's happening at all."

"You don't?"

"No, and you know why?"

"I'm sure you're going to tell me."

"Because I don't harbor any romantic feelings for you, and I feel the same way about Sebastian. The man has pulled your focus away from the case. You're with him more than you're here. And I think he's doing it on purpose. Rebecca told me he wanted you to give up your job and move here. I think he's threatened by your job, and he's doing everything to make himself the center of your attention."

Deep down, she knew Matthew was right, but also, she was sort of resentful. "Stop profiling me."

"I'm not."

"You are. You even put on your profiler voice. I'm your friend and your coworker. I need you to act like it."

"Just because I'm your friend doesn't mean I'm going to just tell you what you want to hear. I'm going to tell you the truth."

"And that's what? That now that I'm with Sebastian I'm not good at my job?"

"I didn't say that. You're twisting my words. I'm saying that now that you're with Sebastian, you're distracted from your job."

"I'm not. I'm here, aren't I? Didn't I just interrogate a suspect with you? I've been at the crime scenes so much I can probably draw them from memory."

"And every night, you go off with Sebastian, and we don't see you again until the morning."

"How is what I'm doing any different from what you did with Rebecca?"

"I didn't go to her every night I was there. I tried, but the case took priority. And I rarely spent the full night in her room."

Hot tears rose to Millie's eyes, but she refused to let them fall. Matthew must have noticed, because his posture relaxed, and he let out a sigh.

"Look, I know it feels like we're all ganging up on you, but we wouldn't be very good friends if we didn't say something, you know? Just please be careful. And think about what I said, okay?"

Not trusting her voice, Millie nodded.

"You said you're seeing him again tonight?"

"Yeah, he's taking me out somewhere nice to apologize for the fight we had last night."

"You'll keep your phone with you?"

"Of course."

"That's all we ask." He looked at his watch before rubbing his hand down his face. "I'm going to go grab some food and see if I can talk to Becks for a few minutes. You okay?"

Millie nodded. "Yeah, I'm fine."

He gave her a small smile before walking off toward the kitchen.

Millie looked down at her phone and sent off a quick heart-faced emoji in response to the text from Sebastian before tucking it back away in her pocket.

Glancing off in the direction Matthew walked off in. That's two people she's close to who have told her to be wary of Sebastian. Was she really prioritizing him over the job?

Maybe?

But that was mostly because their time together was limited. Right?

She sighed. Some things for her to think about later. First, she had to see how tonight went.

Sebastian told her to wear something nice. It's probably a good thing she brought that burgundy dress.

Chapter Twenty-Eight

TREVOR

October 13

Visions of summer and children running happily around the pool deck flew in front of Trevor's eyes. It took him three tries to find a camera with a decent angle. This one, directed toward the sizeable area where most of the umbrellas and chairs were situated, gave him the best view of faces. All the other angles mostly gave him tops of heads. He would have to mention to the pool that if they hoped to identify a thief, they would need to fix where their cameras were located.

Normally he would watch videos at top speed, but since the quality of the video from the pool was really poor, he was forced to watch it only slightly sped up.

And it. Was. Excruciating.

It also didn't help that since they didn't have an exact date, he started in early August. And so far, it had been a bust. An excruciatingly boring bust.

He stared at his phone, willing it to ring. Maybe someone will have some new information for him to work on. Maybe it will be Brad, and he had miraculously remembered something, anything.

There was a light knock on his door, and it opened to reveal Logan.

"Hey," Logan said as he moved into the room. "I just finished talking to Matthew and Millie. They questioned Bobby, and turns out that guy is suspicious as hell."

Trevor perked up. "Really?"

"Yeah, apparently the asshole was fidgety as hell. The only consistent thing about him was he insisted he didn't kill Jamie. But his rage certainly was there."

"Do they think he's good for all the killings? He's not an exact fit for the profile."

Logan shrugged. "Don't know. They think he's possibly good for the first one. And if we know anything about serials, it's that they get a taste for the killing, and then can't control themselves. And we all know the profile could be off a little."

"But what's with the two-week window?"

"Maybe there was a girl in his past who dated him for two weeks and then dumped him?"

"I guess, but that feels too easy. Too cliche."

Logan laughed. "I mean, serial killers aren't anything if not cliché."

"Touche."

Logan pulled out an extra chair and sat next to him. "What are you working on?"

"Pool footage."

Logan looked at the screens. "Are you sure this isn't Bigfoot footage? It's grainy as hell."

"Pool is only open for the summer months, and so they skimped on the surveillance equipment for budgetary reasons. And they also suck at camera placement. Three cameras at the pool, only one of them you can see faces clearly enough to make out distinct features."

Logan let out a low whistle. "Wow. I would rather sit through fifty safety training refreshers than do this."

Trevor laid his head down on the desk in front of him, the surface cool to his cheek. "I know. This case is the worst. Just. The. Worst."

"How about we take a break from the footage for a minute and talk about our friend Bobby?"

Trevor lifted his head from the table. "What about Bobby?"

"Have we thought of comparing his texts to Jamie to the other texts we have?"

"Millie and I did that earlier. It's why they called in Bobby to talk to him."

"Any evidence of Bobby being tech savvy enough to spoof numbers?"

"Random number generators are pretty easy to use. There was a mom who used one to harass her daughter and the boy she was dating a few years back. That's the easiest part of the entire case to do, technology-wise."

"What about the rest of the stuff? The hacking to change the files?"

"Well, if he has a friend on the inside, they could just change the files for him. No hacking necessary."

"Does Bobby have a friend on the inside?"

Trevor shrugged. "I don't know. Did Matthew and Millie ask him?"

Logan shook his head. "I don't know. They didn't mention it if they did."

"I think you've found something we can work on." Trevor started typing on his computer, pulling up different tabs.

"What are you doing?"

"I'm pulling up Bobby's phone records. Maybe if we go through his contacts list, we can see if there is anyone here at the precinct in it."

"Good call."

Silence fell as they scrolled through the contacts Bobby regularly texted with.

"There is nothing here that would implicate anyone here in the building." Trevor pushed back from the table and ran his hands through his hair.

"Not through here. Maybe they communicated in another way?"

"Or maybe Bobby isn't our guy."

"When you and Millie went through the messages, did you only compare the texts between Bobby and Jamie to those of the UNSUB and the other victims?"

"Yeah."

"What if you pull some of Bobby's other texts and see if they match the ones we have?"

Trevor pulled up a random text between Bobby and what appeared to be a client. He pulled up a text from the UNSUB to Sarah, victim number four. His eyes moved between the two screens.

"Look here." Logan pointed between two different messages. "The syntax is the same. Both he and the UNSUB used the same misspellings, the same sentence structure."

Trevor looked where Logan was pointing, and sure enough, the two different taxing conversations were incredibly similar. "How did we not notice this before?"

"I don't know."

"This is gold."

Trevor began taking screenshots of all the different messages. He and Logan spent the next hour annotating the different messages and noting similarities. Once they were finished, Trevor shared the files with the rest of the team, submitting it as evidence.

"This is not concrete proof," Logan noted.

"Yeah, but it's a start. It will probably be enough to get a warrant out for the guy."

"Do you know where Millie is going on her date with Sebastian tonight?"

Trevor whipped his gaze up to Logan, getting whiplash from the random change of subject. "I don't. I'm not even sure if she knows. Said Sebastian was going to surprise her."

Logan nodded and hummed.

"What?"

"Nothing."

"That's not a nothing look. You're trying not to say something."

"It's just, Matthew told me they kind of got into after the interrogation. Have you noticed Millie acting differently during this case?"

"Of course I have. But we're not exactly talking a lot right now."

"Because of Sebastian?"

"Yeah. I don't know. He's got her convinced I'm jealous, but I'm not."

Logan finally turned and looked at him, tilting his head. "You're not?"

Trevor sighed. "I'm not. Okay, maybe a little, but it didn't start off that way. I'm more jealous of Rebecca than I am of fucking Sebastian."

Logan turned his chair fully to face him, folding his arms across his chest. "That's interesting. Tell me more."

Trevor gave up trying to work on what he was working on and turned his chair toward Logan. "Millie is my best friend, and usually we tell each other everything. Everything. And suddenly she meets this guy and after a couple of days she's pushing me away. She's picking fights and saying hurtful things she never would have before. Which, fine, whatever? But last night she and Sebastian had a fight, and she called Rebecca. And it fucking hurt, because I used to be the first one she called when something like that happened."

Logan leaned forward, resting his elbows on the knees with his legs spread. "Listen, man, you saw how close and how quickly Millie and Rebecca got when we were in Iowa. She can have more than one close friend. And things are weird between you right now. If it weren't, I'm sure she would have come to you. Tell me about the fight between the two of you?"

Trevor groaned. "It was really stupid. Sebastian was here, and he did some posturing, and after he left, I told her I had a bad vibe from him."

"Did you really have a bad vibe from him, or were you just upset about his posturing?"

"I honestly get a bad vibe from him."

"You'll be happy to know you're not the only one."

Trevor sat up straighter. "What do you mean?"

"The general vibe from the group is there's something off. Matty said that she told Becks Sebastian wants her to transfer to Albuquerque and give up being a profiler. And she's really been slacking off on this case to go disappear off with Sebastian, not answering her phone, all of which are completely out of character for her."

"Not answering her phone?"

"Yeah, and honestly we don't think she's doing it on purpose."

Trevor leaned forward in his seat. "You think he's manipulating things."

"I do."

"I would believe you."

"She told Matty that she was going to keep her phone on her tonight."

"Good. Because if we break this case, we're going to need her."

"Think she'll leave her special date to come back?"

Trevor nodded. "Absolutely. She felt a connection to Laura. She's committed to solving the case and finding justice for her."

"So, what are our next steps with Bobby?"

"You should go back to the team and try to see if the texts we found are enough to get a warrant to search his properties. I'm going to go back to the fucking pool videos to see if Bobby shows up in any of them and has contact with Laura and her family."

Logan pushed up from his chair. "Good luck. Drink lots of caffeine."

Trevor lifted the container of espresso beans. "Millie took care of that earlier."

Logan gave him a half-smile. "And you're worried about your friendship. That girl has your back."

Trevor watched as Logan left the room, their conversation replaying in his head. Logan was right. Millie had his back. And he really shouldn't be jealous of Rebecca. Millie could totally have two close friends, and he really liked Rebecca. She brought them all food. A lot. She was an honorary member of the team.

But he wasn't going to change his opinion of Sebastian. That asshole was manipulative as fuck. He needed to figure out how to talk gently to Millie about it, without it coming off as jeal-ousy.

Of course, that would have to wait. He had hours of footage to search through, and a Bobby-shaped needle to find.

Chapter Twenty-Nine

MILLIE

October 13

Millie glanced at the clock in her motel room. There wasn't much time left before Sebastian was supposed to pick her up. Turning back to the mirror, she picked up her mascara wand and went back to applying it to her eyelashes. It had been a long time since she had dressed up, and she was pretty giddy about the whole thing.

After leaving the precinct, she had stopped at a CVS to buy some makeup before coming back to the motel. She had taken a shower, and she toughed it out, using the subpar blow dry-er to dry her hair so it fell in soft curls down her back. Her burgundy dress stood out beautifully against her alabaster skin. Sometimes she hated how pale she was, especially in the summer when she would burn easily in the sun. However, when she took the time to apply her makeup like tonight, she loved it. Setting down the mascara wand, she picked up a burgundy lip color and carefully applied it. The color was as close to her dress as she could find at the last minute. And it stood out against her skin fantastically.

She looked at herself one more time and couldn't help the wide smile that spread across her face. Damn, she was pretty. She couldn't remember the last time she had felt this pretty.

Honestly, she couldn't even remember the last time she took the time to dress up for a date. Years, more than likely.

Rebecca had asked her to be a bridesmaid in her wedding, which still didn't have a date set, and really, Millie figured that would be her next opportunity to dress up and look pretty.

She never anticipated meeting Sebastian, and everything that has transpired. There really was no predicting the future, was there?

Walking over to the bed, she sat down and slipped on the heels she had brought with her. Again, she thought she was just packing stuff and taking up room. Who would have thought she was actually going to use it? Definitely not her.

As she buckled the straps on her shoes, what Matthew had said to her after Bobby's interrogation came to her mind, and guilt began filling her stomach. Was she doing exactly what he accused her of? Choosing Sebastian over the case? Setting her foot back on the floor, she closed her eyes and thought back over the case. It was true. She hadn't been as involved as in past cases. She was on her phone more, texting with Sebastian during the day, and gone every night over to Sebastian's place to spend time with him.

Fuck.

She was letting her job slip.

Unbidden, Laura's face flashed in her mind, and she could feel the tears welling up behind her closed eyes. She was failing these women by being distracted by a man. Hell, she was letting feminism down by letting a man distract her from her job. Whenever she brought up maybe she should be at work, he would distract her. Usually with orgasms. She was letting her lady parts control her, and that was not good. Yes, they were getting more attention lately than they had in months, but that was no excuse to let them run the show. Her brain needed to be in charge again.

Millie opened her eyes with new determination. Tonight, while on whatever fantastic date she was going on with Sebastian, she would put her foot down. No more distractions.

Her phone vibrated on the bed, and she picked it up.

Trevor - Logan and I have a lead. They're getting a warrant for Bobby's place.

Millie - What?! Was he at the pool???

Trevor - Not sure. But his texts to non-victims match the language and syntax of the texts from the UNSUB to the victims. Judge said it's enough to get a warrant.

Millie - I'm leaving my phone on. Call me if you find anything. I'll tell you my location, and you can come pick me up.

Trevor - Sounds like a plan.

Trevor - ....

Trevor - Have fun tonight.

Millie smiled down at her phone. She knew Trevor's feelings about Sebastian, and for him to tell her to have fun was a huge step. She could feel the rift between them healing in real time.

Millie - Thanks. Good luck with the footage.

Trevor - GIF of Man banging head on table.

Millie laughed before double-checking her phone ringer was on, and tucking it into the pocket of her dress. Yes, her dress had pockets. It was her favorite part of the dress. Also, it made her breasts look fantastic.

There was a knock on her door. Standing from the bed, she smoothed the skirt of her dress down and walked cautiously to the door. She was out of practice walking in heels. Opening the door, her smile widened when she saw Sebastian standing there.

He was wearing a button-down shirt, unbuttoned at the collar, his long hair slicked back away from his face, but still down. His eyes were lined with his typical kohl liner, and his face still sported his stubble. In his hand, he held a dozen multicolored roses.

When he saw her, his gaze scanned her up and down, and he let out a low whistle. "I thought I liked you best when you were wearing nothing, but I think this is my new favorite look."

He took a step forward, capturing her lips with his in a searing kiss. She brought her hands up to either side of his face, pulling him closer to her.

He pulled back and rested his forehead against hers. "We'd better go, or we won't leave this room tonight. I have a few different stops for us tonight." He moved and kissed her cheek before moving his mouth to her ear, whispering, "But, later, I'm going to fuck you against the wall while you wear this dress and those heels."

Millie's face warmed, and she could already feel herself reacting to his words.

Suddenly, all her resolve was gone, and she found herself looking forward to later that night.

The first stop of the night ended up being what was probably the fanciest restaurant in Calico Rock. Sebastian mentioned he needed to make reservations, and they were lucky it was a Tuesday, because otherwise it was almost impossible to get in.

The atmosphere was dim, and the tables were covered in red tablecloths, but compared to some of the exclusive and "fancy" restaurants in D.C., it was a little underwhelming to Millie. But she didn't say that to Sebastian. Of course, a restaurant in a small town in New Mexico wouldn't compare to anything in the bustling metropolis of the nation's capital, but they were acting like this was L'Ardente, when in fact this place was a step up from an ordinary family restaurant.

Not wanting to make a mess of herself, she ordered a salad, and he ordered some chicken parmesan, and a bottle of red wine.

"How's your salad?" Sebastian asked.

"It's fine."

"You don't have to eat stereotypically in front of me, you know. You could have ordered pasta."

Millie laughed. "Oh, I know I could have. But I'm wearing my nicest dress, and so Murphy's Law would indicate that I would spill red sauce all over said nice dress if I had ordered it. You said this was a multi-stop date. I don't want to mess myself up during stop one."

Sebastian gave her his lopsided smile that always made her weak in the knees. "If you had made a mess of your dress, we could have just skipped to the end."

Millie shook her head. "No. I'm looking forward to a night out with you. Outside the bedroom."

"But I like our time in the bedroom. I get some of my best work done in there."

Her cheeks grew warm. "Yes, well, I think if our relationship is going to work, we need to spend some time outside of the bedroom. Have actual conversations. With our clothes on."

He chuckled. "You make a fair point. What do you want to talk about?"

Millie picked about her salad for a minute before gathering the nerve to bring up what had caused them to have a fight last night. "I'm thinking, maybe, we try long distance for a little bit before either of us commits to moving near the other."

Sebastian stopped mid-slice through his chicken breast and looked up at her. "You want to try long distance? I thought we agreed it would be easier if we lived near each other?"

Millie shook her head. "We never agreed to anything. We fought, and then I left."

Sebastian shook his head. "No, I distinctly remember us talking about it, and then you getting upset about having to give up your job to move near me, since I can't give up my job, because long distance just wouldn't work between us."

She frowned. She honestly did not remember that part of the conversation. But it could have happened. Right? Shaking her head, she locked her gaze on his. "Regardless, after thinking about it, I really think long-distance would be a good first step for us. We've only known each other for a week, and committing to moving is an enormous step for us right now."

"You said your friends met in May, and she moved for him after a few weeks. How is that any different from what we have now?"

Millie sighed. "Rebecca was already planning to move away from Cove Creek before she even met Matthew. And she didn't move right away. They did long distance for three months before she moved."

"They did?"

"They did."

Sebastian set his fork and knife down on the table and leaned forward, pushing his plate forward with his arms as he folded them on the table in front of him. "So, when you're proposing long distance, you're proposing it for a short time, with an end date?"

Millie nodded. "Yeah. We can set a date where we can re-evaluate the situation and adjust as needed."

Sebastian stared across at her and narrowed his eyes. Millie fidgeted under his scrutiny. She couldn't read his expression. After a few minutes, his trademark half-smile spread onto his face. "I think that's a fair deal. How long should we try long distance for?"

A genuine smile spread across Millie's face, and her shoulders sagged in relief. "Well, it's mid-October now. How about we reassess after the new year? That would give us about two and a half months?"

Sebastian nodded. "I like that timeline. And maybe we can spend the holidays together?"

"I am planning on going home to California for Christmas this year to see my nieces and nephews."

"Meeting your family? I wouldn't be opposed to that."

Millie's heart warmed. Rebecca was right. Communication was key. Things were working out wonderfully between the two of them. It was just what she needed in order to feel better about everything. She picked up her fork to eat again, suddenly having her appetite back.

Just as she was lifting her fork to her mouth, she felt her phone buzz against her thigh. Setting the fork down, she pulled out her phone.

"Am I so boring you need to get on your phone?" Sebastian joked.

She shook her head. "We had a big breakthrough in the case, and I promised I would keep my phone on in case there was a development."

Sebastian nodded. "Makes sense. Sorry for making a joke. Sometimes I forget why you're really in town."

Millie swiped open her phone, expecting a text from someone on her team. However, that was not what she found.

UNKNOWN - Tick Tock. Your Time Is Up.

A chill ran down her spine, and her smile slipped from her face.

"What's wrong?" Sebastian's voice was full of concern, but Millie hadn't told him about her being stalked by the killer, and she wasn't going to tell him now.

She shook her head. "Nothing, I just, uh, need to forward this message to Trevor."

"You've gone pale. Are you sure you're okay?"

Millie finished forwarding the message to Trevor and tucked the phone back into the pocket of her dress. She took a deep breath and schooled her features into a smile. "I'm fine."

Sebastian looked at her like he wanted to say more, but he shook his head, and gave her another crooked smile. "If you say so. Let's finish eating so we can get out of here, go to our next location."

"Still not going to tell me where it is?"

"Why would I want to ruin the surprise?" Sebastian grinned at her before picking up his fork and knife and getting back to eating.

Millie tried to match his enthusiasm, but a pit settled in her stomach. Hopefully, Trevor could trace this number. She didn't want to think about what would happen if he couldn't.

Chapter Thirty

TREVOR

October 13

Trevor stared at the message from Millie for a few minutes longer than normal. His heart rate quickly escalated.

UNKNOWN - *Tick Tock. Your Time Is Up.*

Such a simple message, but it held so much. He looked at the calendar.

The UNSUB was either moving up his timeline, or he was giving Millie fair warning. Either way, Trevor didn't like it. And he didn't like that it was yet another randomly generated number. It made him want to break something.

His best friend being targeted by a serial killer was not an ideal situation. The fact that he couldn't do anything about it, made him feel helpless.

Well, there was one thing he could do. He brought his gaze up from his phone, returning it to the computer screens.

The fucking pool footage.

Turns out, when there's a pool open and it's summer in a climate that gets really hot during the summer, lots of people frequent it. And when the footage is absolute shit, that doesn't make things any easier.

Trevor resumed the footage he had been watching and had to force himself to focus so his eyes didn't glaze over. It took a lot of willpower not to click away from the screen and work on something else.

Like tracing this number who sent a threatening message to Millie.

Trevor shook his head.

Focus.

His gaze locked onto the grainy screen. There were dozens of people milling around, and most of them were children. Which actually helped narrow things down. However, he had to keep a photo of Laura and her family pulled up on a screen to make sure he had their faces fresh in his mind. Otherwise, they all sort of started looking the same.

He really needed Brad to remember what date they went to the damn pool.

Trevor glanced at the time. It had only been twenty minutes since Millie had sent him the text. She was still on her date with Sebastian. Trevor tried to comfort himself with the fact that the UNSUB wouldn't do anything while she was with someone else. The UNSUB lured his victims out, and that's when he took them.

Millie was too smart to lure, so he would probably take her, but not when she was with someone else. He would wait until she was alone and then take her.

As long as she was with Sebastian, she would be fine.

She would be fine.

But he fits the profile.

Trevor shook his head silencing the voice in his head.

Millie trusted him, so he would trust him.

Trevor had just turned back to the computer when his phone started ringing. His heart began to jackhammer in his chest. Was this the call that Millie had been taken?

He flipped it over and frowned at a number that hadn't been saved in his phone. "Ford?"

"Hi, um, yeah, this is Brad Hutchins, Laura's husband."

Trevor sat up straighter. "Yes, hi. How can I help you?"

"So, I was sitting here rocking the toddler to sleep, and it came to me."

"What did?"

"The date we went to the pool. I don't know what clicked into place, but it all just sort of rushed back to me. Like one of those scenes in the movies, you know?"

"Yeah, yeah. We told you that it would come to you. It'd just take some time."

"I don't know what did it. But we went to the pool on August twenty-seventh. It was a Thursday. We got there maybe an hour or two before the pool closed. But how shortly I don't know, I can't exactly remember."

"No, no, just you narrowing down the day is probably the most helpful thing you could do. You don't even know how helpful this information is."

Brad let out a breath. "I'm so glad it's helpful. I've been wracking my brain ever since you two left my house last week."

Trevor began exiting out of the videos he had pulled up, and he was scrolling through to find August twenty-seventh. On the date, he was going to look at the footage from all the cameras. He was going to be fucking thorough. "And you're one hundred percent certain this was the date?"

"One hundred percent. I went back to my work calendar once it came to me, and that was the date I had almost nothing on, so I knew I would have left early."

Trevor raised his gaze to the ceiling and mouthed a cheer. The night was turning around. He couldn't have asked for better news. If he could ID the UNSUB at the pool with the Hutchens family, they could break the case tonight.

Before the killer got close to Millie.

"Thank you so much for calling me and letting me know."

"Yeah, it's so weird that last week the day was sort of fuzzy, and now it's clear as day. We were walking in from the parking lot, and Laura dropped the bag carrying all the towels and sunscreen. Before either of us had a chance to pick it up, this man came up to us and picked it up. He walked with us to the counter and even paid to go into the pool so he could help us carry our stuff. I thought it was strange, because we had never met him before, and he wasn't dressed for the pool. But he was being genuinely friendly. And he stayed and talked to Laura for a few minutes at the chairs before he left."

"Did anything else stand out about him other than his not being dressed for the pool?"

Brad was quiet on the other line for a minute before he spoke again, and what he said next sent a chill down Trevor's spine. "Yeah, he had stuff around his eyes? Black stuff. You know what I'm talking about? He kind of looked like the Winter Soldier, you know what I'm saying? I don't know if I'm describing it right. I'm not very good at this stuff."

"Yeah, no. You're describing it perfectly. I know exactly what you're talking about. Thank you so much for calling me, but I need to go look at the footage. You've just given me a huge lead."

"No problem. Let me know if you need anything else."

"I will. Thank you again, Mr. Hutchens."

Trevor pressed the button on the phone, hanging up, not even waiting for a reply.

His heart was jackhammering in his chest. There was one very specific man who he knew fit that description, but Trevor didn't want to jump to conclusions. There could be a few men in Calico Rock who wore guy liner and sort of looked like Bucky Barnes.

At least, he really hoped there was.

He pulled up the footage of the pool. As it played, his knee bounced up and down rapidly. He hoped he was wrong. There they were. The Hutchens family. They had gotten there shortly before closing. He watched as Brad led the girls to some chairs under an umbrella. Following close behind was Laura, and she was talking to a man who was carrying a basket. He could only see the back of his head, but he had dark hair, pulled back into a ponytail.

"Turn around," Trevor muttered under his breath, his leg picking up speed, his heart beating so fast he was sure it was going to burst out of his chest.

He watched Laura say something, and then the stranger laughed, and then he turned around.

Trevor paused the video on the man's face and zoomed in as close as he could without jeopardizing the quality of the video. His stomach dropped.

"Mother. Fucker."

Staring out from the screen was fucking Sebastian Sable.

Trevor ran his hand through his hair and tried to calm himself down. It wouldn't help anything if he was panicking.

But everything made sense.

The asshole was here. A lot. Checking in on Millie.

Fucking over the case.

Trevor shoved himself away from the desk and stood up, pacing the room. He was here so much at the beginning of the case. Everyone knew him as Millie's situationship, and so they probably wouldn't have thought twice about letting him in.

Sebastian knew when they were in the building or not, Millie was constantly talking to him and keeping him apprised of her location, so when they went to talk to Brad, he probably came in and put in the memory stick with whatever it was he used to scramble his computer.

He said he worked in construction, but that was probably a cover.

Fuck. Fuck. Fuck.

Trevor looked around the room and tried to figure out what he needed to do.

He needed to tell the team.

He needed to call Millie.

She was with him right now.

Trevor pulled his phone out of his pocket and quickly dialed Millie.

The phone rang once and then went straight to voicemail.

Trevor frowned.

She wouldn't be screening her calls. She told them to call her if something happened with the case.

Something was wrong.

Chapter Thirty-One

MILLIE

October 13

The car rolled down the road as Sebastian sang along with the radio. He had it on the classic rock station, and Led Zeppelin blasted through the car. He still hadn't told her where they were going, but Millie was excited. She needed something to take her mind off the message she had received.

Millie glanced at Sebastian out of the corner of her eye. He was rocking out to Stairway to Heaven, tapping the drumbeat out on the steering wheel. She closed her eyes, letting herself get lost in the song. It was one of her dad's favorites. Her foot started tapping along with the beat as the music ramped up to the guitar solo.

You're on a date with a wonderful man, she told herself. You need to relax. Enjoy it. The killer won't try anything while you're with Seb. You're safe.

Relaxing into her seat, she started singing along with Robert Plant and Sebastian. She opened her eyes and turned them toward Sebastian, who turned to look at her at the same time. A wide smile spread across his face. She returned it.

This was fun.

They sang together until the last note. Once the song was over and it switched to a song Millie wasn't quite sure she knew, she reached over and linked her hand with Sebastian's. Her night was turning around. They were going to go to wherever it was he was taking her, and she was going to forget about everything else.

Sebastian returned his full gaze to the road ahead of him, but kept holding her hand. Millie turned her head so she could look out the window to see if she could get a hint of where they were going and frowned.

The lights of Calico Rock were long gone, and they were somewhere where the only lights were the lights lining the highway.

"Hey, where are we going?"

Sebastian laughed. "I told you. It's a surprise."

"You didn't say we were going to leave town. What if my team needs me?"

"Then I'll drive you back. It's fine."

"It's not fine. I would have really liked a heads-up about driving out of town."

"We're not going that far."

Millie tried to see where they were going, but the sun had long set, and the desert was pitch black. The shrubby bushes that covered the sand were barely visible if not for the headlights. "There's nothing out here."

"That's not true. There is plenty out here. You just have to wait and see."

Millie shook her head, uneasiness settling in her stomach. All of her instincts were telling her something was wrong.

She brought her gaze back to Sebastian. His eyes were still on the road ahead of them, and he didn't look any different from before. So why did she feel anxious?

"Relax." Sebastian looked over at her and gave her a smile. "I promise if your team calls, I'll drive you back. They know you're out with me. They're not going to expect you to show up immediately. You'll just tell them you need some time to get there."

Millie brought her bottom lip between her teeth and looked out the window. Despite his telling her to relax, it was impossible for her to do so. She turned back to Sebastian. "I think I would feel a lot better if you would just tell me where we're going."

"And I told you; it's a surprise." His voice was light, but it held a harshness below the surface, one that told her she would not get anymore answers. The subject was closed.

She tried to take her hand back, but his grip on it tightened, so she gave up.

They drove for only another five minutes before Sebastian made a right turn off of the highway.

The road was dirt, and as they drove, Millie desperately tried to see something, anything, in the dark, but there was nothing.

Just darkness.

Anxiety bubbled in her stomach, and she was concerned her salad was going to make a reappearance.

After a few minutes, Sebastian made a left turn, the car bouncing on the unevenness of the desert floor. The shrubby bushes she couldn't make out before were coming into focus outside of her window as Sebastian navigated the car around them, making sure not to hit any.

Maybe we're going somewhere to stargaze, Millie reasoned with herself. Stargazing was romantic. Wasn't it?

And then, suddenly, they were stopped.

Millie leaned forward to see if she could get a closer look out of the windshield and froze.

They were in the middle of what had to be a ghost town. There were several buildings on either side of the road, and they seemed to be parked in front of what was once a church. It was completely dark, so there must not be any electricity out here.

"Where are we?"

Sebastian gave her hand a squeeze before letting go. "Isn't it cool? It's an abandoned mining town. I think they were mining silver here before it dried up and they left. The best part? These buildings are still in amazing structural shape." He went to open the door to his car, stepping out.

Millie didn't move to leave. She just continued to stare out of the window, trying to make sense of what was going on. Why would he bring her here? At night?

Her door opened, and Sebastian held out his hand to help her out of the car. She let him, and they stood next to the car staring at the church. It was hard to tell what its shape was in the dark, but it was your typical late nineteenth century church. It looked to be white, but it could have been cream or even gray. There was a short set of stairs that led to the doors of the church, and from the doors, the building stretched up into a steeple.

"Are we stargazing here?" Millie couldn't help the tremble in her voice. It took a lot to scare her, and between this and the message she received earlier, her nerves were definitely jagged.

Sebastian laughed. "No, we're going in there. Come on!" Without waiting for a reply, he grabbed her hand and dragged her up the stairs of the church, and through the front doors.

The inside of the sanctuary was lit with strategically placed lanterns throughout. They must have been solar powered, because the church itself didn't seem to have electricity.

"What's going on?" Millie looked around the room, her skills kicking into overdrive.

"This is one of my favorite places in the world. I wanted to share it with you."

Millie's gaze moved around the room, taking everything in, and froze.

Over where the altar would have been was a wall, covered in paper. Unable to stop herself, she began walking toward it. As she got nearer, she could see what it was. They were photos of the women they were investigating the murders of. In every photo, the women were screaming, pressing against something. Millie couldn't tell what.

She whipped around and looked at Sebastian, who was standing in the middle of the room, his hands in his pockets, a smirk on his face. "What the fuck?!"

Sebastian shrugged his shoulders. "I told you this was my favorite place."

Millie felt bile rise in the back of her throat. All this time she was looking for the killer, and she was fucking him. Falling for him. Unable to hold it in, she fell to her knees, vomiting.

Sebastian's footsteps echoed in the nearly empty space as he moved closer to her. "I knew since you were so smart it wouldn't take you very long to put everything together. I will say I'm a little disappointed you couldn't figure it out sooner. Although I'm kind of glad you didn't. I've never fucked a mark before. I kind of enjoyed it. I'll have to try it again with the next one."

Next one. The words echoed through her head. Next one...

"Was everything between us a lie?" Millie's throat was raw from getting sick.

Sebastian laughed. "Of course it was."

"Why?"

"When I saw you outside the pool, I knew what I needed to do. You fit my mold so nicely. You were the perfect pawn. And you made it so easy. So. Easy." There was mirth in his voice. He was having fun, and he was gloating. Millie knew he was monologuing because he was not planning on keeping her alive. That's why he brought her to his second location.

She fucking went with him to a second location.

He successfully lured her away.

She turned from where she was on the floor to look at the faces of the women. Jamie, Sharon, Laura, and Sarah all looked down at her from the wall.

The trophies.

They thought he was taking something from each victim.

No.

Instead, he was taking pictures of the women and their fear and keeping those as tokens. Which is why the families couldn't find anything missing from the bodies. There wasn't anything.

Swallowing back her emotions, Millie calmly stood up from where she was sitting. She needed to get out of the building and call her team. In that order. Standing on shaky legs, she squared her shoulders and started walking back down the aisle.

If she just acted cool, she could walk right past him and get out of here.

Sebastian just stood there, hands still in his pockets. Smirking.

Millie would have to get around him.

She felt confident she could. She was trained for this. He was scrawny. She knew it was coming, unlike the women before her.

Millie held her breath as she walked past Sebastian, who still stood there, hands in his pockets, unmoving. It was too easy. Why was he just letting her go? As soon as she got to the door, she realized why he hadn't moved. She tugged on the door, but it wouldn't budge.

Locked.

She would have to keep him talking. Her team would find her.

"Why did you kill all those women?"

Turning slowly to face her, Sebastian shrugged. "Did you know, when I was a boy, my mom dropped me off at a friend's house. Said she needed to just run out and get a few things from the store. Never saw her again."

"Wait. You told me you were with your mom all summer as she died from cancer."

Sebastian shrugged. "I lied. I don't know why you're shocked at this point."

"How old were you?"

"Ten."

"How old was she?"

Sebastian gave her the crooked smile she used to love, shaking his head slowly. "So fucking smart. Your brain is always working. Putting pieces together. She was forty-two."

"Why now? Why start killing these innocent women?"

"I decided to track down my mom this summer. Confront her about why she abandoned me. Turns out she's dead. Couldn't confront her. I was walking through town and I saw Jamie coming out of the art gallery. I overheard them talking about their futures. How she was going to leave her husband for him. She needed to be punished for ruining their family."

"But what about the other three? They weren't cheating on their husbands. You've robbed their children of their mothers. You made those children just like you."

"All women are the same."

The text messages from the killer came flooding back to her. When she asked what she could have in common with these women. It was simple, really. She was a woman. That was it. All it took. A woman who had connections to the case. She was a means to an end. A convenience.

And she had caught real feelings.

Was she really that desperate for a relationship that she could be blinded so easily?

"Let me go."

"No."

Millie turned around and started pulling at the door again. She needed to get out. She tried to rack her brain to think about what she had that would help her leave. Why didn't she use bobby pins or something in her hair?

She was so in her head that she didn't hear Sebastian approach her until it was too late. His hand clasped around her bicep, and he dragged her away from the door. She tried to find purchase with her feet, but her shoes couldn't get firmly on the ground, thanks to the heels.

Because she couldn't get a firm plant of her feet on the ground, she couldn't use any of her tricks to get out of Sebastian's grip. As she struggled, he brought his other arm around her body, pulling her taut against him.

He brought his mouth close to her ear and he whispered, "You look just like her."

His hand came up and placed a cloth over her nose and mouth.

And then, she knew nothing.

Chapter Thirty-Two

TREVOR

October 13

By the time Trevor made it to the conference room where the rest of the team was gathered, he was out of breath, having sprinted the entire way between his closet office and the room.

Flinging the door open, he watched every head in the room swivel toward him. He opened his mouth to talk, but nothing came out.

Thomas stood so quickly that the chair he was sitting in slid across the room, crashing into the wall. "What's going on? Did you find something?"

Trevor nodded.

"What'd you find?"

Trevor tried to talk again, but his throat was tight, and he was pretty sure he was going to hyperventilate.

Logan stood from his chair and walked over to Trevor, putting his hand on his back. "Breathe in and out, slowly."

Trevor tried to do as Logan said, but his breaths were still coming in jagged.

"Think of something that you can see, something you can hear, and something you can feel."

Logan's hand on my back. The beige tile on the ground. Logan's voice telling me what to do.

As he thought of everything Logan told him to identify, Trevor's breathing normalized.

"Are you better?" Logan's voice was calm in his ear.

Trevor nodded. "Yeah. I think so. Thanks."

"Panic attack. My husband gets them all the time. I have experience. Now that you've calmed down, why don't you tell us what triggered yours?"

"Millie is in trouble."

That caused Matthew to leap from his seat, pulling his phone out of his pocket, more than likely trying to call her.

"It's no good. It's going straight to voicemail," Trevor said.

Matthew dropped his hand, his phone hanging helpless at his side. "Did she get another message from the killer? Did Sebastian call you?"

Rather than say anything, he walked over to the TV in the room and flipped it on. He then grabbed Thomas's tablet and pulled up the screenshot he had shared into the evidence folder.

The photo of Sebastian with Laura and her family filled the screen.

The men in the room erupted. They were all shouting over each other.

"QUIET!" Thomas's booming voice sounded over the noise, successfully causing everyone to stop. Thomas turned to Trevor, pointing at the screen. "Explain."

"Brad called me. He said he remembered the date they had gone to the pool. Even the time. It came to him tonight. And before he hung up, he said he remembered that the man who helped them resembled The Winter Soldier. The second I hung up, I went to the footage, and there they were. And Sebastian fucking Sable is the guy who helped them."

"Fuck. This entire time, the UNSUB was here." Logan shoved a chair, so it slid under the table, creating a loud thud in the room as the two connected.

"This is typical though, isn't it? He integrated himself into the investigation in order to control it. He supposedly works for construction, but he's probably tech savvy, and actually did alter the files from the outside, but he didn't need to do anything drastic to fuck up Trevor's files, since he had an in with Millie." Matthew's voice cracked as he said her name.

"What are the chances of whatever was going on between Sebastian and Millie being authentic? Like, does he have genuine feelings for her?" Logan asked.

Trevor shook his head. "She is out on a date with him, and she is no longer answering her phone. Earlier this evening the UNSUB, who we now suspect is Sebastian Sable, sent her a text stating her time was up."

"So, it's pretty much given he's truly an asshole and used our Millie," Thomas concluded.

"And she is currently out with him, and not answering her phone. We should move forward with the assumption that she is currently in danger," Logan stated.

"What do we know about Sable?" Matthew asked.

"Only what Millie has told us. He's in his early thirties. He works in construction and lives down the street from the pool. I promised Millie I wouldn't background check him, and I stupidly did what she asked." Trevor could feel his body heating, and his heart rate picking back up. He was a fucking idiot, and his best friend was in danger because of it.

"You didn't do anything wrong," Logan reassured him. "We all had our reservations, but we ultimately decided to trust Millie. Which was a normal thing to do."

"Well, I had a bad feeling about him, and I confronted Millie about it tonight," Matthew spoke up. "She was really defensive, but I think she was listening. She probably went on the date on high alert."

"Okay, here's what we're going to do," Thomas clapped his hands together, getting everyone's attention. "You three are going to Trevor's room and running a trace on Sebastian. I will go to the local law enforcement and talk to them about this update. We will put an APB out for Sable and his car. Does anyone know where Millie was going tonight?"

Three blank faces looked at him.

"No worries. We will find them. This is top priority." Thomas dismissed them, walking out of the room toward where the chief of police was located.

The rest of the men moved out of the room and toward Trevor's closet.

Throughout the entire walk down the hallway, scenarios sped through Trevor's mind, and he prayed none of them would come true.

Chapter Thirty-Three

MILLIE

October 13

Everything was damp.

That's what Millie noticed first as she came to. She tried to open her eyes, but they felt heavy, so she stopped trying for a moment. Instead, she used her other senses to try to figure out where she was.

Everything around her was wet, and the air was cold. Moving her hand across the surface she was lying on, she could tell it was either really dusty or made of dirt. Considering where she was, she was going to go with dirt. Damp and dirt meant she was probably in a basement of some kind. More than likely the one under the church.

Millie breathed in deeply before letting it out slowly and silently. If she kept her eyes closed, she could buy herself some time. Her arms and legs could move freely, so she wasn't bound.

That was either a good thing or a bad. She wasn't sure yet. But she could work with this. Her first order of business was to take the shoes off. She really regretted wearing heels. They had seemed like such a good idea earlier in the night, but she had learned her lesson.

She would never wear heels again.

After getting them off, she would make a run for it. And as she was running, she would call her team.

Trevor.

Tears sprang to her eyes. She would call Trevor first. And he would come and get her. He would find her. They were on each other's Find My Friends. He would come here, and they would arrest Sebastian, and she would see justice for all the women he stole from this world because of his mommy issues.

And she would never date again. Ever.

With a plan in motion, Millie tried opening her eyes again. This time it worked. Instinctively, she braced herself to be blinded by bright lights, but she should have known she wouldn't be. There was no electricity here. Instead, it was dimly lit with the same sort of lanterns Sebastian had set up upstairs.

Millie pushed herself up into a sitting position and immediately regretted it. Her head swam. She had to close her eyes again to stop the world from spinning. The chloroform he dosed her with must have been laced with something else. Something a little stronger in order to incapacitate her longer, or he had drugged her while she was out. She shook her head. She could get through this. Her plan was still feasible. She would just have to push through the muddiness in her brain.

Opening her eyes again, she frowned. There was a wall maybe two feet in front of her. Carefully turning her head around, she noticed she was surrounded by walls on three sides, with only a narrow passage out in one direction. This was not at all what she had been expecting. What the fuck was happening?

"Oh good, you're awake." Sebastian's voice sounded through the room, from a speaker somewhere above her. "I was worried I got the dosage wrong."

"Where am I?"

"The basement of the church."

"This doesn't look like a basement."

"Oh, it's the basement. You're just in the middle of a maze."

Millie blinked slowly, her brain trying to catch up with what was happening. "A maze?"

"A maze." Sebastian repeated. "There are two exits out of the maze. I'm coming in from one of them. If you find your way out, that's it. You can leave. You live. However, if I find you first, well, you're smart. You know what will happen."

"You know this maze. You're watching on video. This is unfairly balanced in your favor."

"I'm not going to be watching you once I'm in the maze. The thrill of the hunt is the best part. And as far as my knowing the layout of the maze goes, guess that means you better run. Running from your problems is what women do best."

Before Millie could fully process everything, he said, an AI-generated voice began counting down from ten. "Fuck." She scrambled with the buckles on her shoes, her fingers struggling to find purchase on them as she rushed to rid herself of the disadvantage. She flung her last shoe to the ground as the disembodied voice hit three.

Millie scrambled to her feet, ignoring the swimming in her head. There was only one way out of this part of the maze, but who knew how many twists, turns, and dead ends she was going to encounter on the way.

A few years ago, the team went to Minnesota to visit Logan's family, and he took them to a corn maze. They split up to make it more fun, and Trevor taught her that if she followed the right wall, it would lead her to safety.

Trevor.

She wished he were here with her now. That she had listened to him when he told her he had a bad feeling about Sebastian.

Taking a deep breath, she pushed those thoughts down. She needed to focus, but it was difficult. All she really wanted to do was lie down and sleep.

Tears started streaking down her face, a sob breaking the surface. Up until now, she had figured she could get out of this. She was trained. She was intelligent. She had people who could find her. But now, as the AI voice announced the number one, she knew she didn't have this. She was in over her head. There was no way she was going to make it out of here alive.

A loud buzzer echoed through the church basement, and before she had a chance to even think about what she was doing, her feet started moving. It wasn't quite a run, but she was moving. As soon as she cleared the wall and entered the maze, she found herself with three choices of directions to go.

She froze.

Which way?

Making a split-second decision, she went with her gut and did what Trevor had told her to back in the corn maze. Follow the right wall. He had never led her astray before, so she would trust him now.

So, turning to the right, she ran.

Chapter Thirty-Four

TREVOR

October 13

"I should have done this a week ago." Trevor scrolled through everything he found after running a trace on Sebastian Sable.

Years in foster care before aging out at eighteen, followed by years of moving around the state before settling in Calico Rock two years ago. In each city, he took a job in construction, but he had attended community college, getting his associate's degree in computer programming.

And the asshole didn't have a record, per say. Nothing he did required him to be booked, but he had some complaints filed against him. Harassment. Stalking.

None of these things pointed to a serial killer by themselves, but the blueprints were there when you put everything together.

Combined with the interactions he had with him, Trevor felt comfortable labeling Sebastian as a textbook predator. If he had done a background check before, he would have tried harder to convince Millie not to date the guy. He was sick to his stomach knowing she was somewhere out there with this asshole, and he couldn't have prevented it with one fucking search.

"Hindsight is twenty-twenty and completely unhelpful at this juncture," Logan said from the corner of the room where he was going through property owned by Sebastian.

"You didn't do anything the rest of would have done," Matthew piped up. "We can't go around and background check everyone one of us goes out with. It's unethical."

"Logically, I know that. But I still can't help but think about how we've dropped the ball." Trevor pulled out his phone and opened up his Find a Friend app for the fifth time. "Millie's phone is still off. Something's wrong."

"We don't know that." Logan's tone was gentle.

"She wouldn't turn her phone off in the middle of the case. Especially after receiving that message from Sebastian."

"We're assuming he scheduled that text to send, right?" Matthew asked.

"Yeah, I would think he did. There's no way he would have done it right in front of her. She's too smart. She would have picked up on it." Trevor replied.

He was sick to his stomach with worry. And he knew that if something was wrong, and Sebastian revealed himself, Millie would beat herself up over not seeing it earlier. And if she was fine, and they found them, she would still feel like an idiot for not seeing it. She was not kind to herself. She was still learning how to forgive herself for killing Rebecca's father in May. They would need to make sure they rallied around her. She was going to need it.

"This guy rents, right?" Logan was still scrolling through property records.

"Yeah, Millie has been going to his apartment every night," Matthew said.

"Well, back in July, right before the murders started, Sebastian Sable bought some land about twenty miles outside of Calico Rock. When I went to look up the property, it looked like it's an abandoned mining town."

"Secondary location." Matthew said.

"Exactly. This guy isn't killing these women in his apartment. He's taking them out to the middle of fucking nowhere to do it."

"Utilities?" Trevor asked.

"None. There's nothing really tying this guy to this land other than the deed. And he got it for a steal, since there are no real utilities even out there."

"Let's go fill Thomas in on what we found, and get ready to head out there and investigate." Matthew moved toward the door.

"Do you think he's taken Millie there?" Trevor asked.

Matthew shrugged. "I don't know. Hopefully not. But we need to go out there and check it out. If it is the secondary location, it will be what we need to nail the son of a bitch."

"All day we've been chasing after Bobby Tucker. We were so sure he was our guy," Trevor mused.

"Well, Sebastian has probably been keeping tabs on our investigation, saw we were leaning toward him as a suspect and then manipulated the evidence. It's probably what he was doing when he had your computer scrambled. That's why the text messages that didn't seem so similar last week suddenly matched. The bastard was framing Bobby to take the heat off of him." Matthew's voice was filled with venom. Trevor couldn't blame him. He knew Matthew wanted to go home to his family, and Sebastian had been manipulating the case, keeping them in New Mexico longer than possible.

And the bastard messed with one of their own. Which, as far as Trevor was concerned, was a step too far.

Trevor stood up from his chair, ready to follow them out.

"What are you doing?" Logan asked.

"I'm going with you."

Matthew frowned. "You never come with us. You always say the best part of your job is that you don't have to go out in the field and confront the bad guy."

Trevor shook his head. "I can't sit here and wait. I need to go out there. I need to make sure Millie is okay."

Matthew nodded. "I get it. If it were Rebecca, I would do the same. Since you're rusty, stay behind us. No rushing ahead."

Trevor nodded. "Absolutely. I'll come in as the tail. And I'll control my emotions."

Inside, though, Trevor's mind was going through every possible scenario right now, and he wasn't sure he would be able to fulfill his promise to control his emotions. Visions of finding Millie somewhere, dead...He shook his head. Not. Helping.

"If at any time you feel you don't think you're in control, you tap out. If you're in over your head, tap out. We don't know if we're approaching an abandoned town or if he's holed up there with Millie."

"She got that text earlier saying her time is up. We don't know how long he keeps his victims alive before killing them." Bile rose to the back of Trevor's throat as he thought of all the things they still didn't know. Were they too late?

"You're right, we don't," Logan's tone held no room for negotiation, and that was enough to ground Trevor back in the present. "That's why we need to focus on what we know. And we know he owns this property. We are going to go out there, and act accordingly."

Logan turned back to the door and walked out, Matthew following close behind.

Before he followed, Trevor took one more deep breath and said a silent prayer that they weren't too late.

Chapter Thirty-Five

MILLIE

October 13

"FUCK!" Millie screamed as she hit another dead end. She quickly whipped around and started running back the way she had come.

The maze was larger than she expected, which led her to believe it covered more ground than just the basement of that church. Sebastian had to have dug out and expanding it. That's the only explanation she had for how much ground she had covered and how long she had been running.

Or, she was backtracking a lot and covering ground she had already covered.

Honestly, it could go either way. She had lost track of time and where she was. The bottoms of her feet were torn up, and she was pretty sure they were bleeding. She hadn't paused long enough to investigate. She just knew they hurt. A lot.

Reaching up, she wiped away the tears that were running down her cheeks.

Another corner.

Another dead end.

Both hands against the wall, she screamed her frustration to the sky.

There was a camera.

Did all the dead ends have cameras? Was he taping this?

Dread filled her when she remembered the photos of the other victims he had hanging on the wall upstairs in the church. They were all screaming while pressed up against something.

Stills from the videos he took while they were running the maze.

His trophies.

Slowly she backed away from the wall and flipped off the camera with both her middle fingers before turning and running again. She stopped at the intersection and whipped her head both ways.

Fuck.

Millie couldn't remember which direction she had come from.

Somewhere in the basement, she could hear whistling. She couldn't tell which direction it was coming from, but it was there nonetheless.

Standing there, frozen in indecision, the tune he was whistling became clear in her mind. And she didn't know whether she should laugh or cry.

He was whistling a song about how he was never going to give her up, but not at the normal tempo. It was slow, and almost haunting. The sound echoed in the basement. He was fucking Rickrolling her as he chased her down to kill her.

He was fucking deranged.

She could never listen to this song again without having nightmares.

The whistling sounded like it was getting closer, so she made a split-second decision and turned left, immediately making a beeline for the right wall. As she ran, she kept her hand on the wall.

Follow the right wall. Follow the right wall. Trevor's voice echoed in her mind as she ran, never letting go of the wall. This was where she had gone wrong. She should have been doing the entire time. Turn after turn after turn, luck was finally on her side. No more dead ends.

Follow the right wall.

When she got out of here, she was going to tell Trevor he was the one who saved her. The one who got her out. She was going to apologize for doubting him. Tell him she would listen to him forever.

One more corner turned, another open corridor. She was doing it. Her feet hurt and her legs were tired, but she would not slow down. Another corner, and she saw it.

The exit.

Millie let out a sob of relief. Letting go of the wall, she sprinted. She just needed to make it five more feet. Five feet to freedom.

A shadow crossed into the opening. She skidded to a stop.

"No," she breathed out.

"Yes," Sebastian growled.

She shook her head rapidly. "You said you weren't watching."

"I wasn't watching. But you haven't exactly been quiet. You said it yourself... I know this maze. I knew where you were, I knew the shortcuts, and I got here first. I. Win."

"No. I. Win."

Millie gathered all the strength she could muster and ran directly toward Sebastian. She thought about the women whose lives he ended. The children whose mothers he stole. She thought about her own broken heart, her survival.

She was going to do it.

She was getting out of the maze.

A growling scream ripped from her as she neared Sebastian. A split second before Millie collided with him, she could see his eyes widen, and she was pretty sure he said the words 'oh shit,' but honestly, she couldn't hear anything over the blood rushing in her ears, and a scream her ancestors would be proud of.

Hands extended out in front of her, her palms collided with Sebastian's chest, and the full weight of her body caused him to tip backwards, falling to the floor, with a curse on his lips.

Her momentum had her following him down, landing on top of him. For a second, the impact disoriented her, but because his body broke her fall, she could recover quicker than him. Pushing herself up, she moved her body until she was straddling him, putting all her weight on his stomach.

She knew from their time in bed, he could easily maneuver her as if she weighed nothing, so she needed to incapacitate him. She stared down at his face as clarity came back. His lips formed that half-smirk that had caused her heart to beat quicker just a few hours ago.

Millie pulled her right arm back and, just as she practiced in the gym with Trevor every week, she put all her weight behind it as she smashed her fist against his face.

His nose crunched against her knuckles. "Fuck!!"

"That's for Jamie." She brought her arm back and smashed it into his face again. "And that's for Sharon." And again. "That one was for Laura. Beautiful Laura and her beautiful babies." She was sobbing as she brought her arm back again. "And this is for Sarah." One more time, she brought her arm back, and smashed it against his smarmy little face. "And that is for me, you fucking asshole."

Her hand was in pain, and she was panting as she looked down on Sebastian. His face bloody, and his nose crooked, eyes swollen closed.

He started laughing. "Got it out of your system, sweetheart?"

"Fuck you."

"Funny, you were basically salivating for me to earlier tonight."

Something shiny glinted out of the corner of her eye. Millie shifted her gaze to her right.

A knife on the ground.

Probably the murder weapon.

Definitely the murder weapon.

With a quickness she didn't know she still had, Millie snatched it up.

"What are you going to do with that?"

Millie immediately pressed it against his throat.

Sebastian's laugh turned into a cough. "You don't have it in you. I know you, Millie. You're not a killer."

Millie closed her eyes and immediately the scene from the basement back in May came flooding back to her. Her rushing down the stairs of Rebecca's parents' house, seeing Guillermo hovering over her friend, how she didn't hesitate to pull the trigger, killing him.

Reopening her eyes, she set her gaze on him. "You're wrong."

"I'm never wrong. But I have to admit, this is turning out way better than I imagined it would. I love it when they fight back, and you, my love, you're giving me one hell of a fight."

Millie pressed the knife firmly into his neck. "I'm not your love. You're a fucking liar!" Her voice was raw as she screamed out her words. "You're a liar and a killer, and you don't deserve to live."

"Do it," Sebastian dared. "Kill me."

Millie looked down at him. The man she had been convinced she was falling in love with just a few hours ago. A man who she was making plans for the future with.

And it was all a lie.

He had tricked her.

Made her believe everything.

All. Lies.

Sobbing, she pressed the tip of the knife further into his neck, a drop of blood pooled there.

Arms wrapped around her body, pulling her up and off of Sebastian's body.

Screaming, she flailed her arms and legs, trying to get away. Did Sebastian have an accomplice they didn't know about?

"Hey," a voice she would recognize anywhere spoke into her ear, and she immediately stopped fighting. "You're okay."

Trevor set her down, and she immediately turned and flung her arms around his body, the knife clattered to the floor. Without hesitating, he wrapped her up in his arms, holding her tightly against him. And she started crying. Relief flooded through her.

His lips pressed against the top of her head as he squeezed her against him. "You're okay. You're okay."

Millie didn't know if he was saying it more for his sake or hers, but being surrounded by him, she allowed herself to believe his words.

Lifting her head from his chest, she turned to look behind her as local PD pulled Sebastian off the ground and cuffed him. Standing behind them, the rest of her team were there, guns drawn, in full tactical gear.

They had found her.

Trevor had found her.

She was safe.

But Trevor was wrong. She would not be okay.

Chapter Thirty-Six

TREVOR

October 14

Trevor stared at Sebastian as he sat at the table in the interrogation room. The man was sporting quite the black eye and his nose looked like it could possibly be broken. Trevor couldn't help but feel proud of Millie. She really gave it to Sebastian good. Saved him from having to rough the asshole up.

Trevor pulled open the door to the room and stepped inside.

Sebastian's mouth curled into a smirk. "Wondered when you would show up."

Trevor walked over and pulled the chair out from across the table and sat down. "You're going away for a very long time."

Sebastian shrugged. "Worth it. Although I kind of wish I had been able to finish that last kill. I was all worked up and everything. Such a shame. You should have heard her screaming."

Trevor *had* heard her screaming. They found the footage of the maze, and he spent all night watching it. He'd heard all the women screaming.

It was something that would haunt him for the rest of his life.

"Why?" Trevor asked.

"You're going to be more specific than that. Why did I choose her? Why did I kill? Why did I fuck her?"

"Why did you make her believe you were falling in love with her?"

Sebastian's mouth spread into a full smile. "Because it was fun. With all those other women, I pretended to be someone else in order to convince them to come to me. With Millie, I could be myself, mostly. And she bought it, hook, line, and sinker. She was *so* desperate to find someone to want her, all I had to do was lay on some charm and pull her away from you."

Trevor clenched his jaw and looked away. He wasn't going to let the man get to him. But apparently, Sebastian wasn't finished.

"The best part? I've ruined her for other men. She's never going to trust anyone again. I may not have been able to finish the job, but she's going to be fucked up for the rest of her life, and that may be a little better."

Trevor stood from his seat. "She's not going to be fucked up for the rest of her life, because she is surrounded by people who love her. People who will help her through this."

"You mean you? A man who can't even admit to himself how he feels about her?"

Trevor smiled. "That's where you're wrong. In fact, I should be thanking you. I know a few weeks ago, I told you I only cared for her as a friend, but you were right. I was lying. But this whole ordeal has made me realize life is short, and I need to own up to my feelings. I *do* care for Millie deeply, and I'm going to make sure every single day she knows it. And if she doesn't return the feelings, who cares? And you? You will spend the rest of your life rotting away in prison. Alone."

Trevor didn't wait for a response. He turned and walked out of the conference room. Even though he was exhausted, he needed to go to the hospital and see Millie. To make sure she was okay.

Epilogue

MILLIE

November 1

"Did you see the pictures Rebecca sent in the group chat?" Trevor's voice echoed out of the Millie's phone that she had set on the dresser so she could video chat with him while she unpacked.

Following the events of Calico Rock, as she spent a few days in the hospital recovering from the injuries she sustained while running the maze, Millie concluded she needed some time off. Internal Affairs and Thomas both agreed with her and immediately signed off on an indefinite sabbatical. She could return when she was ready.

With the sabbatical in place, she did what any woman in her position would do. She went home to her mom.

"I did. Benji made an adorable Fozzy Bear."

Trevor laughed. "I was going to say Matty, as Kermit, will forever be the background on my phone."

"I think it's cute that they had a family costume. It's their first Halloween together. Let them have their fun without you mocking it."

"I'm not mocking it." He paused. "Okay, fine, I am a little, but Rebecca suggested next year we do a department-themed costume. What do you think?"

Millie smiled. "I think it would be a lot of fun. I'm looking forward to it."

Silence fell between the two friends as Millie hung up another blouse in the closet of her room.

"Did you um, get the report Thomas sent?"

"Yeah. I did."

A week after they closed the case in Calico Rock, the Blooming Butcher had killed again. This time in northern New Jersey. He must have caught wind of the nickname, because he signed it on his message.

Thomas had sent Millie the file containing everything about it so she could stay on top of the case. In it, there were pictures of the crime scene. The victim was another woman in her early 20s, stabbed multiple times and strangled. Dumped in front of a white wall. She was covered in tansies, which Millie learned symbolized a declaration of war. On the white wall, the killer had scrawled in the victim's blood: "You're right. I need a better Batman villain - I choose Poison Ivy. - The Blooming Butcher."

Now that he had adopted the name once only used by an obscure blog, the media was running with it. He was getting the notoriety he craved.

It made Millie sick.

"I miss you." Trevor's voice broke her out of her reverie.

"I miss you, too."

"Are you settling in okay?"

Millie looked out her window at the Pacific Ocean as it crashed against the beach of her hometown, Sunset Harbor. "Yeah. As you can see, I'm unpacking right now."

"I know why you need to do what you're doing, but I just wish you could do it here."

Millie picked up the phone and carried it with her to the bed. She sat on the edge before flopping back. "I know. But I need some time away from everyone."

Trevor closed his eyes and bit his lip before he spoke again. "Are we okay?"

"Yes," Millie answered without hesitation. "We're more than okay."

Trevor let out a breath. "Good, because I don't know what I would do if we weren't."

"Honestly, you and Becks are the only two people I look forward to talking to, other than my family."

Trevor smiled. "I'm glad to hear it. Do you think you'll be home for Christmas?"

Millie shook her head. "I was always planning on spending Christmas here. You know that."

Trevor's face showed his disappointment as he nodded. "Yeah, you're right. I must have forgotten after..."

After the case upended her life.

Millie rubbed her eyes. Nightmares of that night plagued her every time she fell asleep. And when it wasn't nightmares about her ordeal, it was of her killing Rebecca's father. She was a mess, and she hoped being away from work and Washington would help fix her.

"You could come here?" Millie held her breath.

Ever since the maze, her feelings for Trevor had been a little mixed up. Somewhere as she ran, and used his maze advice, something shifted. And as time passed, and she had all that time in the hospital to reflect on everything, she realized at some point, maybe her feelings had changed.

The problem was she didn't know if he still felt the same way. They had spent all their time defining their relationship as best friends, and *only* best friends, that she feared she had missed her chance.

Even so, she knew she wanted him with her. She wouldn't be able to fully heal with him on the other side of the country from her.

"What?"

"You can come here for Christmas. Spend it with my family."

Trevor smiled. "Really?"

"Yeah, and if you're worried about your mom, she can come, too."

"I'll talk to my mom and get back to you. Are you sure you're okay? You know you can talk to me."

Millie simply nodded, a lump forming in her throat. "Yeah," she choked out. "I'm fine."

"I've got to go, but we'll talk soon, yeah?"

"Yeah. Give Benji a hug for me when you see him."

"Of course. I love you."

"I love you, too. Let me know about Christmas."

"I will, but you already know, we'll be there."

As she hung up the phone, knowing she would see Trevor soon gave Millie hope she hadn't had since before Calico Rock. She didn't know what would fix her, if anything could, but being around Trevor would make things better for a while. After all, he was her best friend.

LOVE'S
DEADLY
GAME
PROFILING THE HEART 3
Stephanie R. Caffrey

CHECK OUT THESE OTHER GREAT HEAs FROM ROWAN PROSE:

Stephanie R. Caffrey is a romantic suspense author who lives with her family in the Midwest. When she's not working on her books, she's a substitute teacher, and loves to write fanfiction. She is a proud marginalized voice in the Mexican-American community. Besides writing, she enjoys sewing, knitting, and cross stitching. www.srcaffrey.com